MYSTERIOUS LOVER

Crime and Passion, Book 1

Mary Lancaster

ARE YOU SIGNED UP FOR DRAGONBLADE'S BLOG?

You'll get the latest news and information on exclusive giveaways, exclusive excerpts, coming releases, sales, free books, cover reveals and more.

Check out our complete list of authors, too!

No spam, no junk. That's a promise!

Sign Up Here

www.dragonbladepublishing.com

Dearest Reader;

Thank you for your support of a small press. At Dragonblade Publishing, we strive to bring you the highest quality Historical Romance from the some of the best authors in the business. Without your support, there is no 'us', so we sincerely hope you adore these stories and find some new favorite authors along the way.

Happy Reading!

CEO, Dragonblade Publishing

Additional Dragonblade books by Author Mary Lancaster

Crime & Passion Series
Mysterious Lover

The Husband Dilemma Series
How to Fool a Duke

Season of Scandal Series
Pursued by the Rake
Abandoned to the Prodigal
Married to the Rogue
Unmasked by her Lover

Imperial Season Series
Vienna Waltz
Vienna Woods
Vienna Dawn

Blackhaven Brides Series
The Wicked Baron
The Wicked Lady
The Wicked Rebel
The Wicked Husband
The Wicked Marquis
The Wicked Governess
The Wicked Spy
The Wicked Gypsy
The Wicked Wife
Wicked Christmas (A Novella)
The Wicked Waif

The Wicked Heir
The Wicked Captain
The Wicked Sister

Unmarriageable Series
The Deserted Heart
The Sinister Heart
The Vulgar Heart
The Broken Heart
The Weary Heart
The Secret Heart
Christmas Heart

The Lyon's Den Connected World
Fed to the Lyon

Also from Mary Lancaster
Madeleine

CHAPTER ONE

G RIZELDA LIKED TO lose herself in opera, in the exquisite music and the inevitable tragedy. Unfortunately, there was little chance of that tonight, since her mother was restless and needed someone else to be running around for her.

"Don't you find it too warm in here?" the duchess whispered audibly to her son as she rummaged in her tiny reticule. "Where is my fan?"

"You gave it to Griz," Forsythe replied without taking his gaze off the stage. Grizelda suspected he was pursuing one of the chorus girls—which may have been what made their mother so restless, since she was trying to promote a match between Forsythe and their youngest guest, Miss Watters.

Griz intercepted her mother's glare, and remembered where she'd put the fan. "I'll fetch it," she murmured, and slipped from her chair. To her surprise, Miss Watters's brother smiled at her as she hurried past. Disconcerted—for she was used to being the invisible member of her noble family—she settled her spectacles more firmly on her nose and walked out of the private box into the quiet corridor.

It took only a minute to reach the cloakroom and retrieve her mother's fan from the pocket of her cloak. With a word of thanks, she left, so lost in thoughts of *Fidelio*, that she walked straight into a large, solid object. The object was traveling with such speed that she was sent sprawling into the wall. It felt, she imagined, like being hit by a railway train.

However, this particular train, a tall man with a dark green cloak falling from one shoulder, halted abruptly, reaching out to stop her from falling forward again.

"Forgive me, are you hurt?"

Dazed, Grizelda stared up at the most handsome male face she had ever seen. Raven hair fell forward over a nobly high forehead. Dramatic black brows arched perfectly over a pair of long-lashed, melting brown eyes. High cheekbones, a thin nose, and generous mouth lent him a deceptive air of delicacy—there had been nothing delicate about the force of the hard body slamming into hers. He was so lean that had he been less handsome, he might have looked cadaverous, but as it was, his ridiculous good looks snatched at one's breath.

Fortunately, she was immune to young men's charms and well past the age of being enslaved by a pretty face. Though it was true, his voice did have an intriguing effect on her. It must have been the foreign accent.

"Just winded," she replied hastily. "Like falling off a horse."

His lips quirked upward. A hint of amusement overlayed the relief in his eyes. His grip on her arm loosened, and he stepped back. "May I escort you somewhere, madam?"

She shook her head, and at the corner of her eye, glimpsed a familiar figure flitting down the steps from the foyer to the front doors. Surely that was Nancy, the housemaid? What the devil was she doing here?

"No, thank you," she replied, dragging her gaze back to the handsome stranger.

He bowed with considerable grace and hurried on his way to the door. Grizelda, oddly disappointed, moved more slowly toward the staircase, touching the fan to be sure it still dangled from her wrist.

Her wayward mind could not help wondering why Nancy was at

the theatre. It was not her evening off, and she really had no business being out of the house. Normally, Griz would not have troubled about a servant slipping away for a few hours. She did not grudge them the extra time, and in any case, it was not her business but her mother's or the housekeeper's. But Nancy had been acting recently as her lady's maid, helping her fasten and unfasten gowns, and dressing her hair in a manner that didn't annoy Their Graces. And she had seemed distracted that evening as she'd helped Griz dress for the opera.

Griz had taken three steps up the staircase before she changed her mind and hurried back down. She did not bother with her cloak since she only meant to glance outside and see if Nancy was still there. If the handsome stranger was still outside, she might even ask him if he had noticed which way Nancy went.

The liveried doorman asked in some surprise if he could help her.

"Oh, no, I just want a moment's air," she replied, sweeping outside.

The road in front was well lit, and carriages lined the roads. A few coachmen had gathered for a gossip nearby. But there was no sign of either Nancy or the foreign gentleman until she spun around to go back inside and was sure she saw a skirt vanish around the side of the building.

It could have been anyone's skirt, but on impulse, she followed it, walking the length of the building quickly and around the corner, where there were only more carriages and coachmen. She crossed the road and, hearing quick footsteps to the left, turned into a dimly lit alley. Since she could still be seen by the coachmen and an old couple were waddling toward her, arguing, she did not hesitate. There was still no sign of anyone who might have been Nancy.

She paused and cast one glance up the next opening before she meant to return to the opera house. There was no lighting here. And she could hear no footsteps in that direction, only the snorting and shifting of horses closer to the theatre, and some distant, raucous coughing followed by a stream of male and female laughter. A faint sound of scraping stone reached her, but she could not tell the direction. Nothing moved in the dark passage ahead.

But as she stared, it seemed to her there was a blacker heap of something on the ground. A wink of moonlight glinted on an object closer to her, perhaps a coin. Griz cast another glance to either end of the back street she hovered in and then darted up the darker, narrower opening. She had no intention of lingering. Apart from anything else, the smell was unpleasant. She didn't like to think what she was walking on, merely held up her voluminous skirts as much as she could.

Something skittered off the toe of her shoe, and she bent to pick it up. The glinting object. As she grasped it, the heap she had discerned resolved into a troublingly human shape. She straightened, took a step nearer, and the moon blinked down again. On a woman lying on her back on the ground, a woolen cloak barely covering the black dress she normally wore under an apron. And the face was only too familiar.

"Nancy!" She bent over the girl in alarm, but even before clouds blocked the moon once more, she had seen the open, staring eyes of death. *Please let me be wrong, please!*

Her movements suddenly clumsy, she tore off her glove, touching the girl's hand, her face, both reassuringly warm. Abruptly, a swinging lantern light swept up from the direction she had just come.

"Please, can you help her?" Griz called urgently. The light moved faster, rising higher to reveal the handsome face of the stranger she had walked into at the opera house.

Immediately, he dropped to a crouch on Nancy's other side, setting the lantern in the filth beside him without looking at it. His attention was all on the maid. He took her wrist in his hand, then pressed his long slender fingers to her neck.

And then she saw the terrible, red stain on Nancy's chest, blooming from the small tear in her dress.

Everything inside her seemed to lurch in horror. Especially when the stranger took hold of Nancy's face and bent over her. For a bizarre moment, she thought he would kiss the dead girl, but it seemed he was trying to give her his own breath.

Appalled, she could only watch as he straightened and sat back on his heels.

"She is beyond anyone's help," he murmured.

"Except God's," Griz whispered, touching Nancy's hair. Her bonnet had been pushed back, crushed under her head.

The stranger did not respond. When she glanced at him, his gaze was on her other hand, the one that held the glinting object she had picked up. A dagger.

A Renaissance Italian dagger with a jeweled hilt, remarkably like the one in her father's collection.

She stared at it with ominous fascination.

"Perhaps you should give that to me?" He had risen and stood holding out his hand over Nancy's body.

Instinctively, Griz leapt back. After all, she did not know this man, who could have followed her, or, worse, Nancy. He could have come *back* to Nancy, perhaps to find the dagger with which he had killed her...

He moved quickly, stepping over the body and grasping her wrist. Before she could cry out, let alone flee, he had wrested the dagger from her.

At least he released her immediately, leaving her glaring at him.

"Here! Stay where you are!" shouted a voice from the end of the alley. The sound of a policeman's rattle ensued, summoning his colleagues, and a tall-hatted policeman, lantern in one hand, truncheon in the other, ran toward them.

His lantern shone in her eyes, blinding her until he lowered it again. He looked very young and very determined.

"Nancy is dead," she said, a sudden wave of grief catching at her voice.

The policeman shone his lantern over the dead girl's body. Briefly, Grizelda closed her eyes.

"She's been murdered," he uttered grimly.

"With this, I imagine," the stranger said, holding out the dagger.

The policeman snatched it from him. "And you just happen to be holding it," he said with satisfaction. "Name!"

"Tizsa, Dragan."

"Foreign," the policeman accused. "What are you doing here, and what are you to this poor, dead young woman?"

"I was passing, and I am nothing to her."

"She's my maid," Grizelda blurted. "Nancy Barrow."

The policeman stared at her, no doubt taking in her opera finery wildly out of place in this squalor. "And *your* name, ma'am?"

"Grizelda Niven." Her eyes flickered to the young man, Dragan, who was watching her intently. He had very intense eyes.

"What happened here?" the policeman asked her. "Did you see this man murder your maid?"

By then, another, older constable had run up from the opposite end of the passage and now halted beside them, panting.

"No," Grizelda said. "I just found her here, already dead, and then..."

The older policeman walked around the body portentously, while the younger told him all that he had learned.

"My lady!" exclaimed the second policeman, suddenly interrupting as he recognized her. With an effort, Grizelda remembered him from last month's dog and meat-barrow incident. "What in the world are you doing in this place?"

"I was at the opera with my parents."

"But it hasn't finished yet," the first policeman pointed out. "And you shouldn't be out here alone. 'Specially not dressed like that!"

"Were you looking for the maid?" the older constable asked, suddenly enlightened. "Then followed her out here, I daresay?"

"Yes, that was it," Grizelda said with relief at telling at least partial truth. Though she did not look at Mr. Dragan, she could feel his gaze boring into her. More policemen came running from either end of the alley.

"Come, we'll escort you back to the theatre," the older constable said kindly. "Send someone to Her Grace..."

"Oh, no," Grizelda said quickly, "there is no need. I'll go back myself. Only Nancy..." She blinked rapidly down at the dead maid who would never scold, pry, or serve her again.

"Don't you worry, my lady," the constable soothed. "We'll see she's taken care of and her family informed. Now you," he added in quite another tone to Dragan, "had better come to the station with us."

At his nod, two officers seized hold of Dragan, who made an instinctive jerk to throw them off.

"No, no," Grizelda protested, perversely annoyed because they shared her initial suspicion. "He arrived *after* me. I very much doubt he did this."

"He was holding the weapon, my lady," the first policeman said dryly.

"I picked it up *there,* and he took it from *me*," she retorted.

Several constables stared at her, frowning.

"How long have you known this man?" the older policeman demanded, as though he suspected an assignation.

"I've never met him before tonight," Grizelda said indignantly.

"Good, because I'm very sure His Grace would not approve! Take him away."

To her surprise, Dragan cast her a quick, sardonic smile over his shoulder. Somehow, he brushed the policemen's hands off his arms, and they let him walk freely between them, a tall, straight figure that made her think of battered but unbowed nobility.

She stared after him, helpless, for once, unable to think, to cope.

"Shall I bring your lantern, my lady?" asked one of the policemen.

She blinked, turning to see him picking up Dragan's spluttering lantern that stood on the ground beside Nancy. "It isn't mine," she observed.

The older constable urged her to walk with him out of the alley and back toward the opera house. At some point, before she walked back inside, her body began to tremble. Her head pounded, and wherever she looked, Nancy's expressionless, dead face swam before her eyes.

There seemed to be even more people in her parents' box when she reentered it. The final act was in full swing. Since someone else now sat in the chair that had once been hers, she murmured an apology to two gentlemen as she brushed between them and dropped the fan over her mother's shoulder into her lap.

The duchess looked up quickly. "Did you have another made?" she asked with heavy humor.

Grizelda smiled dutifully and stumbled her way to a vacant seat at the back of the box beside her brother Forsythe and Miss Watters.

Forsythe wrinkled his nose and glanced at her in some surprise. "Is that you?" he hissed, raking his gaze from her no doubt white face to the soiled hem of her gown. His expression changed. "What's wrong, Griz? Has something happened?"

Grizelda nodded, trying to smile while she distractedly rubbed the side of her hand over her aching forehead.

Her brother's erratic kindness kicked in. Without asking any more, he leaned forward and murmured in their father's ear. His Grace lifted one impatient hand, which may or may not have been permission. Forsythe seized Griz by the hand, murmured an apology to Miss Watters, and dragged her outside.

"Nancy's dead," she blurted. "Nancy, the housemaid. I thought I saw her leaving the theatre. She had no reason to be here, and she certainly didn't seem to be looking for us, so curiosity got the better of me, and I followed her. I found her dead in an alley close by. She'd been murdered, stabbed to death."

"Dear God," Forsythe uttered, staring at her. "Have you told anyone?"

"The police know. They've arrested someone, though I don't think he did it."

Forsythe flung a brotherly arm around her, urging her toward the staircase. "You're shaking like a leaf. Come on, I'll take you home in a cab, and we'll leave the carriage for Their Graces. They won't like this, by the way. They'll take it as a personal insult. Especially since you found her."

"She'd still be dead," Griz said flatly, "whoever found her. The police would still come to us since she is—was—our servant." She swallowed. "But I do wish I hadn't been quite so curious…"

CHAPTER TWO

D RAGAN SAT ON a wooden chair in a bare room, his gaze fixed on the austerely painted wall in front of him.

As a student, he had frequently run afoul of the police in his own country for saying, writing, and doing the wrong thing. The London police, concerned with *actual* crime, had never worried him until now. In fact, hemmed in by two constables, he had walked away from the scene of the murder with a weird sense of familiarity that had nothing to do with Nancy Barrow's death, from which he still felt oddly detached.

On the other hand, the police were definitely connecting him to it by means of his presence and the dagger. When, shortly after arriving at the police station, they took him out again, the first twinge of unease had taken him by surprise.

"Where are we going?" he had asked the constable beside him.

"Headquarters, Great Scotland Yard. Matter for the plainclothes lot. Detectives," the policeman had added for the benefit of the foreigner. "They'll get to the bottom of this, and you'll be banged up all right and tight in no time."

Dragan had sighed. "I hope they do. That should stop me being— er—banged up."

The constable had stared at him with distaste. "You're mighty cool for a man who just murdered a respectable young woman."

"Consider the possibility that I didn't murder her, and my demeanor will make much more sense."

"Ha! You're all bloody innocent, aren't you?"

Perhaps, he reflected, he should not have removed the weapon from the possession of the young lady. In his defense, he had no way of knowing whether or not she had killed Nancy, and if she had, if she would turn next on him.

Besides, it would have made no difference who held the knife. In a choice between a foreign nobody and a wealthy lady in silks and jewels, being constantly addressed as "my lady," there was only ever going to be one outcome.

Without warning, the door crashed open, and a man in a grey suit strode in, kicking the door shut behind him. He was probably only a few years older than Dragan.

"Inspector Harris," he introduced himself briskly, throwing a notebook onto the table. "Sorry to keep you waiting, Mr. Dragan?"

"Tizsa."

Inspector Harris blinked, sat down, and opened the notebook. "Did some idiot get your name wrong?"

"Just the wrong way round. My surname is Tizsa, my Christian name Dragan."

"Ah. Where are you from, Mr. Tizsa?"

"Hungary."

"And what brought you to London?"

"The promise of execution in my own country."

Harris cast him a more piercing look. "For what crime?"

"Patriotism."

"You were on the wrong side in the late revolution," Harris translated.

"Oh, no, I was on the right side. Unfortunately, it turned out to be the losing side."

"So, you sought refuge here?"

Dragan shrugged. "Eventually, yes."

"And how long have you known the deceased, Miss Nancy Barrow?"

Dragan smiled faintly. He hadn't said he knew her at all, and there had been no time for the police to find out, but he allowed Harris the point. "Two, maybe three months."

"What was your relationship with her?"

"Friends. Of a sort."

Harris cast him a longer look. "Not a good sort, I might guess."

"What makes you think that?"

"You show no overt signs of grief at her passing. I understand you showed no horror either at the scene of her violent murder."

Dragan almost laughed. "Inspector, I have seen far too much violent death to faint at the sight of a little blood. I am sorry she is dead, but I cannot bring her back."

"Did you kill her?"

"Of course not. Why would I do such a thing?"

"A lover's quarrel?"

"I was never her lover."

Harris sat back. "How did you meet her?"

"At the house of a friend."

"May I have the name of this friend?"

"Dr. Cordell, in Caroline Place. I have a room in his house."

"And where does Miss Barrow live?"

They already knew that. It was some trickery to see how much he would admit to. "In the house of her employer, I imagine. She is in service to some nobleman."

"The nobleman whose daughter was with you tonight?" Harris asked innocently.

"I have no knowledge of her. I never met her before."

Harris sighed. "You had better tell me what happened."

"I attended the opera as the guest of a friend," Dragan said impatiently. "While I was there, I received a note. From Miss Barrow."

"Was that usual?"

"No. Unprecedented, to be honest. The note asked me to meet her at the interval, at the front door of the theatre. Which I did, only she was not there. I looked around, eventually into the surrounding streets, and that was when I found her dead."

"And the other lady?"

"She seemed to have found her first."

Harris frowned. "She was there when you arrived on the scene?"

"Yes."

"She did not come with you?"

Dragan stared at him. "No."

"How did the weapon come to be in your hand? Did you remove it from the body?"

"No, I removed it from the living lady."

"Why?"

"Because I didn't know she hadn't killed Nancy Barrow," Dragan said frankly.

The policeman looked skeptical. "Do you know who that young lady is?"

"She said Nancy was her maid, so I can only suppose she is a relation of the duke Nancy worked for."

"And you want me to believe Lady Grizelda Niven killed her maid?"

Dragan sighed. "No. I don't think she did. She was too shocked. And besides, if the girl had annoyed her, she only needed to dismiss her, not stab her to death."

"Then what in the world was she doing in a Covent Garden back alley—Mudd Lane, to be precise—decked out in silk and jewels?"

It was a very good question. "You would have to ask her. I had the impression she was curious by nature. Eccentric."

"An impression based on, what, ten minutes acquaintance?" the policeman asked in disbelief.

"Less," Dragan said with a shrug.

"If you had an assignation with the lady, you had better tell me now. Unless it is germane to the inquiry, the information won't be released."

Dragan stared at him. "She's a duke's daughter. I'm a refugee revolutionary without a penny to my name. Why would she look at me?"

Harris met his gaze. He seemed almost...amused. "Perhaps she really *is* curious by nature. Perhaps you were blackmailing her. With Nancy's help."

Dragan stood so quickly his chair fell over. "Sir, I marched in the streets, fought in the army for nearly two years in defense of my principles. Why would I abandon them now?"

Harris had stood with him but did not call for help. "You mean to imply that blackmail is beneath your principles?"

"Well beneath," Dragan said between his teeth.

"Please sit down."

Dragan picked up his chair, all but throwing it upright before flinging himself back into it.

"Do you think it was beneath Nancy's principles?" Harris asked innocently.

Dragan curled his lip. "Probably. Either way, there was no harm she could do to me. Nor have I anything to pay a blackmailer." He drew in his breath. "Inspector, if she was in trouble, I would have done my best to help her. I most certainly did not kill her. But if you release me, I will do my best to find out who did."

RISING EARLY THE following morning with new determination, Grizelda dressed without help and went immediately to the breakfast parlor. There, as she had hoped, she found only her second-eldest brother, Horace, who was preparing to face the day at his Whitehall office with a newspaper and a huge plateful of bacon, eggs, sausages, and toast.

"Good morning," she said cheerfully.

Horace grunted without looking up.

Grizelda helped herself to toast and jam and sat down opposite him. "Horace, where would the police take someone they had arrested for murder?"

His eyebrows flew up, dragging his gaze off the paper to her face. "Headquarters at Whitehall Place and Great Scotland Yard, probably. Why?"

"Are you in charge of the policemen there?" she asked, ignoring his question.

His frown deepened. "Not as such…"

"Then your name carries no weight with them?"

"I wouldn't go as far as that," Horace said with dignity. "My influence is broad."

She smiled. "I thought so."

In fact, Horace had come into his own during the panic of 1848, when revolution had swept through Europe and London had been shaken by the Chartist riots. Of course, unrest in Britain had been a pale echo of what had happened abroad, but with hunger and unemployment high, people were nervous. Now, Horace "kept an eye" not on crime as such but on threats to the government and to order. His authority appeared to be vague, yet everyone, including her politically active father and eldest brother, took it seriously.

Horace returned to his paper, only to look up a moment later. "Griz, are you up to something?"

"Lord, no. Just preparing for an argument." She took a gulp of coffee. "I must dash. Vicky needs her walk. Have a pleasant day at the office!"

ALTHOUGH HE HAD never been accused of murder, there was nothing else new to Dragan's situation. He had been arrested before and questioned by the police. He had even spent a night in the cells once, in Pest. And another night locked up with his men in Transylvania when they had been captured by Austrian forces. On the first occasion, without evidence, they had let him go with dire warnings. On the second, he had taken matters into his own hands and escaped with his men.

This morning, he didn't hold out much hope of either eventuality. Unless he could somehow get a message to a lawyer friend. He supposed he would go to court this morning, but the chances of him being granted leave to await trial out of prison were remote unless someone would vouch for him.

At the sound of rattling keys, he looked up from his hard, wooden bench. As did everyone else.

"Tizsa!" a policeman called, turning the key. "Inspector's got some more questions for you."

Dragan stood and wrestled himself into his coat, then snatched up his cloak as if quite confident of leaving.

"Bloody gentlemen," someone growled. "Always get special treatment."

"He ain't a gentleman," scoffed the man beside him. "He's foreign!"

Which entertained Dragan all the way back to the bare room he had left only a few hours ago. This time, a pale beam of sunshine shone in through the small window, but it did little to alleviate the dreariness.

Inspector Harris laid a dagger on the table and glanced up at him. "Recognize this?"

"No." He frowned. "Perhaps. Is that the dagger that was found beside Nancy last night?"

"It's the one you handed to Police Constable Porter," Harris said

16

dryly.

"I didn't really look at it. But yes, it could be." He grimaced. "Pretty thing for such a grizzly purpose."

"Valuable thing for such a grizzly purpose," Harris corrected. "I'm told these jewels are real."

"If you say so." Dragan sat opposite the inspector, without being invited. "A simple inquiry should acquit me of any possibility of owning such a thing."

"But you own a sword and a pistol."

Before he could answer, some growing commotion in the corridor suddenly exploded into the room in the shape of a speeding dog, no more than a streak whizzing past Dragan's eyes as it ran twice around the room and jumped on the table, sniffing the dagger.

Harris leapt to his feet, reaching out to rescue the weapon. The dog snarled, and Harris snatched back his hand.

Dragan laughed.

Another, bigger whirlwind in a wide-skirted blue gown flew into the room, closely followed by two bewildered-looking policemen.

"My lady, you can't go in there!" one expostulated, much too late.

"What is the meaning of this?" Harris thundered.

The bespectacled young lady, resplendent in a fine Paisley shawl and wide-brimmed bonnet of precisely the same shade of blue as her gown, lifted the dog off the table and held it in her arms. It appeared to be a small, Italian greyhound, with fur of a rare, deep grey that was almost blue. It gazed up at her adoringly, as though saying, *Would I growl at a policeman?*

Over its head, she met Dragan's gaze and smiled. Oh, yes, she was the same girl as he had all but knocked over in the theatre, and whom he had found bending over Nancy Barrow, clutching the dagger that now, probably, lay on the table between them. Unless the dog had swallowed it.

"Naughty Vicky," she scolded the animal without heat. "I am so sorry, sir," she added to Harris. "I don't know how she came to escape me! But it has worked out excellently, for I was just telling these men I wished to speak to Mr. Dragan, and here he is!"

She bestowed such a brilliant smile on him that he was dazzled, even knowing she was acting. Even not knowing her purpose.

"This," Harris said, heavily sardonic, "is Mr. Tizsa."

"He looks," the girl said firmly, "like Mr. Dragan."

"We are the same man," Dragan said, rising belatedly to his feet. "My surname is Tizsa. How can I help you, madam?"

Harris, scowling heavily, tried to break into an illicit conversation over which he seemed to have lost control, but the girl's laughter drowned him out.

"How gallant you are! But of course, it is I who came to help *you*. It bothered me so much that they had arrested you over poor Nancy that I told my brother all about it." She swung on Harris. "You will probably know my brother, sir? Lord Horace Niven? When I told him how Mr. Dragan—Mr. Tizsa, whatever his name is—could not possibly have done it, he said I must come immediately to Scotland Yard and give you my statement."

Harris, whose mouth had dropped open, now closed it with a gulp. "Me?" he uttered. "He gave you my *name*? Is his lordship with you?"

She waved that aside as a matter of no moment, merely caressing the dog and addressing Dragan. "I have been thinking about it, you see, and though I wasn't perfectly sure last night that you hadn't killed Nancy, I quite see now that you couldn't have."

"And how is that, my lady?" Harris asked, pulling himself together while Dragan held his chair for her. "You are, I take it, Lady Grizelda?"

"How clever of you," the girl marveled, with a smile of thanks cast to Dragan as she sat. "Let me tell you how it was. We were at the opera. My mother asked me to fetch her fan, which I had foolishly left in the pocket of my cloak, and when I retrieved it from the cloakroom, I walked straight into *this* gentleman. Or he walked into me. Either

18

way, I was nearly knocked over. It isn't important, except for the fact that I saw him at the same time as I saw Nancy leaving the theatre. Mr. Tizsa left, too. And then it occurred to me that Nancy had no business to be there, and so I ran out after her. I saw no sign of Mr. Tizsa, but I thought I saw Nancy vanish around the side of the building, so I followed until I found her in the alley."

"Was she alone?"

The girl nodded, and a muscle twitched beside her eye. She was acting, but this, the horror of discovering the murdered body of her maid, was still with her.

"Mr. Tizsa appeared a few moment later. I'd kicked the dagger as I walked toward Nancy and picked it up without thinking what it was. Mr. Tizsa told me that she was dead and took the dagger from me. And then the policeman came. But the thing is, in the time between them leaving the theater and me following them, there just *might* have been time for him to kill her. But there could *not* have been time for him to kill her, run to the end of the alley, run around and come back into the alley from the opposite direction as he did, only seconds after I got there."

Harris and Dragan both stared at her.

Perversely, Dragan said, "I could have run out the nearer entrance just before you got there and hidden."

"Where?" she asked. "There was enough light to see, and I looked very carefully before venturing into the dark alley. Well, one would, wouldn't one?"

"One would," Dragan agreed. He began to like her, whatever she was up to.

She smiled as though satisfied and turned back to the scowling Harris. "My brother, Lord Horace, said that if I made a statement to that effect, you could not charge Mr. Tizsa but would have to go out and discover the true murderer."

"And are you prepared to make a statement to that effect?" Harris asked faintly.

"Of course," she said in surprise.

Harris snapped his fingers, and the constables fell over each other trying to get out of the room, presumably to fetch the paper and pen that appeared only moments later.

"One question," Harris said to him while Lady Grizelda's pen scratched busily across the paper. "Why do you keep a sword and a pistol in your room?"

"Because they are mine. I was an officer of the Hungarian cavalry."

The girl's eyes flickered up to his face, but only briefly. She didn't stop writing.

CHAPTER THREE

A S THEY STEPPED out onto Great Scotland Yard, she heard his sharp intake of breath, as though he relished the fresh air—well, fresh by London's grimy standards. Or perhaps he had just noticed the ostentatious carriage on the other side of the street, emblazoned with the Duke of Kelburn's arms.

"Sometimes, it helps to impress," she murmured as a policeman leapt forward to open the carriage door. Vicky hopped in and took possession of the forward-facing seat. "Home, John, if you please," Griz added cheerfully to the coachman.

"Allow me to drop you somewhere," she said pleasantly and murmured under her breath, "I want to talk to you."

"It would hardly be proper to travel alone with you," Dagan said.

"Oh, no one cares about that," she said impatiently. "No one will see—or care."

She thought curiosity flashed momentarily in his eyes. At any rate, he climbed in after her and sat down on the opposite seat. The horses stepped forward, and the carriage rumbled over the cobbles toward Charing Cross.

His hair was rumpled. A dark stubble shadowed his jaw, and his clothing looked as if he'd slept in it. Which, presumably, he had. Amazingly, none of this detracted from his good looks. In light of this, his steady gaze on her face might have disconcerted her, had she not been such a down-to-earth kind of woman.

"Was any of that true?" he asked abruptly.

"Most of it," she said cautiously.

"But *she*—the Lady Grizelda in there..." He jerked his head back toward Great Scotland Yard. "*She* is not real."

"No," she admitted. "She's a mixture of my sister, my sister-in-law, and a gushing friend I once had. To be honest, I wasn't sure I could pull it off, but it was actually easier than being myself."

"And your dog just happened to slip her leash?"

"It was loose." She gave him a quick, conspiratorial smile. "And I did just happen to notice the open door. All the policemen looked in that direction when I mentioned you."

"And the bits about your brother?"

"Horace? Oh, yes, he is real, and he *is* my brother. He has some kind of authority in the world of law and order."

"Mostly matters of political unrest and sedition."

So, he knew that much. It was not difficult to pick up the distaste in his voice. His mesmeric dark eyes were like agates.

She lifted her chin. "Is that a problem for you?"

"Not for me, no. At least, not yet. Did he send you?"

"Lord, no," she scoffed. "He had no I idea I would come here, though I daresay he will do soon enough. But I *did* ask him where you would be, and he told me. I have to say his name worked like a charm."

A breath of laughter shook him, softening the sudden hardness in his eyes. "You have my gratitude, Lady Grizelda. But why did you do it?"

She sighed, idly stroking the dog's elegant head. "Because when the police took you away last night, it was for the wrong reasons. Something about you made me doubt you had done it, and when I considered it—I couldn't sleep for thinking about Nancy—I realized you *couldn't* have done it. So I resolved to make them release you."

Again, that spark of amusement flared in his eyes, quirked the corner of his mouth. "I may not remain released," he pointed out.

"True. That's one of the reasons we have to find out for ourselves who killed Nancy."

That seemed to deprive him of speech for a moment. Then he asked curiously, "What are your other reasons?"

She looked away, struggling to find the words. "It isn't fair," she said at last. "She shouldn't have died, not like that."

"No one should. And yet it happens all the time."

"I know," she said restlessly. "And I can't do anything about most of it. But Nancy was *ours*. She dressed my hair for the opera."

"She did it beautifully," he said with unexpected gentleness.

"No, she didn't. She wasn't a very good maid, but she was kind, even when she scolded and pried." Her voice cracked, and she stopped talking, staring fiercely out of the window. "Will you help me?"

He leaned forward, and the dog's head lifted warily, watching him, though it was interesting she didn't growl. Dragan didn't seem to notice. "You don't know me. The police are the proper people to find out the truth."

"The police arrested you," she pointed out.

"To be fair, I was standing over the body with a dagger in my hand."

"So was I."

"You are a duke's daughter. I'm a foreign refugee from a failed revolution."

"Exactly!" she said eagerly. "We cannot be influenced by status or names. Even though Horace's was quite useful today."

He sat back. "You should give Inspector Harris a chance. He is not an idiot, by any means."

"I cannot stop Inspector Harris, even if I wished to, which I don't. Besides, Horace will cut off that contact once he knows what I've done."

"Have you considered that it will hardly be safe for you to poke your aristocratic nose into filthy alehouses and rookeries? Which, to be frank, are the likeliest places to discover the murderer."

"Poke my aristocratic nose?" she repeated in outrage, though she spoiled her attempt at dignity by a smothered giggle. Straightening her face to severity, she frowned at him. "Have *you* considered that since she was not robbed of so much as her boots or bonnet, that thieves or beggars are unlikely to be responsible?"

The lack of surprise in his expression told her he had indeed considered the matter. But he said only, "Nevertheless, your thieves and beggars could have seen or heard something, or even been paid to do the killing. Or your arrival scared them off before they could take anything from the body. She was only just dead."

"And we won't know until we ask. Look, we are home. You had better come in for a little to discuss the matter."

He gazed at her in disbelief. "I am in no condition to visit anyone, let alone dukes and duchesses."

"Oh, you won't see *them*," Griz assured him as the carriage came to a halt outside the large house at the corner of Park Lane and Upper Grosvenor Street. "My mother ordered the carriage for midday, otherwise I would let it take you home. Everyone else will have gone out ages ago."

He opened his mouth as if he would dispute the propriety, then he only shrugged and got out, turning to help her. James, the footman who had descended the steps to perform this duty, stood to one side, wooden faced.

Dragan—*Mr. Tizsa*—presented a curious yet dashing figure, hatless and rumpled, but moving with grace and manners, handing her down and escorting her up the steps to the open front door. Vicky, trotting between them, did not appear to object.

Inside, Grizelda took off the leash and her hat, which she gave to Peter, the other downstairs footman, and pointed to a door on the left of the staircase. "We'll just go in there… Could you bring us some tea?

24

And perhaps a sandwich? And scones."

Her main aim was to get out of the way before her mother descended to the carriage, and Dragan was obliging enough to walk quickly in her wake.

The room she had chosen was not used as a public reception room, more of a private meeting place for guests her parents did not wish to come into contact with anyone else. It was small and not terribly well lit from a side window, but it was furnished with a small sofa and two chairs and a low table between.

Dragan, who had not given his cloak to the waiting footman, threw it over the back of a chair.

She sat on the sofa. "You think I am mad."

He shrugged, taking the seat in front of his cloak. "I don't mind insanity. Dishonesty is another matter."

She stared at him. "You don't pull your punches, do you? What exactly are you accusing me of?"

"The weapon on the table in Scotland Yard. You dodged Harris's question, but you *did* recognize it. I think the dog did, too."

Vicky, currently sniffing delicately at his boots, offered a slight wag of her tail as she looked up at him.

Grizelda's stomach twisted. "I hoped I was too scatterbrained for anyone to notice that."

"I don't think you are scatterbrained at all."

"Actually, I am. But not, I hope, about things that matter."

"And why does the dagger matter?"

She considered not telling him or making something up. But she had a feeling he would fall for neither and simply walk away. Lying was not the way to achieve his cooperation.

Fortunately, Peter appeared with a tray of tea, sandwiches, and scones that were still faintly steaming. Fussing with them and waiting for Peter to leave the room gave her time to think. Dragan took something from his pocket—a notebook and a stub of pencil. He opened the book and rested it against his crossed leg. From the corner of her eye, she saw the tiny pencil move, guided by his long, busy fingers. He focused on whatever he was writing while Peter arranged things. They were both silent.

But as the door closed behind the footman and she placed a cup of tea on the table in front of him, he was still waiting for an answer, for his gaze lifted to her face and lingered, steady and expectant.

Without laying down the pencil, he accepted a ham sandwich and rapidly consumed it without breaking his gaze.

"The dagger matters," she said, low, "because it is my father's. He collects antique weapons. When I saw it the lantern light last night, I thought it looked like the one he bought in Rome five or so years ago. I looked at his collection this morning, and the dagger was not there." She frowned with defiance. "He may have taken it to be cleaned or lent it to someone. I have not yet asked him."

"So, what is it you want?" he asked flatly, returning his pencil to paper. "To find the truth of Nancy's murder, or to protect your family?"

She threw up her chin. "You would protect your family, too!"

"For all the good it did them. What do you propose to do?"

Grizelda, her mind caught on the first sentence, had to bite back personal questions. "I think we should start by sharing what we know about Nancy and about last night. How do *you* know her?"

The pencil stilled. He searched her eyes, an oddly disturbing experience. Then his lips curved into a faint, rueful smile. "This is the problem when we neither know nor trust each other. I am not sure how much I can safely tell you."

"I won't repeat it to my brother Horace if that's what worries you."

His brow twitched, as though she had surprised him, though he retorted quickly enough, "How can I know that?"

"I suppose you can't," she admitted, deflated. "You do not care that I am a duke's daughter, or even a lady because you do not believe that confers any special virtue upon me. Being an egalitarian."

He snatched up another sandwich, almost angrily. Half of it vanished in one bite, and he returned to the notebook.

"I lodge with a friend," he said abruptly, without looking up. "A good man. A physician. I met Nancy in his house one afternoon, among several other guests."

"She was his guest?" Griz said, startled, then nodded. "Ah, I see. This good doctor shares your egalitarian views. Was this a political meeting?"

"It was a discussion about improving the health of working people and giving them more say in how they are governed."

Distractedly, Griz picked up a buttered scone and took a bite. He followed the movement with his dark, oddly beautiful eyes.

"Is that not how your revolution began?" she asked.

"Sort of. But acquit me of fomenting revolution in the country that has given me refuge. Such methods failed all over Europe in 48, and I cannot see the British adopting them at this stage. Everything discussed was within the law of your country."

"I did not know Nancy had such political or social awareness," Griz admitted. "In fact, she…"

"She what?" he encouraged, reaching distractedly for his teacup.

Griz frowned. "I asked her just last week, before her afternoon off, if she was still stepping out with Jack Payne—he's the son of one of our tenant farmers in Sussex. She laughed and said *Bless you, no, my lady. I have a* gentleman *going to marry me now.* She was in a hurry to be off, and I forgot to ask her more later. She never introduced the matter again either."

"Do you have any idea who she meant?"

Griz shook her head and sopped her tea. "No. I thought she meant she had met some clerk in London or an affluent upper-servant, but I…" She fixed him with her gaze. "Was it you?"

His lips twisted. "Lord, no. I have nothing to bring anyone in marriage."

There was nothing coy or arch in his denial, a simple, dismissive statement that she was inclined to believe. She wasn't quite sure why it pleased her. "Perhaps your good doctor?" she suggested.

"He's married already. With four children, three of them grown-up."

"I'll ask the other servants," Griz decided.

He nodded, glancing up from the book. He seemed to be drawing rather than writing. "When did you see her last? When she dressed your hair for the opera?"

"Yes."

"How did she seem? Was she happy? Anxious?"

"I think she was a little anxious," Griz admitted. "Certainly, she was distracted." She swallowed. "I didn't ask her why." She straightened her shoulders determinedly. "Why were you there? In the alley?"

"I was looking for her. She sent a note to me in the good doctor's box at the opera, asking me to meet her outside the theatre at the next interval. I was worried enough to go early, which is when I ran into you. But she wasn't outside, so I went looking."

"She left the theatre just ahead of you. I saw her."

He frowned, shaking his head. "Perhaps she was hiding in a doorway? Or around the other side of the theatre? I walked to one side, then came back. When I glanced up the other, I saw a woman's figure disappearing around the corner. That must have been you, but I followed in case it was her."

"Why would she ask you to meet her and then hide from you?" Griz demanded.

"I have no idea. Unless she had seen someone who frightened her. Perhaps she was hiding from *you* because she knew she should not be there."

"Oh dear. I hope I did not cause her to run into danger. She never seemed frightened of me before. To be honest, it was more in her nature to brazen it out."

"Did you let her?" He seemed genuinely interested.

Griz shrugged. "I told her Mrs. MacKenna—our housekeeper—would dismiss her if she caught her. She is a lot more terrifying than I."

"I'm not sure I can imagine that. You broke me out of prison single-handedly, surrounded by policemen."

She regarded him suspiciously. "Are you making fun of me?"

"Far from it. I am wondering how many people underestimate you."

She wasn't quite sure what to make of that, so she asked bluntly, "Do you have any idea who might have killed Nancy, or why?"

"Unless it was a random attack by thieves who ran off when they heard you and I blundering about, no."

"Random thieves who just happened to be in possession of my father's dagger?"

"Don't you think it more likely that Nancy took the dagger?"

"Nancy would not steal!" she exclaimed.

"But she might have borrowed it for her protection. But we are speculating without evidence. We don't even know if it was the dagger that killed her."

"Was there blood on it?" she said, jumping to her feet in agitation.

He rose with her, the open notebook and pencil in his hand. "I don't think so. But it could have been wiped clean by accident or design. Or any blood there might not even have been Nancy's."

The sheer weight of what they did not know crushed her for a moment. But Nancy's poor, dead face was still there before her eyes, awaiting justice, not just from the law, it seemed, but from Grizelda, who should at least have asked the maid what troubled her.

"Will you help me find out?" she asked.

He stared down at her, a shabby, unshaven stranger of dangerous political persuasions. Conflicting emotions swirled in his eyes, among them, surely, a hint of desperation.

"Yes," he said reluctantly. "But not until I wash and change my clothes."

She grinned at him. "Thank you! Do you have a card?"

"A card?" he asked, apparently baffled.

"With your name and address," she explained.

His lips twisted. "No."

"Oh." She darted across to the table, where she showed him paper and pen. "Then write it here, if you please, so that I can find you if I need to."

He hesitated, then did as she asked, leaning over the desk to scrawl the few words. The notebook lay open on the table in front of him.

She watched his face while he wrote, wondering what sort of an ally he would make. Behind the masculine beauty and the self-confessed revolutionary, she recognized both intelligence and pain. A man who had suffered in ways she could only imagine. At this moment, he presented as much of a mystery as Nancy.

It might yet prove to be a mistake—using him to learn about the part of Nancy's life she had no knowledge of.

He pushed the paper toward her, glancing up in time to catch her staring.

"Thank you," she said hastily, picking up the piece of paper and folding it twice. As he reached for the notebook, she saw what he had been drawing.

A likeness of Nancy, her head held at just that angle that could be submissive, mischievous, or coquettish, depending on her mood and her company. She looked peculiarly classless, almost mysterious, her thoughts hidden behind an enigmatic half-smile.

It brought a lump to Grizelda's throat. This was how he had seen her. Still familiar to Griz, but secretive, a young woman with a life beyond the household she had served.

"That is an extraordinary likeness," she said, her voice hollow.

He picked up the notebook and slid it into his pocket. "Thank you. I cannot help thinking, you know, that your family will not approve, either of your quest for justice for Nancy or your alliance with me."

"They won't notice," she said, stuffing the paper with his address into the hidden pocket of her gown.

He looked somewhat startled, but if he meant to comment, she gave him no chance.

"Good," she said briskly. "So, I will speak to the servants, and you will investigate among your radical friends, and then we may meet—tomorrow, perhaps?—and share what we've learned."

He inclined his head, which she took for agreement.

CHAPTER FOUR

D RAGAN FOUND HIMSELF in the unusual position of being manipulated, and yet, too intrigued to object. Besides, had he not already offered this service to Inspector Harris? Who had treated it with the contempt it no doubt deserved.

It was not just the tragic murder of Nancy Barrow that puzzled him now either, but the small, aristocratic girl in the spectacles, whose smile was unexpectedly dazzling.

As he followed her back into the entrance hall, a man leapt down the stairs three at a time and skidded to a halt when he caught sight of Lady Grizelda.

He was, perhaps, about Dragan's age—twenty-four—and sporting a rather fine mustache and an excellently cut coat worn carelessly open to reveal the colorful waistcoat beneath. His expression was amiable but distracted, his features similar enough to Grizelda's to betray a relationship, although his hair was lighter, almost blond.

"All well, Griz?" he said cheerfully. "Because if so, I thought I might go away for a few days, just to slow Her Grace's matchmaking train—" He broke off as he caught sight of Dragan, who refused on principle to hover in the shadows of doorways.

Dragan meant merely to bow distantly to them both and depart, but the newcomer greeted him with careless civility.

"Sorry, didn't realize we had guests!" he said, advancing and holding out his hand.

"Mr. Tizsa," Lady Grizelda said in tones of resignation as they shook hands. "My brother Lord Forsythe Niven. But Forsythe, I don't think you should go away just now. The police will come about Nancy and—"

"Yes, but they won't want to talk to me," Lord Forsythe intervened.

"They may want to talk to all of us," his sister said, lowering her voice. "One of His Grace's daggers was found at the scene."

Lord Forsythe dropped Dragan's hand, staring at his sister. "So were you, Griz."

"And I," Dragan said, feeling her family had better be aware of the worst.

"Well, I'll be damned," Lord Forsythe said, gazing from one to the other. "This is more of a tangle than I thought."

"So you see why you had better not run off very far?" Grizelda said anxiously.

"His Grace," Lord Forsythe said heavily, "will not be pleased."

"Look on the bright side," Grizelda said wryly, "your marriage prospects will plummet."

Lord Forsythe grinned. "Oh well, I daresay Horace will be able to hush it all up, anyhow. Got to dash, but a pleasure to meet you, Mr. Tizsa!"

Lady Grizelda seemed to see nothing odd in this behavior, as her brother had appeared to see nothing unusual in Dragan's presence, for she merely walked on to the center of the hall while the door banged shut behind Lord Forsythe. One of the liveried footmen shot out from the back of the house and took up position beside the front door.

Lady Grizelda turned and extended her hand. "Goodbye, Mr. Tizsa."

He took her hand politely. Ungloved, it was soft and birdlike, unexpectedly frail. He bowed over it and released her. "Goodbye."

She gave a small, uncertain smile as he strode past her to the door.

The servant appeared perfectly wooden as he let him out, but Dragan was sure he had an opinion about ill-dressed, ill-shaven foreigners.

LETTING HIMSELF INTO Cordell's house with his key, Dragan fully expected the wrath of his kind hosts to descend upon him at some point. He was not prepared for the explosion of three people out of the kitchen door at the end of the hall or to have his hands grasped by both Mrs. Cordell and her second daughter, while the third grinned at him from behind with unfeigned delight.

"Dragan, thank God!" Mrs. Cordell exclaimed. "The police were here, searching your room! I have never been so mortified in my life. *Has that poor young man not suffered enough in his own country?* I said to them. *Must he suffer persecution in our supposedly civilized country, too?* You can be sure they left much more shame-faced than they arrived, and I made sure they took nothing with them!"

"I'm so sorry you were subjected to that," Dragan said seriously, allowing himself to be dragged into the parlor.

"They said Nancy Barrow was dead," Annie, the middle daughter, burst out. "They said you had been arrested for her murder!"

"Both are true," Dragan allowed. "I found Nancy, you see, but I could not save her. She was already dead."

"Oh, my dear," said Mrs. Cordell, pressing him into a chair. "Poor Nancy. What in the world happened to her?"

"We'll know more soon," Dragan said evasively. "At least they are aware I did not do it and so will look for whoever did." He stood up again. "Forgive me, I spent the night locked up with several other miscreants, and I can't imagine I am pleasant company. Excuse me, while I change…"

To his relief, they let him go, although they seemed avid for his story. He was reluctant to speak of Lady Grizelda's part in the tale for many reasons.

Only when he had washed thoroughly from head to toe, shaved, and dressed in a clean shirt and his only other trousers and coat did he notice his hat placed on the center of his bed. He smiled, for he had left it at the opera last night. Cordell must have picked it up.

Clapping it on his head, he picked up his small, battered medical bag and walked quietly downstairs.

"Just going to the clinic!" he called and hastily let himself out of the house.

By now, he had made the journey so often that his feet knew the way without any interference from his brain, which spent the time mulling over Grizelda Niven and her connection to the murder.

Dragan had seen enough violence in the last three years to know that given the right circumstances, anyone was capable of anything. As far as he could tell, Grizelda was the only person he knew of with the time to have killed Nancy. And the weapon belonged to her family. She was undoubtedly troubled by last night's events, a disturbance not unfree of guilt.

But guilt was not necessarily an emotion of truth, and for the life of him, he could not imagine her killing her maid. She was not so stupid or so ill-disciplined. And she really did not seem the kind of person to hurt someone beneath her, a dependent of her family. She did not even care that Nancy hadn't been very good at her job.

Exactly what sort of person was Lady Grizelda Niven?

Pretty, eccentric, an idle, aristocratic lady with too much time on her hands. With acting skills that seemed to surprise even herself.

He came back to his own surroundings with a start, to realize he was already in the waiting room of Dr. Cordell's surgery. It was several months since he had lost so much time in his head. But at least he had been thinking of only one death and one very much alive young woman. He hadn't abandoned himself to the horror and grief of war.

He nodded to the waiting patients, some of whom he recognized. They smiled at him. Someone greeted him by name.

"Good afternoon, Dr. Tizsa," Mrs. Johns said in surprise. A respectable widow, she acted as their secretary three days a week. "Dr. Cordell didn't think you would be here today."

"Neither did I," Dragan said cheerfully, "but here I am."

The afternoon passed in a flurry, as their clinic often did, situated as it was on the boundary of Kensington's relatively affluent neighborhood and the poorer streets beyond. There was neither time nor inclination to talk to Cordell about anything other than medical matters until they were walking home together at the end of the day.

"What happened?" Cordell demanded bluntly, his bushy brows contracted, his piercing blue eyes fixed on Dragan.

Dragan told him, ending with an apology for ruining his family's rare treat to the opera and causing the indignity of a police search, both of which the doctor waved impatiently aside.

"Why the devil did Nancy Barrow want to see you?" Cordell demanded. "What was so urgent that she had to drag you out of the opera?"

"I have no idea. I cannot even guess, for I know nothing about her life. How do you know her?"

"I don't, really. She came the first time with Mrs. Fisher, from curiosity, I always thought. It never seemed to me her heart was in the cause. In fact, I assumed she came back because of you."

"Me?" Dragan said, startled.

"You stepped out with her, did you not?"

"No," Dragan said, scowling. "I took her for tea once and to the theatre once because she asked me to take the place of a friend who had let her down. I was *not* her lover."

"Annie thinks you were."

Dragan blinked. "I can't think why. Apparently, she—Nancy—told her employer she was about to marry a gentleman. Who could that be?"

"You?"

Dragan waved that impatiently aside. "I hadn't even seen her for a month."

"And yet, whatever trouble she was in, she came to you."

Dragan mulled over the oddity of that, not for the first time. "I need to go the inquest, discover how she died, and if the dagger they found was the one that killed her. Would the coroner even look to see if the weapon matches the wound?"

"I hope so. Since she worked for the Duke of Kelburn, I imagine they will pay a little more attention than for some homeless stray."

"Hmm... What do you know of the duke? Or his family?"

"Nothing," Cordell replied dryly. "We don't exactly move in the same circles."

"But you know Lord Horace, do you not?"

"Goodness, no, not personally. It was one of his assistants I met once. Gabriel. Colorless individual yet full of his lordship's importance, came by especially to remind me of the laws and my responsibilities."

"Then do you think Lord Horace knew of your group? Was his office watching Nancy?"

Cordell frowned at him. "Imperfect as this country is, it is not the Austrian Empire! Of course, they were not watching her! Or me. I am well aware of the law *and* my responsibilities."

"I know," Dragan said mildly. "What of the rest of the family? Do you know of a Lord Forsythe? A Lady Grizelda?"

"Have you ever seen me read the society pages?"

Dragan sighed. "No. But you do live in this town. Nancy was a housemaid, but she seemed also to act as lady's maid for Grizelda. Grizelda—found the body, you know."

"Ah. I see." Cordell lapsed into thought. "Do you know Jeremy Battsby?"

"No."

"Patient of mine. His brother was a friend at university. He asked me to take another look at his arm, which got broken in a hunting accident. We could go over there after dinner if you like. He will know the Kelburns. For whatever his opinion is worth…"

"NOT REALLY FRIENDS of mine," Mr. Battsby said cheerfully, two hours later, while Cordell examined his arm. "Their society's a bit rarified for an old wastrel like me. The duke's a huge political figure, of course, and his eldest, the Marquess of Monkton, seems to be following in the footsteps. Bit of a stuffed shirt, to be frank."

"What about Lord Horace?" Dragan asked.

"Ah. Different kettle of fish." He thought about it. "Much more substance, but one never quite knows what that substance is. Don't find him comfortable company. Forsythe, now, is a pleasant young fellow. And Lady Azelea…" He smiled and kissed his free hand expressively.

"A beauty?" Dragan hazarded.

"And some. They all are, of course. Lady Rosemary and Lady Athena both took London by storm. And Paris."

"And Lady Grizelda?"

"Don't know her," Battsby said regretfully. "I suppose she must have done the Season, though I don't recall her. But if she is anything like her sisters, she will be dazzling."

GRIZELDA FELT EXHAUSTED by the end of the day.

It was harrowing, talking to the shocked servants, explaining about Nancy's death, cutting through their grief to warn that the police would probably wish to speak to them.

"There is nothing to worry about," Griz assured them as they gathered around her in the servants' hall. "Just answer their questions truthfully, because it is their job to discover who did this to Nancy. I know we all want the culprit found." She turned to Mrs. MacKenna, the housekeeper, who stood beside her, pale and tight-lipped. "Shall we talk in your room, Mrs. MacKenna?"

"Over the last few days, did Nancy seem unusually distracted or worried to you?" she asked the housekeeper as soon as they were seated in her cozy room.

"She never really had her mind on the work in hand." Mrs. MacKenna blew her nose defiantly. "But maybe, yes, a little."

"Did you ask her what was wrong?"

Mrs. MacKenna shook her drooping head.

"Neither did I," Griz confessed. "Whatever bothered her didn't necessarily lead to her death, though. Did she ever mention to you anything about marrying a gentleman?"

The housekeeper snorted. "No. I make sure the girls know their place, which is *not* thinking they can marry gentlemen! Only trouble comes from such delusions."

"But did she have a young man? Did she go out and meet him on her day off?"

"She was always rushing off somewhere. Late back, too, often enough. But who she saw and what she did, she never confided to me."

"Did you know she had gone out last night?"

"No. She went to her room when the work was done but promised she would wait up for you."

Griz sighed. "Who were her closest friends among the staff? Janet?"

Mrs. MacKenna nodded. "And Emmie."

"None of the footmen?"

"I don't allow fraternizing with the male staff."

"Of course not," Griz said hurriedly. "But she did work beside them."

"I think they flirted a little," Mrs. MacKenna said reluctantly. "But there was never anything in it. In fact, in recent weeks, if anything, she was more aloof. Almost looking down on them."

"Because of her more gentlemanly suitor?"

The housekeeper shrugged. "I couldn't say, my lady. I really couldn't."

Griz walked to the window, which looked out onto the kitchen garden, and back again. "Mrs. MacKenna, was she liked belowstairs? Was there ever any trouble with her? Between her and any of the other staff?"

"She was liked well enough. I grumbled at her occasionally, told her off for gossiping. She was always too interested in everyone—"

"The other staff?" Griz interrupted.

"Yes. And the family and their guests. But never in a nasty way. She was just...*interested,* as I said. I don't think she was malicious at all."

"I never thought so," Griz agreed. "Look, can you send Emmie and Janet in to me, here? I'd like to talk to them before the police come."

Two minutes later, the two maids edged nervously into the housekeeper's room and stood before her.

"Sit down," Griz invited, indicating the two stools she had already pulled forward for the purpose. "And don't look so worried. I'm only trying to work out what happened to poor Nancy, and anything you can tell me might help. Did you know she left the house yesterday evening?"

The maids glanced at one another, then Janet nodded miserably. "She asked us not to tell. Said she'd be back before you came home."

"Did she say where she was going?"

Both shook their heads.

"Do either of you have any idea?"

Another exchange of glances. Then Emmie said, "We thought she was away to meet her fancy man."

"Her fancy man?" Griz pounced on the scornful phrase. "Do you mean this gentleman she was expecting to marry her?"

The maids nodded, looking relieved that she had heard of this personage.

"Do you know his name?" Griz asked.

"I don't think she ever said it," Janet replied.

"But did you guess?" Griz persisted.

"Not really," Janet said grudgingly.

"Unless she went back to the foreign gent," Emmie volunteered.

Grizelda's stomach twisted. "What foreign gent?"

"Someone she had high hopes of at the beginning of the year," Janet said, "but she'd given up on him."

"You don't know that," Emmie argued.

"I do. She spoke differently about this new man."

"Maybe she just had the foreign gent more securely attached. After all, who has time to meet all these so-called gentlemen?"

"Do you know the foreign gentleman's name?" Griz asked. She found she was crossing her fingers in the folds of her gown. Because she wanted the name and didn't want it to be Dragan Tizsa's.

"No." Both maids shook their heads.

"But she went on about him being the most handsome man," Janet volunteered, "and how we would all envy her."

"Did she say where she had met him?"

Again, they shook their heads.

"And this new man," Griz pursued. "Did she describe him in such glowing terms?"

"Don't think she described him much at all," Emmie offered. "Which is why I kept thinking he was the same man."

Griz sighed. "Very well. Don't be afraid to tell the police any of this, should they ask. Oh, one last thing. Did you find her a bit troubled over the last few days? Do you know what was bothering her?"

"No, my lady," they chorused, jumping up and curtseying.

For the first time, Griz suspected they were not telling the truth. She was wondering how best to persuade them when their whispering at the door caught her attention.

"You had better tell me," Griz advised.

"We promised not to," Janet said miserably, coming back into the room. "But I suppose it doesn't really matter now she's dead. Except for her family. But you'll know what to do for the best, my lady." She lowered her voice. "Nancy was going to have a baby. She was pregnant."

CHAPTER FIVE

UNTIL SHE WANDERED from habit into the library just before the dinner hour, she had forgotten that she had yet to face her parents—and Horace. Annoyed for failing to have invited herself to dine at her friend Annabelle's house, she almost turned back to request a tray in her room instead. However, since this was both craven and unlikely to diffuse the situation, she quickly gave up the idea and peered around the door.

Her heart lifted to find neither of her parents there, only her brothers Horace and Forsythe. And, she saw with happiness, a guest—Horace's colleague Mr. Gabriel, whose presence, she hoped, would rein in Horace's anger. Not that she was afraid of Horace, but it was tedious and distracting to endure one of his lectures.

"What are we celebrating?" Forsythe asked as Horace handed sherry glasses to him and Mr. Gabriel. "Have the police caught the swine who killed poor, little Nancy?"

"Oh, no, this is a much more important case," Horace said, "concerning the whole country. Gabriel has proved to be something of a genius, following whispers to a very unlikely source, and the result is we've brought down a whole gang of treasonous dogs in the rookeries. Why—" He broke off as his gaze fell on Griz wandering into the room, and he frowned as though trying to remember why he was cross with her.

Luck appeared to be still on her side.

"Lady Grizelda," Mr. Gabriel greeted her with a civil bow. A serious man of middle height and mild if gentlemanly appearance, he was a frequent and comfortable guest at Kelburn House.

"Good evening," she replied cheerfully, nodding to the three men in careless fashion. "How do you do, Mr. Gabriel? I hear you are to be congratulated on your recent engagement!"

Gabriel, who had always appeared to her a rather cold fish, actually blushed, which was rather endearing. "Thank you, ma'am, it is a matter of great happiness to me."

"As it should be," she said warmly. "I look forward to meeting the lady."

"I shall be honored to introduce her. Lady Trench has been kind enough to invite us both to her soiree next week."

The invitation was, Griz thought, pleased, one of her eldest sister's random acts of kindness to those beneath her on the social scale.

"Excellent," she approved, smiling, and turned to her brothers. "Are Their Graces out for the evening?"

"Dining with the Russells," Horace replied. "So, you get to play hostess, God help us. Griz, what the devil do you mean by going to Great Scotland Yard and bandying my name around?"

She should have known better. Of course, he had not forgotten, whatever major success had momentarily distracted him.

She shrugged. "Well, I thought they were more likely to listen to me if I said I was your sister. And I really did feel obliged to give my statement when I discovered they had arrested the wrong man for poor Nancy's murder." She dropped onto the nearest sofa and smiled vaguely. "I wanted to do the right thing."

Horace stared at her. "Very laudable. But how the devil do you *know* he was the wrong man?"

"Didn't you read my statement?" she asked innocently.

Horace narrowed his eyes. "Harris showed it to me. I had to agree you were a truthful person, but wild to a fault. It is not easy to explain to someone why one's sister was gallivanting in dark alleys in the neighborhood of Covent Garden!"

"I was at the opera."

"I have yet to discover they sing outside," Horace said with heavy sarcasm.

"You know I was trying to speak to Nancy," she said reproachfully.

"She meant it for the best, Horace, let her be," Forsythe interjected. "She was pretty shaken, you know."

"Exactly!" Horace exploded.

"Lady Grizelda," Mr. Gabriel intervened, "must be unaware of the many dangers lying in wait for an unprotected lady in such areas. If you knew the world as we do, my lady, you would never venture into such places as Mudd Lane, alone or otherwise."

"I understand," Griz said meekly.

"You should have come to me," Horace added, scowling. "Don't go behind my back to policemen."

"Very well." She jumped to her feet with relief as Berry, the butler, announced dinner.

⫸⫷

SINCE CORDELL'S PRACTICE was not normally busy on a Saturday, Dragan had the day to himself. He used most of it to follow a trail of Nancy Barrow's known acquaintances, which led him to some more interesting places than he expected.

At last, he dropped into the coffee house in Tottenham Court Road, where he often met friends, particularly those who had escaped Hungary with him. He almost didn't go in, for it was always a bittersweet experience, reminding him of home and all he had lost. But it seemed he couldn't wean himself off the habit. They were the only people who truly understood.

As usual, he left them both recharged and melancholic.

Almost as soon as he walked out of the shop, he had to side-step someone running hell for leather down the road.

"Sorry!" the runner yelled, then skidded to a halt. It was a lad whose broken wrist he had set not long after arriving in London. "Will you come?" he gasped. "I was looking for Dr. Cordell, but it turns out you are closer!"

"What has happened?" Dragan asked, resigned.

"Old Marty at the soup kitchen was taken ill."

"I know the way."

The soup kitchen in St. Giles was a brave charity run by a Mr. Wells, a clergyman who seemed to be vaguely attached to the parish church. Wells appeared to be a good man, apparently unworldly by his speech, and yet he was responsible for many practical good works among his poor and often dangerous flock, including the running of a soup kitchen in a not quite derelict building close to the church.

To Dragan's surprise, the lad, who he thought was called Bill, strode along beside him.

"I work for Mr. Wells now," he said proudly. "And the vicar."

"Good for you," Dragan said, surprised but pleased. "How did that come about?"

"Couldn't thieve with my wrist broken, could I? Couldn't work at much either. Ended up in the soup kitchen, and I cleaned the tables one-handed, just for something to do. Helped him more as my wrist got better. Like it better than thieving. Here we are."

The place smelled of over-cooked food and unwashed humanity. Once, it might have offended Dragan. Now, he had smelled much worse.

The tables were still set up in the kitchen, though most of the diners had gone, save for a group standing in a huddle to one side. Between then, Dragan glimpsed a man stretched out on the floor.

"I brought the doctor," Bill said, and the vicar turned toward them.

"Excellent." Mr. Wells held out his hand in a welcoming plea. For a moment, his expression was baffled, then his face cleared. "Ah, you are the assistant, of course! Here is your patient. He just collapsed, clutching his chest, clearly in pain."

The solemn watchers, who appeared to be a mix of the vicar's diners and his charitable helpers, parted to let Dragan through. A rough-looking old man in a coat tied with string lay on the floor with his eyes shut. His head was pillowed on a rolled-up cloak or blanket, and one of Mr. Wells's charitable ladies knelt beside the patient, stroking the pock-marked old forehead.

"He is still breathing," she said anxiously, twisting around to face him.

Dragan gazed down at the bespectacled beauty of Lady Grizelda Niven. Her smooth, brown hair was pinned rather more severely than on their previous meetings, and her garments were old and drab, her skirts narrow to the point of unfashionable. Lady Grizelda incognita?

He would have laughed at her ludicrous expression of surprise, except that he suspected his own face mirrored it. And in any case, he was in a hurry to reach his patient. He crouched on the other side of Marty, dropping his bag and finding his stethoscope by feel. Only when he had listened to the old man's heart and was taking his pulse did he murmur to Grizelda, "This is becoming a habit."

"You are a doctor?" she exclaimed with unflattering astonishment.

"Opinions vary." He released Marty's wrist and gazed at the tranquil face. "Feeling better?"

The eyes opened, watery and a little muddy. "Am I dying?"

"No, you seem to be recovering. Is the pain gone?"

"Yes, but—"

As he lifted his head, trying to get up, Dragan held him down by the shoulder. "No, no, stay put for a little. The strain on your heart has been considerable. Where do you live?"

"He don't live anywhere," Bill supplied. "Sleeps rough, wherever he can."

"That is part of the problem," Dragan murmured. "Marty, is there anywhere you can stay even for few days? Somewhere comfortable you can rest up?"

"Got no family left," Marty said matter-of-factly. "Don't worry, though. I'll take my chances on the street, as I always do."

"An alternative would be better. Even a hostel at night."

"He could stay with me for a week in the outhouse," Bill suggested, looking at Mr. Wells. "I can make him up a bed and look after him until he's back on his feet."

"Excellent plan," Mr. Wells beamed.

Dragan took a large bottle from his bag and poured about a quarter of it into a smaller bottle he handed to Bill. It was merely a general tonic when what the man needed, what the man truly needed was impossible—a complete change of diet and way of life.

"Give him a little of this night and morning. It should help a little. But Marty, no more spirits. I'll come by your house tomorrow, if that is allowed, sir?" He glanced at Mr. Wells, who nodded enthusiastically. "Just to be sure he doesn't lapse. Can he lie here for another hour? And then, perhaps return with Bill? He must rest for several days."

"It shall be just as you say," Mr. Wells assured him.

Dragan packed away his bag and stood, slinging it over his shoulder. "Until tomorrow," he said to Marty and stepped over him, just as Grizelda sprang to her feet. She smelled of orange blossom and fresh air, an unexpected delight to his senses.

He couldn't help smiling at her, which seemed to take her completely by surprise.

"Goodness, look at the time!" Mr. Wells exclaimed. "Billy, run and fetch a hackney for her ladyship. Her family must be worrying by now."

"Oh, no," Grizelda said in apparent surprise. "Bill, you stay with Marty. Mr. Tizsa can take me to the hackney stand." She bolted away from him into a back room, from which she emerged with her bonnet and cloak.

At least she wasn't insane enough to walk these streets alone.

She was dressed, he realized, with more plainness and less style than on either of their two previous meetings. Perhaps she had hoped to blend in with an old dull grey gown and cloak with a plain, unadorned bonnet.

"What on earth are you doing here?" he murmured as he held open the front door for her to precede him into the street. He followed quickly, letting the door fall shut behind him while he scanned the street for lurking dangers. "Did Nancy come here? Did she know Mr. Wells?"

"Oh, no. I always come here on Saturdays. And Tuesdays."

He glanced at her with a different sort of appreciation. "You are quite remarkable, are you not?"

She laughed, a low, pleasant sound, short but genuinely amused. "Lord, no. It's almost obligatory for a lady to be involved in charitable works."

"Then your parents approve?" he asked in fresh surprise, taking her arm and crossing the road to avoid unsavory shadows in a nearby doorway. "Of you coming to *St. Giles?*"

She considered. "I'm not perfectly sure that they know. I am more interested in your presence. You are a physician as well as a soldier? What else do you do?"

"Believe, me, no one is more aware of the moral conflict." Although he spoke lightly, she cast him an unexpectedly piercing look. "But no, I am not actually a physician," he added hastily. "The revolution got in the way, and I did not sit my final exams. So, I don't practice here as such. I merely assist Dr. Cordell."

"Did you practice on the battlefield?"

"I was often all they had." To his relief, they were emerging from the narrow, threatening streets of St. Giles and approaching the stand where several carriages were waiting, and he found he was reluctant to let her go. "Why are you traveling by hackney?"

"My mother always uses the carriage at this time of day," she said blithely.

"Does she not expect you to accompany her?"

"Lord, no, not since I was twenty and was accidentally rude to a marchioness. Have you discovered much about Nancy?"

"Nothing very helpful." Reluctantly, he opened the carriage door. "Have you?"

"A little, but we can't talk comfortably here. Can I drop you somewhere?"

His temptation had little to do with saving his shoe leather. She intrigued him too much, and that annoyed him. He did not wish to be at her beck and call.

"I'm going in the opposite direction," he said curtly, "but I thank you."

She showed neither disappointment nor disapproval, which made him feel unreasonable. "Oh. Well, can you come to Hyde Park around half-past five? I'll be close to the Exhibition building." She climbed into the hackney, and he closed the door.

Perversely, he found himself ridiculously glad that he would see her again today after all. For some reason, she made his world brighter.

"Kelburn House," he told the driver. "Park Lane."

>>><<<

Promenading in the park at the traditionally fashionable hour had seemed to Grizelda the perfect cover for meeting an acquaintance "by chance." On the other hand, the park was likely to be full of people who knew her family, so she could hardly go unaccompanied.

Before she changed her dress, she scribbled a note to her married friend Annabelle and sent a footman scurrying across to Brooke Street to deliver it.

When she had changed her dress to a full, cambric gown embroidered with lavender, over several wide petticoats, she brushed out and repinned her hair in a still plain but less severe style.

Without warning, a pang for Nancy hit her. To have lost everything, and in such a way... She must not lose sight of that. Her excitement should be for discovering the truth, not for encountering the intriguing Mr. Tizsa again. But if they went hand in hand... well, she would rather like him for a friend. He wasn't like anyone else she had ever met. His words were rarely serious, and yet his eyes were never anything else.

Blinking away the vision, she stood, donned the matching mantle and the new hat her sister Azalea had given her. Then, she picked up the leash, much to Vicky's delight.

Half an hour later, she and Annabelle made their way toward Hyde Park on foot, Vicky alternately tugging at the leash and trying to hide among Grizelda's skirts.

"So, am I assisting at an assignation?" Annabelle asked hopefully.

"Don't be ridiculous," said Griz, who had expected just such a comment at some point in the expedition. "We're meeting someone who is helping me find out what happened to Nancy."

Annabelle frowned. "Yes, that was terrible, horrible. But Griz, finding her does not make you responsible. The police will catch whoever did this horrible thing. It isn't up to *you*."

It is. She blinked several times to dispel the emotion.

"Griz—"

"Look, it's quite busy," Griz interrupted brightly, nodding ahead. They entered the park by the Grosvenor Gate and turned down the path toward the Serpentine.

Annabelle said nothing for some time, then, "I suppose I understand and am even willing to help. But Griz, have you considered, this could be extremely dangerous?"

"That is why I have Mr. Tizsa," Griz said.

"Hmm. I look forward to making his acquaintance, but frankly, one of your footmen would make a better bodyguard."

"Mr. Tizsa is a soldier."

Annabelle squared her shoulders as though ready to do battle, which amused Griz and caused a rush of affection for her old friend.

"How are the Timothies?" Griz asked, covering Annabelle's husband and son in one question, and for some time was able to lose herself in the happy anecdotes of her friend's household.

However, behind everything, she was aware of a faint tension, a worry that Dragan would not come. She had sensed a distance in him when she had suggested the meeting, as though he regretted their alliance.

"I have to say," Annabelle broke off to comment as they approached the Exhibition Hall, "this is the most extraordinary building I have ever seen. I thought it would look ridiculous, but somehow it doesn't."

It was, indeed, a spectacular structure of steel and so much glass that the newspapers had dubbed it the Crystal Palace. It was to be a temporary building only, to house the Great Exhibition due to open next month. A few bits of scaffolding remained, but it was more or less ready.

"If the exhibits are half as fun as this edifice," Griz remarked, "I shall enjoy coming here."

"Timothy says there will be so much to see that we will need to come several times to take it all in."

Grizelda's gaze was darting around the passers-by. "I think I shall buy a season ticket so that I can drop in whenever I... Ah, there he is." The last words spilled from her as she caught sight of him. Carelessly, shabbily elegant, he held his hat in his hand, his head tipped up to examine the structure before him. The spring sunshine glinted on his raven hair, emphasizing the sharp, sculpted lines of his face. Her heart gave a funny little leap.

"*That* is your Mr. Tizsa?" Annabelle hissed. "Oh, my dear, he may not be respectable, but he is...*gorgeous!*"

"I thought it was just me," Griz said, relieved.

"You and every other female with eyes."

Griz wasn't quite sure she liked that. While it seemed to lessen her own reaction to him as merely normal, the idea of every woman ogling him was somehow distasteful.

However, there was no time to dwell on that, for as they approached him, he brought his gaze back to earth and saw them.

His lips quirked, and he walked immediately toward them. Vicky began to scrabble in his direction. He bowed with drawing-room grace.

"This is Mr. Tizsa, Annabelle," Griz said. "Sir, my friend Mrs. Worth."

"How do you do?" Dragan said politely.

"Delighted to make your acquaintance," Annabelle replied faintly.

Unexpectedly, Dragan dropped to a crouch and held out his hand to the skittish Vicky, who deigned to sniff the long, bronzed fingers before actually pressing into him.

"She seems to remember you," Griz observed, watching Dragan stroke the dog's head. She felt oddly breathless.

"I'm not surprised," Annabelle murmured, adding hastily, "I hear you are one of Mr. Kossuth's heroic Hungarians."

He glanced up at her, his eyes narrowed against the sun. "I don't think of myself like that." He rose, and Vicky, abandoned, crept back to Grizelda's skirts.

"But you held out so long against the emperor," Annabelle enthused. "Who we all know to be a great tyrant. We were all cheering for the Hungarians here in Britain, weren't we, Griz?"

"Most of us were sympathetic," Griz muttered, allowing Vicky to pull her on along the path. The others followed close behind.

"Did you rank very high in the Hungarian army?" Annabelle asked, and Griz began to suspect her friend's ploy was at least as much to discover his background as to simply admire.

"I was a mere captain of cavalry."

"How exciting," Annabelle murmured, and Griz could tell she was relieved that he had been an officer. "And your family? Did they flee with you? Or are they still in Hungary? Are they safe?"

"I have no close family."

"And I suppose you must have lost everything, your land...?"

"I had no land."

Griz didn't know whether to laugh or cringe at this blatant interrogation.

"Forgive me," Annabelle said brightly. "I assumed you were of the nobility."

Griz spun around to put a stop to the questioning and found him regarding her friend with tolerant but sardonic humor.

"I was a true revolutionary who marched in the streets to *scare* the nobility. But for what it's worth, my elder brother had the land, such as it was. He died defending it."

Whatever Annabelle would have replied to that was lost as someone hailed her by name, and she was forced to turn and greet people Griz vaguely recognized. In a flurry of bows and greetings, Annabelle introduced Dragan.

Griz was able to stand back and observe, as she often did. Annabelle clearly assumed everyone else was acquainted by name and did not introduce the newcomers. But the recognition was clearly only vague. Had they known she was the Duke of Kelburn's daughter, she would never have been able to stay on the fringes of the group, watching as both the older lady and the younger vied for Dragan's attention. One of the men, perhaps a brother, got deliberately in the way of that, and in the more general discussion, Dragan, too, stepped back beside Grizelda.

This was the opportunity she had waited for—Annabelle occupied but still close enough for her to count as a chaperone.

Abetted by Vicky, Griz stepped closer and met his gaze.

"Nancy was pregnant," she breathed.

His eyes widened. "By whom?"

"I don't know. Presumably the gentleman she expected to marry her." Griz glanced at the others and moved further away from the path. "It wasn't you, was it?"

"I?" He stared at her. "I was never her lover."

Griz flushed, more at the word lover than at the impropriety of her accusation. She let herself be pulled by the leash in the direction of the trees and shrubs.

"I only bring it up," she said matter-of-factly, "because her friends had the impression she was... er... walking out with a foreign gentleman at the beginning of the year. Their opinions varied as to whether or not this foreigner was the same person as the gentleman she expected to marry."

Dragan frowned, but he did not look angry, merely as if trying to rearrange his thoughts. "I had not seen her for several weeks before I received her note at the theatre. Before that, we had tea together once, and I escorted her to the theatre on another occasion. She seemed an interesting person, but I barely knew her. I certainly had no thoughts of marriage. I'd be astonished if she had any about me."

"Why?" Griz asked frankly. "Because you are not of the same class?"

He waved that aside. "More because she...lost interest. I don't think I was who she expected me to be. For my part, I found her not to be as thoughtful as I had originally imagined."

"Perhaps she thought you were rich because you are a gentleman. A Hungarian nobleman who is also a hero is quite an exotic prize to show off to friends."

"She never introduced me to friends," he said impatiently. "But if I am the foreign gentleman, whose baby was she carrying?"

"I don't know, but the maids told me her pregnancy was not far advanced. It must have been someone she met after you. In fact, she probably lost interest in you because she met *him*."

"Possible," Dragan said doubtfully, adjusting his course to stay parallel with Annabelle's party. "Did her friends have no clue as to his identity? Even a first name? A hair color?"

"None that they told me. But I don't believe they ever met him, and Nancy seems to have been very secretive for such a talkative girl. I had no idea of her interest in politics or social problems."

"I had the impression she was curious," Dragan offered. "A little like you. But I never discovered what, if anything, was behind it."

"Flirting, probably."

He glanced at her in surprised amusement. "Why would you think that?"

"My dear sir, we women are all but trained to look interested in whatever you men are talking about and to ask questions to encourage you."

"Alas, we are sadly easy to manipulate," he agreed without obvious offense. "However, while *you* might be taught that is the way to catch a desirable husband, I imagine Nancy's education was a little more practical."

Griz thought about that for a little, before her mind jumped back, and she said abruptly, "I hope you did not mind Annabelle's questions. She did not mean to be rude. *Or* to flirt."

"I know. She was trying to find out if she needed to protect you from me. And since we have fallen further behind, we should—"

Without warning, something catapulted out of the trees on their right and cannoned straight into Dragan, knocking him to the ground.

CHAPTER SIX

FROZEN, GRIZ COULD only watch in astonishment as an anguished, furious man reared up, raising his fist, clearly ready to smash it down on Dragan's face. Sudden recognition broke her paralysis, even as Vicky snarled and tugged forward.

Griz clung to the lead. "Jack Payne, don't you dare!"

She didn't even have to shout, for he was barely a foot away from her. His head jerked round, eyes widening in horror, even as Dragan heaved beneath him, throwing him off. Jack went with the momentum, leaping off and bolting for the trees.

Before Griz could say a word, Dragan sprang to his feet and gave chase like a hound after a fox.

"Oh, the devil!" Griz muttered. She spared the time only to glance at Annabelle's group, some yards parallel to her and a little ahead. None of them were looking in her direction. She walked quickly toward the trees with Vicky, trying to appear casual to any observers.

In the admittedly feeble cover of the trees, she broke into a run, but they were not difficult to find. Dragan had caught up with the shorter but burlier Jack, dragging him around to face him. Jack swung a wild punch, which Dragan easily dodged, then caught Jack's wrist as the next blow descended. There was a flurry of skidding feet, and Dragan twisted. He held the furious Jack immobile with one arm wrenched up his back.

"Move, and I'll break it," Dragan said shortly. His gaze fell on Griz.

She advanced, holding her skirts clear of the mud. "I thought you cavalrymen fought on horseback."

"Not always. You know this man?"

"Jack Payne. His father is one of our Sussex tenants. We played together as children. At one time, he and Nancy had an understanding."

Dragan did not relax his hold, although the hard look on his face vanished.

Griz addressed her old playmate. "If Mr. Tizsa releases you, will you talk without fighting?"

Panting, Jack stared at her, then looked away and nodded.

Dragan released him without stepping back. His erstwhile captive shook himself.

"What are you doing in London, Jack?" Griz demanded.

"I came to see Nancy," Jack muttered. "Make her see sense. But when I got to the house, they told me she was dead, killed by some foreigner that *you* knew. I found out his name, where he lived, and I followed him here." He glared at Dragan. "I never knew you were with him here, my lady, but you should be warned against him."

"Well, no, you see, it was I who found Nancy, Jack, and Mr. Tizsa is the one man who could *not* have killed her. In fact, we are trying to find out who did. Though I do think," she added in a different tone, "that it was very clever of you to discover Mr. Tizsa. Um… who told you his name?"

"Peter, the footman," Jack said grudgingly, rubbing his shoulder. "He heard you introducing him to Lord Forsythe."

"And gossip runs amok at Kelburn House," Griz said ruefully. "I suppose it is no wonder. But truly, Jack, you cannot go about attacking strangers because someone tells you they are a murderer. The police already arrested Mr. Tizsa and let him go when they discovered the truth."

Jack swung away. "Who would do such a thing to her? Surely only those who had filled her head with nonsense, trying to entice her up the wrong path?"

"There are many dangerous people in London," Griz said, touching his arm. "It needn't have been anything to do with her or her personal life. She may just have been in the wrong place at the wrong time. But you must leave it to the police to discover the truth." She crossed her finger surreptitiously among her skirts. "His Grace will make sure they do."

Dragan stirred. "How long have you been in London, Mr. Payne?"

"Since Thursday," Jack answered grudgingly.

"Then what have you been doing since you arrived? Where are you staying?" Griz asked, catching on to Dragan's suspicions, although she could not believe that Jack could murder anyone, let alone Nancy.

"Had to find lodgings, and then I slept. If only I'd gone straight to find Nancy…"

"Don't torture yourself," Griz pleaded. "I'm afraid we all have *if onlys* like that. Where did you find lodgings?"

"Near Covent Garden," he replied impatiently.

She didn't look at Dragan. "Will you go home?"

"I'll stay for the inquest." He swallowed painfully.

"Well, don't get into any more trouble," she urged. "Think of your parents. I'll send you word when we learn anything certain."

He nodded and bent to pick his cap off the ground.

Dragan said, "When did you last see Nancy?"

"When Their Graces came to Sussex. November." Jack stared at him defiantly. "When did you?"

"February, I think. In company with other people. Whatever you have heard, I did not seduce your Nancy. She was not interested in me."

Jack looked him up and down and gave an odd little laugh, then tugged his forelock to Griz and trudged off, clapping his cap onto his head.

"Why did he have to stay in Covent Garden?" Griz demanded, walking swiftly back the way they had come. "*He* could have killed her."

"But he would not appear to be the father of her child if he had not seen her since November."

"If Emmie and Janet are correct about her dates."

"Then you think he might be the killer?" He sounded surprised. "For jealousy?"

She sighed, slowing as they emerged from the trees. "No." She snatched up Dragan's hat, which he had dropped when Jack landed on him and began distractedly brushing off grass and dirt with her fingers. "I don't believe he's capable of such an awful crime. Not in cold blood at any rate, and there was no time for an argument before I found her body."

He took the hat from her, startling her. "It could have been the continuation of a previous argument."

"You suspect him?" she asked anxiously.

"Not really. He seemed too genuinely suspicious of me. Besides, I think you're right. We can all kill, given the right circumstances, but I doubt these were his."

"You make up your mind very quickly," she noticed.

He shrugged. "I've had to. And I think your friends have noticed your absence."

Annabelle was abandoning her friends, some of whom gazed after her. Griz waved back, pointing to poor Vicky, as though she were to blame for Griz and Dragan straying from the group.

As she walked toward Annabelle, she said rapidly, "The dagger only vanished on Thursday. Mrs. MacKenna swears it was there when she inspected the maids' dusting before dinner—we always gather in the library, where my father's collection is."

"Then there must be a limited number of people who could have taken it. If it is precious, surely it is locked away?"

"The cabinets are all locked. Mrs. MacKenna has the key and opens them to let the maids dust. But my father keeps his own key in a desk drawer."

"Who would know that?" Dragan asked.

She shrugged. "The family. Any of the servants who might have noticed him put it there at any time, or who heard of it from someone who saw."

"And I suppose it's possible the maid might occasionally forget to lock one of the cabinets."

"Yes," Griz admitted, smiling at Annabelle as they caught up. "So, we're not really much further forward. Sorry, Belle."

"Don't be. Whatever you were up to, you seem to have got away with it unnoticed. The Cartwrights didn't seem to remember who you are, fortunately."

"It's much easier to move around when people don't remember you," Griz said vaguely.

Dragan glanced at her with unexpected perception, and she said hastily, "What did you learn? About Nancy's interests?"

"Griz, I have to go home," Annabelle said firmly. "It's almost time to put Timmie to bed. Come, you can talk on the way, and I will promise not to breathe a word. In fact, it's more than possible I won't understand what you say anyway."

"Nonsense," Griz said dryly, though she nodded to Dragan's questioning look.

"Nancy *was* curious," he said. "I spoke to a trail of people who had seen her at various meetings in parlors, church halls, and inns. Some had introduced her to others. In each meeting, she appeared very interested, asked questions of many different people, and then suddenly moved on to another group, usually introduced by someone she had met at the previous one. Almost as if she was constantly looking for something."

"She always was," Griz realized. "In her personal life, too. But were these groups a danger to her? To anyone? Were they seditious in nature?"

He shrugged. "I don't think so. Some had more radical ideas than others, some were more political, others concerned only with alleviating poverty or providing education. Some were charitable. Her latest printed leaflets, apparently, though I haven't seen them."

"I suppose there were no hints who her gentleman was?" Griz asked hopefully. "Or if she met him at such gatherings?"

"I doubt it, considering how often she moved on."

They were silent for a little, mulling things over as they walked toward the park gates and headed toward Brook Street.

"You must come to tea one day, Mr. Tizsa," Annabelle said.

"You are very kind," he replied politely.

"Actually, that's a good idea," Griz said, brightening. "We can meet there without criticism and discuss developments. If you don't mind, Annabelle?"

"When have I ever minded your presence?"

"I do also have responsibilities to Dr. Cordell," Dragan pointed out.

"Well, come if you can on Monday," Annabelle said. "I shan't bear a grudge if you don't. You will make sure she gets safely home, will you not, Mr. Tizsa?" Clearly returning to her parental role, she ran up the steps, throwing, "Be careful, Griz," over her shoulder.

Griz paused to let Vicky sniff the railings. A thought struck her. "Did your parents have a townhouse something like these?"

"No, we didn't have a house in town at all. When I was at the university, I had far less salubrious lodgings, which I shared with an intellectual peasant and a law student."

"Did you quarrel with your family?"

"Why would you think that?"

"That your accommodation was so poor."

His lips twisted. "We did not quarrel. Merely, my family was not wealthy. We were noble, and so we could vote, and certain other opportunities were open to us, but we had less land and money than many peasants. They called us *sandal nobles* because, often, we couldn't afford boots."

Intrigued, she thought of a lot of other questions, but he had already moved on. Or back.

"Did you have dinner guests on Thursday? Before the opera?"

She blinked. "Yes. Mr. and Miss Watters. My mother is trying to make Forsythe marry Miss Watters—to settle him down, apparently. And Mr. Gabriel, who is Horace's underling. And Lady Beasley, Mama's friend. Why?"

"I suppose they could all have had access to the dagger. Did they all come to the opera with you?"

"Yes. Apart from Horace and Mr. Gabriel, who had to return to work. But the others were all in the box when I left it, and they were all still there when I returned. And honestly, I cannot imagine any of them noticing a housemaid, let alone murdering one with a stolen dagger."

"No, it makes little sense," he agreed restlessly. "What of her family, where are they?"

"Lincoln. My mother has written to them." She cast him a quick glance. "That is, I did, at my mother's request, so I—" As they rounded the corner, she saw a familiar carriage drawn up by the imposing portico of Kelburn House. "Drat."

"Unwelcome visitors?"

"Oh, no." In fact, usually, she was pleased to see Azalea, who, alone of her family, never expected her to be any different, so for a moment, she was at a loss to account for her sinking spirits. Until Azalea alighted from the carriage and glanced in her direction.

In repose, Azalea was stunningly beautiful. When she smiled, as she did now, she was dazzling. Splendidly dressed in layers of forest green, her skirts so wide it was a miracle she could get them in and out of the carriage door, she was fashionable, magnificent, and utterly charming.

"Escaped again, Griz?" she drawled. The indulgent, older sister, amused by the antics of her precocious sibling. Her eyes flickered without interest to Dragan and lingered. Her smile widened. "Won't you introduce your companion?"

"Mr. Tizsa," Griz muttered. "My sister Lady Trench."

Azalea offered one languid hand, her gaze riveted to Dragan's. He bowed over her fingers with one of his rare smiles. "A pleasure, my lady."

Azalea eclipsed most women. She most certainly eclipsed Griz. "Thank you for escorting my sister home."

"Also a pleasure," Dragan murmured, releasing Azalea's hand after what Griz thought an unnecessarily long time.

"Your accent intrigues me, sir," Azalea said with the frankness for which she was famous. "Where does it represent?"

"Hungary."

"Ah!" Azelea's eyes sparkled. "Can you be one of the heroes forced to seek refuge here from the emperor's vengeance?"

"I fought in the Hungarian army," Dragan admitted. Although his tone was not effusive or awed, his gaze never left Azalea, who pressed her hands together with delight.

"How exciting! You must tell me your story—though not perhaps on the doorstep. Will you join us?"

"Sadly, I must decline," Dragan said, rather to Grizelda's surprise, for he had seemed to be falling nicely under Azalea's spell. "I am expected elsewhere."

"Oh, well, another time, perhaps. Griz, you must bring him to see me. Goodbye, sir!" She took Grizelda's reluctant arm, urging her up the front steps and through the open door. "My dear Griz," she said before the door was even shut, "where did you find such a handsome and gallant admirer? At least I imagine he is gallant—is he?"

Griz pulled free. "I have no idea. He isn't an admirer, as you put it, but a friend."

"Good," Azalea said frankly. "Because a man like that will break your heart. Where is Her Grace, Peter?"

CHAPTER SEVEN

G RIZ DID NOT accompany her parents to church the following morning. Instead, she joined Emmie in the tiny attic bedchamber she had shared with Nancy, boxing up the maid's personal possessions.

It didn't take them long, although there were a few surprises, including a silk bonnet and a matching purple gown, stowed in a drawer by themselves.

Griz took them out and handed them to Emmie. "These are rather fine."

"She said they were gifts from her gentleman," Emmie said, placing the fine garments in the box.

But Griz had already moved on, her fingers closing around several banknotes which had been hiding beneath the smart clothes. "Did Nancy not send money home from her wages?"

"Oh, yes, my lady. More than I did."

"Then how did she come by this? There must be two years' wages here."

"Her gentleman, I suppose," Emmie said uncomfortably.

"Do gentleman admirers normally give money to the objects of their affection?" Griz wondered.

Emmie flushed scarlet. "Not unless it's *for* something. Oh dear, you don't suppose she was up to something, do you?"

"Like what?" Griz asked, rising and dropping the money into the box.

"I don't know, my lady. She was a good girl," she added defensively.

"Perhaps her gentleman was not so good." *Perhaps he is not a gentleman at all. Perhaps Nancy only spoke of him that way because he is wealthy...* And there were many ways to acquire wealth in London, not all of them legal. Something tugged her memory, the germ of an idea beginning to form before it vanished.

"It's a cruel waste, my lady," Emmie burst out. "Cruel waste of a life."

"A life she grasped with both hands," Griz agreed, sinking down on the hard little bed, gazing at the box that was all that was left of Nancy's time on Earth. "Emmie, did she ever talk about politics with you?"

"What do you mean, my lady?"

"About the government? About Tories or Whigs or radicals?"

"Oh, no, why would she? It's nothing to do with us."

What a telling indictment. "What about poverty? Was she sympathetic to the poor?"

"Of course, isn't everyone? But she certainly didn't want to be among them. She'd no intention of being in service all her days. She thought she'd be a lady with maids of her own. And do you know, my lady," Emmie added, waving to the box, "I think she might. If only her life had not been taken from her."

It was odd, Griz reflected. Surely a girl involved in so many political meetings would at least have let some inkling of her views drop to those closest to her? Unless she was still searching for a view that made sense to her, as Dragan suggested. But even so, would she not have bounced ideas off her friends? Those same friends she had dropped hints to about marrying a gentleman, whom she had told the secret of her pregnancy.

"Emmie, did she still talk about Jack Payne?" Griz asked suddenly.

"Not really," Emmie said uncomfortably. "I think she'd left him far behind, which is a shame because he seemed a good man who'd have been kind to her." Emmie shifted from one foot to the other. "He came here, my lady. On Friday, looking for her. Someone might have mentioned the foreign gentleman who was arrested. The one who was here. He might have misunderstood."

"He did," Griz said severely. "I've already spoken to Mrs. MacKenna, so you might have heard this before, but I don't want gossip and speculation about poor Nancy. Think of her parents. And Jack, who I think truly loved her. He nearly got himself in a lot of trouble."

"Yes, my lady. Sorry, my lady."

"You may go," Griz told her. "Thanks for helping me."

Emmie scuttled off, leaving Griz alone in the room. She had been disappointed not to have come across any letters which might have given some clue as to the identity of Nancy's lover. Surely there would have been something, arranging meetings and assignations, and surely a romantically inclined girl would have saved such things? But there had been nothing at all, not even letters from her parents. And Griz was sure she had received some of those. Did she just throw them out once she had read them?

On impulse, Griz lifted the pillow, felt inside the case, which had not yet been changed. Then she stood and felt under the mattress. She even went as far as pulling the bed out from the wall in order to reach under the other side, but she found nothing.

Letting the mattress fall back onto the bed, she stared out of the little window under the eaves, then let her eyes drop below, where narrow, painted wooden planks lined the wall. One to the right seemed scratched, as though the bed frame had rubbed against it. And yet the marks were below that level?

She knelt on the floor, pulling scissors from the pocket of her gown, and inserted them between the planks, just where the scratches were. The panel pried away easily and clattered onto the floor.

Griz slid her hand inside and in no time had grasped something, a packet of paper. She pulled it free. It was indeed a little bundle of letters tied with a scrap of ribbon. She stared at them blindly for a moment, then slipped them into her pocket with the scissors and replaced the plank. She shoved the bed back against the wall and left the room.

Descending from the attic, she made her way to her more comfortable bedchamber. Privacy, clearly, had been important to Nancy. She had kept things from her closest friends, like where she spent her time and her letters. Perhaps it was her way of preserving her sense of self among people she was forced to live so closely with. Much as Griz, the youngest of a large and forceful family, had found her own way to hide and still be herself with her own much-valued independence.

She dropped Nancy's letters on her bed. It seemed rude and invasive to read them. Perhaps she should give them to the police. But she had already been selective with the truth she had given Inspector Harris. She should know first what she was giving him.

Sinking on to the bed, she untied the packet. Yes, there were letters from her parents. She put them aside, unread, and turned to the others. One was from Jack Payne, pleading with her to respond and reciting a list of local news in awkward language. She skimmed it and put it hurriedly with the parental letters. Otherwise, there were only a couple of short notes inviting her to tea—one was signed M. Cordell—and a few scraps of paper with addresses written on them. She doubted the latter were in Nancy's writing. The hand looked too bold, too practiced. A man's hand. A little shiver ran up her spine. Was this the work of Nancy's lover? Proposing assignations?

Or political meetings. She stared at one. 12 Caroline Place. Was that not the address Dragan had given her? She pulled up the short note from M. Cordell, also written from 12 Caroline Place.

What did this mean? That someone had *told* Nancy to go there? To the other addresses? Lovers' assignations? Or something more sinister?

Hastily, she seized a sheet of notepaper from the bureau in the corner and scribbled down the addresses on the paper scraps, then the names and addresses of Nancy's unknown correspondents. Then she bundled the letters back up and retied the ribbon keeping back the address scraps, which she put in the drawer of her bedside table.

Taking only her own notes with her, she repaired to the library and hunted down the most recent map of London. This turned out to be one clearly produced for the upcoming Exhibition, because the building was clearly marked in Hyde Park with all the paths and roads leading to it.

She pored over it for some time, tracking down each address on her list. Most of them were in respectable, though not necessarily affluent, areas. Only one was decidedly dubious in the maze of streets close to Mr. Wells's soup kitchen in St. Giles.

She shivered as she remembered where she had found Nancy. With difficulty, she found Mudd Lane on the map and realized Nancy had died not so very far from this address. Sheltered as she was, Griz knew only to go into St. Giles in a carriage and never to walk there alone. The place was a maze of rookeries, a morass of poverty and crime. Had Nancy been involved in something worse than radical politics?

Immediately, the memory she had been looking for in Nancy's bedroom popped up to the surface. Horace and Mr. Gabriel in the library, celebrating an important arrest.

We've brought down a whole gang of treasonous dogs in the rookeries.

Rookeries, as Griz understood the term, were tenements full of thieves and murderers and other dangerous villains. Places that neither the police nor respectable people dared to enter without very good reason. Was the St. Giles address a rookery? Nancy would never have gone near such a place.

Knowingly.

But Horace's words seemed to imply an unexpected connection between sedition and straightforward crime. Could Nancy possibly have got mixed up in such confusion? Perhaps via a wealthy lover she called a gentleman?

Griz jumped to her feet and ran, barely remembering to grab her old cloak and bonnet before she left the house.

><<

CAROLINE PLACE, WHERE the hackney dropped her, was a quiet street of smallish houses with gardens. Griz guessed its residents were better off clerks with a scattering, perhaps, of lawyers and doctors and the like. Number twelve had a bright redpainted front door and a tidy path.

Griz raised the polished brass knocker and rapped.

The door was opened by a slightly harassed looked middle-aged maidservant.

"Good morning," Griz said civilly. "Is Mr. Tizsa at home?"

The servant bridled, but before she could open her mouth, another woman bustled up behind her. "Who is it, Hilda? Are they looking for Dr. Cor..." She broke off as the servant stood back and she saw Griz.

Griz smiled tentatively. "Mrs. Cordell?"

"Yes?"

"Good morning. My name is Niven. I was hoping to speak to Mr. Tizsa."

"I'm afraid he is out on a call."

"Drat, I should have known he wouldn't be in. I should have sent a note instead." She hesitated, wondering what best to do.

"If it is an urgent matter, Dr. Cordell could see you," his wife said reluctantly.

"Oh, no, it is not a medical matter," Griz assured her, becoming aware of the assessing nature of Mrs. Cordell's gaze.

Whatever that lady saw did not inspire her to close the door in her visitor's face. Instead, she stood back.

"Dragan should not be long. Come in and wait, if you wish."

"Oh, thank you, how kind," Griz said in quick relief. "Though I hesitate to disturb your Sunday."

"It is always a pleasure to meet a friend of Dragan's."

Griz felt a twinge of guilt, doubting that Dragan would class her amongst his friends, but she smiled and stepped inside.

Mrs. Cordell ushered her into a parlor, where two girls on the cusp of womanhood sat sewing on the window seat. A craggy but still handsome man rose from an armchair by the fire.

"Miss Niven came to see Dragan, Arthur," Mrs. Cordell explained. "Miss Niven, my husband, Dr. Cordell, and my daughters, Anne and Margaret."

Griz gave an awkward smile, feeling quite unequal to explaining that she was not Miss Niven but Lady Grizelda. The girls curtseyed to her, though the older one, Anne, did not look happy about doing so.

The maid, Hilda, had followed to take Griz's hat and cloak, after which the doctor ushered her to a chair by the fire.

They talked about the weather for a little until Hilda brought tea. The younger daughter, Margaret, carried a cup and saucer to Griz, while the older served her father. But to Grizelda's surprise, the younger girl lingered, gazing at her with open curiosity.

"Are your eyes very bad?" she asked bluntly.

"They're very short-sighted," Griz replied. "But I'm fortunate to be able to compensate."

"With the spectacles. Do you hate wearing them?"

Griz considered. "I think I found them a nuisance when I was small. I recall them falling off when I was halfway up a tree, which made descent somewhat hazardous."

Margaret grinned. "Do you wear them at parties, too?"

"Well, yes. Why?"

"I am short-sighted," Margaret confided, kneeling by the hearth. "My oldest sister says they will make me look clumsy and owlish."

"Well, I think you'd look clumsier tripping over things." Griz considered. "Are owls clumsy?"

"My eldest daughter," Dr. Cordell intervened, "has grown very opinionated since she married. Her main focus is now on seeing her sisters happily married, and she will have it that spectacles are an impediment."

"Do you find that?" the older asked, having returned to her sewing in the window. She smiled innocently but, for some reason, Griz felt it as a barb.

"I never thought about it," Griz replied honestly. "There is more to life than marriage, even for girls."

Margaret's mouth fell open at this heresy.

"Such as what?" Anne demanded.

"Friendship. Education." Griz broke off, acutely aware of her privileged position where an unmarried daughter was no real drain on resources. "To each his own," she said hastily. "And *her* own."

She was relieved as the door opened on her last words. Dragan strode in like a breath of fresh air, windswept and curiously untamed.

"Twins," he pronounced jubilantly. "And all are healthy. The—" He came to an abrupt halt, staring. "Griz?"

She had never heard her shortened name on his lips before, and for some reason, it made her tingle. It was probably relief, because although he looked and sounded startled, he did not appear displeased, let alone angry.

Griz stood. "Sorry to beard you at home on a Sunday, but there is something I wish to discuss with you."

"Use the consulting room," Dr. Cordell offered. "Or the dining room."

Dragan held open the door, and Griz smiled a little hesitantly around the family before walking past him.

"Are we consulting or dining?" he asked flippantly, conducting her toward the back of the house. Delicious cooking smells made her stomach rumble.

"We had better consult since I suspect luncheon is on its way."

Dragan pushed open a door on his right and ushered her into a small, cramped room with a desk, three hard chairs, and several cabinets.

"What's wrong?" he demanded, and she saw with surprise that he was genuinely worried about her, not about annoying their amiable hosts.

"Nothing," she assured him. "But I need to discuss something with you." Hastily, she told him about Nancy's hidden letters and showed him the paper on which she had written down the addresses and names she had discovered.

He frowned. "You think someone told her to come here? To all these places?"

"I'm worried," Griz confessed. "About this gentleman of hers not being a gentleman at all. To begin with, he made her with child, which, if he didn't mean to marry her, would ruin her chances of any respectable position. But what if he was worse than that? What if he was some wealthy thief? Some villain of the underworld?"

He frowned, raising his eyes from the paper to her face. "She would find little in this house to steal."

"Oh, I don't think *she* would steal," Griz said. "I think she might have been the unwitting pawn of this man, only I can't quite think how."

"She is drifting around groups of reformers and radicals. What has this to do with thieves and the underworld?"

"Horace said something the other day," she confessed, "about arresting a gang of thieves who were also involved in sedition. I don't know the details, and frankly, I doubt he'd tell me if I asked—although I suppose I could try Mr. Gabriel..." She became aware he was gazing at her, waiting for her to continue. "That is it. If Nancy had stumbled on some connection between this criminal fraternity and treasonous politics—"

"It's quite a leap," he interrupted. "I can't follow it."

"Nancy had money," she blurted. "More than we paid her. She had a silk bonnet and a dress she could never have afforded. They don't sound like the gifts of a gentleman suitor."

"Gifts to a mistress," he murmured, thoughtfully. "It's possible she did not understand. There was a certain naivety beneath her worldliness. He could have been offering to set her up in her own little establishment, and she mistook this for marriage. But it does not make him a thief."

"I know."

"Nor does it tie reformers or political radicals to the underworld."

"They both have an interest in keeping the law away," she said defensively. "And you need not take it personally. Look. I found all these addresses on the map. None of them are obviously *not* respectable. Except this one, which seems to be near Seven Dials in the back streets of St. Giles. Which is not so far from Mudd Lane, where we found Nancy."

An arrested look came into his eyes. "I did hear talk of the police cleaning out some thieves' den in St. Giles. Did your soup kitchen patrons ever mention it?"

She shook her head. "They would never talk of such things to me. But if Nancy had been somehow involved with people like that," she added eagerly, "it might more easily explain how she came to be murdered. I wanted to at least go and look at this address, but I didn't want to go alone, considering—"

"Dear God, no," Dragan exclaimed.

"Will you come with me, then?"

He regarded her. "Your family would string me up. And rightly so. If anything were to happen to you—"

"Perhaps you should bring your pistol," she suggested.

A breath of laughter seemed to take him by surprise. "Perhaps I should."

CHAPTER EIGHT

SEVEN DIALS, IN the heart of St. Giles, seemed like another world. The hackney dropped Griz and Dragan at the junction itself and left at worrying speed.

At one time, the seven roads converging at the junction had been elegant, the center itself marked by a great sundial with lesser ones facing each street. If one peered under the grime, no doubt the old buildings were fine, but it was impossible to tell.

There seemed to be an alehouse or gin shop on most of the corners, with men and woman spilling out of them, some arguing, some laughing uproariously, most of them drunk, even at two o'clock on a Sunday afternoon.

Dragan plunged down Little White Lion Street—at least that was what Griz worked out from her memory of the map. Even the sky seemed dirty here, hazing the rooftops and casting an unhealthy dimness across the maze of back alleys, the scattering of dingy shops, and the unhealthy yet aggressive looking people who passed them.

There was really no way to avoid the filth on the ground. Griz gave up trying to step around it and merely held her old skirts as far away from the ground as was seemly. And concentrated on not wrinkling her nose at the smell of rotting fish and fruit.

"That is it," Dragan murmured, nodding to his right where two blacked-out windows flanked a closed door.

"What *is* it?" she asked, coming to a halt. A rusty sign hung above it, though it was impossible to read through the filth.

"An alehouse," Dragan replied.

"How can you tell?"

"I can smell it."

"You must have a nose like a dog." Dubiously, she eyed the blank, grimy face of the building, which stretched up several floors at a crooked angle. "Nancy would not have come to a place like this."

"She might have."

"But why?"

"Adventure," Dragan said, reaching for the door. "The same as you."

He walked in first, holding the door to let her join him.

They were inside a gloomy room. A wall of tobacco and the smell of stale beer deprived her of breath—in fact, of any desire to breathe. Silence surrounded them, although she had the feeling it hadn't been quiet when Dragan first pushed the door. Through the fog of smoke, a few still figures seemed to be staring in their direction. Every hair on her body stood up in alarm.

"Ale, if you please," Dragan threw to a man she could barely make out behind a small counter. He took Grizelda's arm, for which she was pathetically grateful, and steered her to a table by the wall.

"Is it my imagination," she murmured as he slid onto the stool opposite, "or is the atmosphere a little tense?"

"It's certainly a little thick. We're spotted as strangers. They will get used to us."

She cast him a long glance. "You seem very…comfortable."

"Do I?" He sounded surprised, but since the potman in his greasy apron plonked down two mugs of ale between them, he said no more, merely delved in his pocket for coins and dropped one into the potman's grubby palm. The man retreated without a word, back behind his counter.

"It strikes me it might not be easy to ask questions in a place like this," Griz said, darting a quick glance at the nearest occupied table.

"Listening might be best," he agreed. "And while they get used to us, it might be good to look as if we have something to say to each other. What has your sister done to upset you?"

She had gingerly lifted the mug, trying not to imagine when it had last been washed. At his words, it slopped, and she lowered it to the table again. "My sister? Which sister?"

"The one we encountered yesterday."

"Azalea doesn't upset me," Griz said with dignity. "In fact, she is my favorite sister."

"Then why did you melt into the railings and turn into a sullen child?"

Her color high, Griz took a defiant gulp of her ale. "I did neither."

"Is she everything your family wishes you to be?"

Griz glared in outrage, then gave in and shrugged. "Of course. I didn't even try. There is no point. Azalea is Azalea, and I am not."

To her surprise, he pushed his glass against hers in what might have been a toast. "You are you." His lips quirked into a smile, and he drank. "I can't imagine your sister coming here for any reason."

"Most people would count that in her favor," Griz admitted, ridiculously pleased that he did not appear to do so. "But what of you? Will you stay here in England?"

He shifted on his stool, instantly restless. "I don't know."

"Perhaps you can go home soon. Is the emperor not beginning to pardon those who fought against him?"

"He will never pardon me." His lips twisted. "And I will never accept that I need to be pardoned. I will never go home."

His voice was carefully flat and expressionless, and yet she knew. She could feel the surge of sorrow and anger leaking from him like blood.

"Could you not sit your medical examinations here?" she asked. "Perhaps go into partnership with Dr. Cordell?"

"He has suggested it."

"But you are not convinced?"

"I could bring nothing material to the partnership." He gazed into the murky depths of his ale. "And it seems I am too...*unsettled* to make such commitments."

A man who had given up his studies to march against his government and create revolution. Who had fought two years in a war to protect that revolution. Commitment did not appear to be a problem for him.

"You're bored," she guessed.

His gaze flew to hers. He emitted a short, bitter laugh. "How could I have the ill-manners to be bored?"

"It isn't really a matter of manners, is it? It used to happen to me a lot. Until I set about finding ways to do exactly as I liked."

His gaze rested on hers, half-amused, half-intrigued. "And what is it you like to do?"

"Lots of things. There are my good works, of course. And I spend a good deal of time in museums and galleries. And bookshops. Sometimes I like to hide in my room and read. Others, I walk, even run with Vicky, though of course, that is much easier when we are in the country. I like music, and sometimes I play with other people or go to concerts. Sometimes it's fun to go to a teashop by myself and observe the other patrons. And the staff."

The smile in his eyes was more pronounced. "And your family have no idea about any of this, have they?"

She considered. "My parents have given up on me and have clearly decided I will be the spinster daughter who looks after them in their old age. My siblings have concerns of their own, but mostly we don't interfere or tell on each other."

"And so you manage to lead an independent life without scandal or husband. I doff my hat to you."

She flushed. "I'm aware that only my privileged position allows me to do so. I have a generous allowance and busy parents, and servants who do not question the daughter of the house." She drew in her breath. "Except Nancy. She was curious, always asking where I was going."

"Did you tell her?"

She shook her head. "No. When I was accompanying my mother anywhere, such as the opera on Thursday evening, she already knew."

He frowned, leaning forward across the crusty table. "That is what I really don't understand. She came to Covent Garden, where you were. She must have known you would help her. And yet it was me she asked to see, little more than a stranger."

"Perhaps she wanted to tell you about the baby." She flushed. "Because you are a doctor," she added hastily. "And perhaps less apt to judge her than others she might know."

He sat back. "Being foreign and revolutionary, and therefore an advocate of free thought and free love?"

"Are you?" she asked curiously because she really wanted to know, and then bit her lip because it was none of her business.

His eyes followed her reaction, lingering on her lips as he said, "I am an advocate of all freedom that does not step on the toes of someone else's."

"For example?"

"For example, in my country, the old freedoms of the nobility severely hampered the freedom of peasants and workers. And for another more nuanced example, I have a friend who led the early days of the revolution in Pest, who thought as I did. He fell in love with a noble lady who gave up her family to be with him without the ties of marriage. The last I heard, they had married in Turkey. Because it was better and safer for her. Because love trumps abstract ideals of freedom. One learns to live with shades of grey."

She searched his haunted eyes. "Is the world just grey for you now?"

His lips quirked. "It has been. Now I see splashes of color. There is nothing grey about you, my lady."

Before she could ask what he meant by that or object to the mockery of *my lady*, she was distracted by a small boy in a brave red cap, streaked with something black that might have been coal. Over his shoulder, he carried a canvas satchel that was clearly too large and heavy for him. But somehow, he heaved it onto the counter. The potman swept it casually onto the floor beside him and put a coin in its place. The boy's hand streaked out, and the coin vanished.

The boy turned, leaning one shoulder casually against the counter in a gesture surely copied from many an alehouse denizen. Only a man would have leaned his elbow; the child couldn't reach. He surveyed the patrons with very adult speculation. None of them paid him any attention until his gaze reached Griz. His little eyes sparkled in the grimy environment.

The potman muttered something, and the boy smiled at Griz, a deliberately winning, charming smile, before sauntering toward her.

"Bring you something, missus?" he offered. "Fetch you gin instead of that nasty ale, for only a penny? Or I can sweep the street in front of you, fetch you a horse or a cab—"

"Where would I get a horse?" Dragan asked with interest.

The boy touched the side of his nose. "*I* know. You don't need to. But it'd be a good horse."

"I'm sure it would," Griz said, feeling inside the pocket of her cloak and coming out with a penny, which she gave to him. "We don't need anything right now, but it's a pleasure to meet you."

The boy palmed the coin with the same speed he had the potman's, though he regarded her with some suspicion. "You talk mighty posh."

"I was well taught," she replied, honestly enough. "What's your name?"

"Nick. What's yours?"

"Griz. Do you work for the tavern keeper, Nick?"

"Lord, no," he said with what appeared to be genuine scorn. "But he pays me for odd jobs, sometimes. Lots of people do."

"Don't you go to school?"

He cast her a look that clearly questioned her sanity. "What would I do that for? No money in going to school."

"Not in the short term, I suppose," she agreed.

But Nick's attention had moved on to Dragan as he asked cheekily, "What do you do then, Mr. Gress?"

Gress? Griz. She almost giggled when she realized the boy had given Dragan her name.

"You a Peeler?" Nick guessed.

Ah. Now Griz understood the boy's approach. He had been sent to find out who the incongruous customers were and, no doubt, what they were doing here.

"A policeman?" Dragan asked, amused. "You have no idea how funny that is. What made you imagine such a thing?"

Nick shrugged. "You look like one of them that wear plain clothes. Worse than the uniforms, they are."

"In that case, I'm happy to say I'm not one."

"He's a soldier," Griz said with sudden inspiration as to how to win the boy's confidence. And she was right.

Nick's eyes sparkled. He drew an imaginary sword from his belt-less, torn trousers and waved it aggressively. "I'm going to be a soldier when I grow up. One that fights on horseback. Did you do that?"

"I did," Dragan replied.

Nick grinned and held out his hand. "Reckon that's worth a shilling, then."

Dragan sipped his ale. "You'll get that from the queen when you join up."

"Don't need her money, anyway," Nick said perversely. "Or yours. I earn plenty."

"Lucky you. What do you do with all that money?" Dragan asked casually.

"I give it to my old mum," Nick said piously. "She's sick, prob'ly dying."

"I can help there," Dragan said at once. "I'm a doctor."

Nick's eyes narrowed with dislike. Clearly, he knew Dragan didn't believe in the sick mother. "Thought you were a soldier."

"I was both. Where is your mother?"

"How should I know? Where's yours?"

"In her grave a long way from here."

Something that might have been shame crossed the boy's eyes before they slid from Dragan's. "So's mine. Prob'ly."

"Then who looks after you?" Griz asked.

"No one," the boy said grandly. "I look after myself."

"How old are you?"

Nick's eyes flickered. "Seven."

Griz wondered. By his height, he could have been seven, but his manner, his quick responses, made her think of her nephew, who was ten. Of course, if he was really alone in these streets, he would have had to develop a maturity beyond his years to survive.

"What d'you want, coming to a place this anyway?" Nick asked, looking from one to the other.

"Just passing," Dragan said, "and wanted a drink."

"You don't seem to like it much," Nick observed, eyeing their still almost-full mugs. "You should have the gin instead."

"Probably," Griz agreed peaceably. "So, where do you sleep, Nick? Is it warm?"

"Warm enough. I got people. Family," he added, in case she didn't understand.

But glancing at Dragan, she rather thought she did. Whoever was looking after him wasn't true family. No doubt someone who kept him away from school and sent him out to beg or work or steal, and took his earnings, too. But gave him a warm place to stay.

In a rookery, perhaps?

"I hope that wasn't stolen goods in the bag you brought here," Dragan said.

"Of course not," the boy said with overdone shock. And yet the pleased innocence of someone who was actually telling the truth. He grinned at Dragan. "Just paper."

Dragan glanced at Griz. "What kind of paper? Blank? Printed?"

"How should I know? Or care."

"Because a bright boy like you would have kept a sheet or two," Griz said conspiratorially.

Nick grinned at her. "Might have."

"Let me see?" she suggested.

The boy considered her, then took a crumpled paper from his pocket. "Have it," he said generously. "I've got another."

"What does the tavernkeeper want with a load of paper?" Dragan wondered.

Nick shrugged. "I dunno. Art don't want it."

"Who's Art?"

"I never said Art," the boy said angrily. "I said Dad. My dad don't want it. What would he want a load of old paper for? My dad's rich."

"Nick!" a man growled. A surprisingly well-dressed man in a top hat stood by a back door. He had clearly been in conversation with the potman, who still stood beside him.

The boy bolted over to them without a backward glance.

"He doesn't have a father, does he?" Griz said bleakly.

"Not alive or functioning as a parent," Dragan agreed. "But someone's feeding him and giving him jobs."

"Art." She scowled. "Who is Art? I do hope he isn't Nancy's gentleman."

Dragan's gaze was on the men by the backdoor.

"Well, *that* can't be him, at least," Griz said of the better-dressed individual. "Nancy would never call such a man a gentleman."

Nick seemed to be giving him cheek, too, for the man aimed an ungentle slap at the back of the boy's head. Nick ducked in what looked a very practiced way, and grinned as he dived out through the back door. The two men turned their attention to Griz and Dragan.

"Do you think we asked too many questions?" Griz asked.

"Yes. And I think we have outstayed our welcome." He pushed back his stool and stood, his gaze darting around the smoke-filled room. Although he didn't take her arm as she rose, he walked very close to her as they made toward the front door. Again, the hairs on the back of her neck stood up. She tensed, expecting some kind of attack from behind.

It didn't come. Dragan opened the door, and she couldn't believe the air of the rancid alley smelled almost sweet. However, her relief only lasted a moment. Two men flanked the door, rough, bullish men with short necks and mean faces.

Dragan took her arm, walking smartly to the left, retracing their earlier route. A boy with a barrow hurried past. A woman with a bundle of washing on her back dipped out of sight, and a door slammed. Coming toward them were two more men who could have been clones of those behind.

Dragan must have seen them, but his step didn't falter. Instead, he leaned his head nearer hers as though to continue a private conversation. "Be ready to run."

CHAPTER NINE

GOD KNEW SHE was ready to run *now*. The direction was the problem, for she could hear the following footsteps of the men from the pub door.

Abruptly, her arm was yanked to the left as Dragan pulled her through a doorway she hadn't even seen. She seized her skirts to avoid tripping and bolted with him along a covered passage into a small courtyard surrounded by buildings and doorways, one of which was almost certainly the backdoor to the alehouse.

Without hesitation, Dragan dragged her to the right and through the first door. A voice objected, though she could see no one. Hand in hand, they ran toward a small seam of light and broke through a doorway, back into the alley they had just left, and pelted on. The men who had been in front had vanished, perhaps through another door, hoping to catch them in the courtyard.

A shout went up just before they flew around the corner at the end of the alley and into the next. Footsteps pounded behind them. Dragan heaved his shoulder at a wooden gate, but it appeared to be locked. From it, a wall about five feet high stretched for the next dozen yards or so.

Dragan seized her by the waist, all but throwing her up the wall. She gasped, clinging with both hands and hauling herself up to straddle it. By then, Dragan was sliding over the top and dropping down. He held up his arms, and she jumped without hesitation.

He caught her, pushing her at once against the stone wall, his finger to his lips.

Someone battered on the wooden gate, making her jump.

"Locked!" the unseen man snarled, and footsteps ran on—two pairs.

A shout went up some distance away, echoed surely by their running pursuers. Griz breathed again, though her heart still hammered, which may have had less to do with fear than with her close proximity to Dragan, still squashing her into the wall. He was very large, warm, and solid. She could feel the rise and fall of his chest with every quickened breath. Did all men have this strangely exciting smell? Something faintly earthy, herbal, and utterly masculine...

"Stupid men always underestimate women," Dragan murmured happily, dropping his gaze to her face as he stood back. "No one would believe you would or could climb that wall."

Griz adjusted her spectacles more securely on her nose. "What made *you* think I could? That I wouldn't just scream as you hurled me over the top?"

He only grinned. "Come on, let's find a way out."

"Here!" yelled a man emerging from what might have been a workshop at one end of the yard. "What d'you want, then?"

With a breath of laughter, Dragan seized her hand again, and they ran like children through the yard, leaping over a much lower wall that led to a fence full of gaps. They rolled through the nearest, and Griz jumped to her feet, gasping with the sudden desire to laugh. But there was no time, for Dragan seized her hand once more, and they ran along the narrow, busy street, dodging carts and people who screamed obscenities after them. At least, Griz supposed they were obscenities.

At one point, Dragan released her hand and leapt over a barrow full of highly fragrant fish, while she sprinted across the front of it with inches to spare. They came together again with the furious yells of the barrow boy ringing in their ears and ran on.

"You're enjoying this," Griz accused breathlessly.

"So are you."

She couldn't deny it. It was the most fun she'd had since childhood games of tag, and somehow that seemed to wipe out the actual danger presented by their pursuers. She could only assume that Dragan, too, missed the adventurous life he had left behind.

Sharing a quick, conspiratorial grin, they rounded the next corner and skidded to a halt. Two men carrying clubs advanced from different doorways.

Dragan swore beneath his breath, possibly in Hungarian, for she couldn't make out the words.

"Psst!" A boy in a red cap hissed at them from the gap in a wooden fence, beckoning wildly.

Griz exchanged glances with Dragan, but there was no other option. They had no idea who they would run into if they ran back the way they had come. As one, they dived across the road and through the plank in the fence.

Nick was already haring into the tumbled-down building behind it, so they followed. At least they were out of sight of the men with clubs.

"Follow me," Nick said cheerfully. "Short cut to the cab stand. You'll be safe there."

"Will you?" Dragan asked bluntly. "If they know you helped us—"

Nick cast him a pitying glance. "Don't be daft. Who'd suspect me? Told you, I can take care of myself." As he spoke, he led them out the other end of the building, through a maze of passages and the remains of buildings that seemed to have been knocked down, with no attempt to replace them. Some of them smelled still of smoke.

"Do you suppose they're still following?" Griz asked nervously, though she could not hear any sounds of pursuit.

"Nah, they'll never come this way," Nick assured her. "Enemy territory, isn't it?"

"Enemy?" Dragan repeated.

"The law got most of 'em," Nick said. "But there's enough left to do our lot some damage if they stray into the wrong place."

"But *you* aren't afraid?" Griz said anxiously.

He grinned. "Who notices me? I'm just a kid."

And then, without warning, Dragan cannoned into her, with far more force than their first encounter. His hard arm at her back, she seemed to fly through the air and land with a thud. The world was exploding, shaking in a rising cloud of opaque, choking dust.

Dazed and winded, her brain too numb to think, Griz flung out her hand to Dragan, sprawled half on top of her, touching his face, feeling his breath.

"Christ!" Nick's childish voice whispered, more like a prayer than blasphemy. "Christ..."

She moved, twisting her head. The boy lay dazed and staring on Dragan's other side. Through the dust, she made out a huge chunk of masonry on the ground, only feet away from them. Almost exactly where they had been, surely, when Dragan hurled them all to safety.

The cloud drifted and parted further. And on top of the nearest half-demolished building, she saw four men peering toward them. Somehow, she understood at once that it had taken all four to push the masonry down on them. That all three of them would have been dead if Dragan had not seen or heard it coming.

She had heard nothing, no warning...

But one of the men was pointing. Angry voices reached her ears as their survival was discovered. And she knew they were not yet safe.

She hauled herself out from under Dragan, staggering to her feet. "Hurry! Nick, run!"

Nick was standing, his eyes wide and staring in his dirty face. Dragan sat up, and she grasped his shoulder urgently. It jerked and trembled but otherwise, he didn't move.

"Dragan!" Terrified for his injury, she crouched beside him, grasping his face between her hands. "Dragan, can you stand? Can you run? They're coming for us."

His eyes stared at her, frighteningly blank. Helpless.

Dear God. "Dragan, get up!" With both hands, she hauled at his shoulder and, at last, he moved, stumbling upright. She grasped his arm in one hand, seized Nick with the other, and lurched away from the building.

"Nick, you have to lead the way," she said urgently. "We're lost."

Nick nodded, and they ran together, stumbling over stones and slates and what must once have been a road of some kind. Dragan moved without her support, but it was almost as if he was not there, which for some reason frightened her more than anything.

At last, they broke into a wider road. Griz glanced wildly around her, searching for landmarks. Behind a loaded cart, a hackney was coming toward them. They should follow it, hopefully to a stand, or at least to civilization. But even as she turned to do so, Nick darted out into the road to stop it.

The horses screamed and reared. The driver cursed, and Grizelda's heart rose into her mouth. But somehow, Nick survived. And the carriage was empty.

"They're hurt!" he yelled to the driver. "You have to take them home."

Which is when Dragan suddenly blinked and strode after him, and, grasping the child by the scruff of the neck, all but throwing him into the carriage. Then, he kicked down the steps for Griz, shouting her address to the driver.

He leapt up after them, and to her relief, Griz saw that the terrible blank look had gone. Still, he was shaking as he cast himself onto the seat beside her and glared at Nick.

Tears were rolling down the child's cheeks. He didn't even seem to notice. Impulsively, Griz reached out to comfort him, but Dragan's cold voice froze her.

"You set us up to be killed."

Nick didn't deny it. He stared back at Dragan from his own haunted eyes. "They'd have killed me, too. *Me*."

Griz, grappling with both vile facts, fell back into her seat.

"There is no honor among thieves," Dragan said harshly. "You are as expendable to them as we are."

The boy did not—could not—deny it. He turned his head away, silently weeping.

"Why did they want us dead?" Dragan asked.

"'Cause you were asking too many questions."

"No," Griz said suddenly. "It wasn't the number. It was particular questions we asked." From her pocket, she took the crumpled paper Nick had given her in the alehouse and spread it out on her knee. But she was still too shaken to read it. The words jumped and jostled before her eyes. "This came from the rookery that the police cleaned out?"

"Art's taken over their business," Nick said dully.

"What business?" Griz asked, folding the paper and replacing it in her pocket.

Nick shrugged impatiently. "Thieving. Fencing. Girls. Boys." He turned his miserable gaze to Griz and then Dragan. "He looked out for me. Sent me with special messages, kept the pimps away from me. Why'd he turn on me, now? Didn't he see me?"

"I don't know," Dragan said. Although he did, he was clearly sparing the child as his anger retreated. "The point is, you've seen too much, now. You can't go back."

Nick dashed his sleeve across his eyes and from somewhere found more brash courage. "You going to give me to the Peelers?" he asked carelessly.

"That depends," Dragan replied after a moment.

Obviously sensing a way out, Nick wheedled. "I can disappear, no bother. Other manors won't know or care what I done. And I'll spread the word no one's to touch you. No one'll thieve from you or burgle you ever."

"It depends," Dragan interrupted, "on what you tell us now. Who is Art? What's his name?"

"Art," Nick said, casting him a familiar, pitying look. "Big Art Dooley."

"Did you ever meet a girl—a young woman—called Nancy?"

"Of course," Nick scoffed. "Lots. Nancy at the King's Head, Little Nance, who works at Flo's. And Old Nancy, who takes in washing and sends it back dirtier."

"None of those. Her name was Nancy Barrow. She'd have looked respectable, about the same age as this lady, but with brown hair and light blue eyes. Short lashes and straight eyebrows. And a little mole on her chin, *here*." Dragan touched a point to the left of his chin, and Griz regarded him with fresh fascination.

He may not have been Nancy's lover, but he had certainly studied her.

Perhaps he had wanted to be.

And abruptly, she remembered. "The sketch in your notebook, Dragan, show him."

Dragan delved into his pocket and dragged out the book. He had forgotten about it, too. He thumbed quickly through the pages until he came to his portrait.

He had even marked the small mole on Nancy's chin.

Nick did them the courtesy of considering the drawing. "No, don't think I know her."

"Did you ever carry messages to a Nancy or a Miss Barrow from Art?"

Nick looked at her as if she had horns. "Big Agg'd have killed me."

"Big Agg being Art's wife?" Dragan suggested.

"Something like that," Nick replied. Losing interest, he gazed out of the window and scowled. "Here, where are we going? These houses are *huge*, like palaces in the middle of a park…"

"We're just dropping off Lady Grizelda," Dragan said. "Then you'll come home with me while we—"

"I ain't going nowhere with you!" Nick declared, glaring with sudden, incomprehensible fear. "I'll take my chances with Art before I'd go with you!"

"Mr. Tizsa saved your life," Griz said, frowning. "Aren't you grateful?"

"Not that grateful," Nick said fervently.

"Don't be ridiculous," Dragan said without heat. "I don't even like small boys at a distance. I have lodgings with a doctor and his family whom I shall try to persuade to let you stay for a little. If you promise not to steal."

"No, he had better stay with me," Griz said, winning an unexpectedly warm smile from the manipulative child. "But they'll stand no nonsense in the kitchen, mind. No stealing or cheek, and you'll get a warm bed and good food."

"Deal," the boy said promptly as the hackney pulled up outside Kelburn House.

As they alighted, he stared open-mouthed up at the houses with their clean windows and gleaming front doors.

"Are you sure about this?" Dragan murmured.

"Nick? Yes. But you are coming in with us, aren't you? We need to talk."

He hesitated, almost as if there was nothing he wanted less, and then he shrugged and delved in his pocket to pay off the driver.

Nick's eyes showed a tendency to pop out of his head as Griz led him toward the biggest house on the corner. She even wondered if he would have bolted had Dragan not been on his other side.

Since it was a Sunday, and fewer servants were on duty, she opened the front door with her key and led the way across the broad hallway to the small salon where she had entertained Dragan before. It still seemed the best place to remain undisturbed by whoever else was in the house.

Stripping off her dirty hat and cloak, she rang the bell.

"Do you really live here, Missus?" Nick asked, awed. He stood in the middle of the room as though afraid to move.

"Yes, I do, but if you are to stay here, Nick, you should call me Lady Grizelda. And this is Mr. Tizsa."

His eyes widened. "What a real *Lady* lady? Damn!"

"It's not polite to swear," she warned him.

Janet stuck her head into the room.

"Ah. Ask Mrs. MacKenna to step in here, please, Janet. Mrs. MacKenna is our housekeeper," she explained to Nick. "You must be respectful to her and do as she says."

Nick mumbled, and Griz wondered uneasily how this was going to work out.

Mrs. MacKenna, entering the room a minute later, eyed Nick somewhat dubiously. But she only said, "Come, then, young man. Cook will give you some dinner, and then we can see about a bath and clothes."

"Remember what we said," Griz reminded him.

Nick only grinned over his shoulder and followed Mrs. MacKenna.

Griz sighed. "I hope he doesn't steal all the silver and bolt."

"It is a possibility," Dragan admitted. He had been moving restlessly about the room, gazing out of the window, picking up and laying down the not-very-interesting knickknacks scattered around. He glanced over his shoulder at her. "Your housekeeper didn't seem very surprised. Are you in the habit of bringing home waifs and strays from the gutter?"

"Not usually the gutter," Griz replied vaguely. "But sometimes people have nowhere to go... Why was he afraid of you, suddenly? Because he thought you might still be angry about him leading us to our deaths?"

He stopped pacing and glanced at her. "Partly, perhaps. A child alone faces many dangers from unscrupulous and perverse adults. It isn't just girls who are sold to pimps and brothels."

Griz sat down abruptly on the sofa. Anger, pity, and revulsion struggled for dominance. "He is used to defending himself," she managed at last. "That's what he meant. Art protected him from that and all the other dangers."

"And turned on him in the end, just to stop us asking questions."

She shivered, feeling the child's betrayal as well as the horror of their near-death.

"Look on the bright side," Dragan said lightly. "We must have been close to something they wanted to hide."

Remembering the leaflet, Griz quickly extracted it from the pocket of her cloak and spread it open on her lap. Dragan threw himself down beside her.

This was no mere urging for political change. This was a call to arms, a denunciation of everyone in power, from the queen to the city corporations and everyone in between.

"Armed rebellion," Griz said, stunned, staring from it to Dragan. "Is this what *you* sought?"

"No. Though we weren't above using the threat of it, using their fear of it, to win what we wanted. Our revolution was bloodless. Until the emperor recovered his nerve." He flicked one scornful finger against the paper. "This is half-baked, illogical nonsense. No political thinker, no social reformer would come out with such pointless, ill-focused anger. There is no goal here, nothing to achieve. Just destruction and violence, as though they were ends in themselves."

"Would it convince people to overthrow their government?"

"To riot and loot and threaten their better-off neighbors, perhaps. Perhaps the aim was just chaos so that the rookery—if this is the leaflet that was found in the raided rookery—could thrive?"

"Nancy would never advocate such a thing," Griz stated. "I don't understand her connection to this. But these people are clearly dangerous. They tried to kill us, so they could quite easily have killed her without a backward glance. Perhaps she was betraying them."

"Perhaps." He didn't sound convinced, and she glanced at him. He was frowning over the paper, every sense, it seemed, focused on the violent words.

Not for the first time, her stomach fluttered at his sheer good looks. But his face was more than handsome, it was expressive and intriguing and as contradictory as the man himself. She was very aware of his shoulder against hers as he leaned over the paper. Her every nerve tingled in novel, secret pleasure.

He looked up suddenly, catching her avid gaze. It seemed cowardly somehow to simply avert her eyes, so she held on, searching for something to say.

"What happened to you?" she blurted.

The corner of his eye twitched, but he didn't look away either. Nor did he pretend to misunderstand. "I'm sorry. There are some things I cannot help."

"You don't need to apologize," she said fervently. "You saved all our lives."

"I only began it. You finished it. Thank you," he added with such difficulty that she covered his hand with hers.

"There is no need," she said.

He searched her face, all but devouring her with his haunted eyes, and then dragged them free at last. Her heart fell because he seemed to have withdrawn from her, but he did not move his hand from her clasp.

"I am not a natural soldier," he said. "My purpose has always been to *save* lives, but I fought to preserve what we had won. It was justice. And I did some good among the horror. I saved some lives, patched up a lot of wounds, even helped in the villages we passed through. In the fighting, I did my part, because I had to because I had to look after my men. And then, toward the end of the war, I was too slow to withdraw. Canon fire came out of nowhere and exploded yards from me. I saw…"

He broke off, his hand twisting and grasping hers. She understood he would not distress her with the details of what he saw.

"Several of my men were killed. My lieutenant, who had become my friend. Perhaps it had been coming for a while, but from then on, sudden noises, like thunder, anything that makes the ground shake…"

She tightened her grip on his hand, raised her other arm around his neck, and pressed her cheek to his soft hair.

"I'm sorry," she whispered.

It was instinct, impulsive compassion for a man who had always shown himself utterly capable. But with a jolt, she realized he was also a stranger, alone with her against all propriety, and she had her arms around him. She wondered how it would feel to brush her lips against his hair, his skin. If he turned his face to her and—

She sprang up, just as Peter walked in with the tea tray, Janet at his heels to arrange things on the table for her.

Perhaps it was the awful possibility of being discovered only a second or so earlier in such a compromising position that made her stomach churn and tingle. At any rate, the familiar fussing with tea gave them both time to revert to normal.

She set a strong cup of tea in front of him and sat on a different chair. "I'll ask Horace about the leaflet," she said. "See if it's the one that inspired the rookery arrests. I wonder if he would know about Art? Or Art's enemy, who was arrested. *He* could have been Nancy's gentleman."

Dragan shrugged. "I think you underestimate her. She worked for years in a nobleman's household. Do you really think she could not tell a genuine gentleman from a rich villain?"

"Oh, no, I'm sure she could," Griz said in surprise. "It's more about what she told her friends, to let it appear, perhaps, that she was doing better than she was."

Dragan was frowning at the leaflet beside him on the sofa. He drank his tea in two gulps and replaced the cup in the saucer. "It just doesn't seem right, though. Something is missing." He stood. "I'd better go. Let me know what you discover."

"Likewise," she said, unreasonably disappointed that he was rushing off. She had probably offended him. Men didn't always like to be reminded of weakness. They would rather pretend they didn't need comfort. Or perhaps he truly didn't... "Goodbye," she added as he strode to the door.

He paused and glanced back over his shoulder. "Griz?" A smile lurked in his eyes.

"Yes?"

"It was a fun afternoon."

CHAPTER TEN

D RAGAN FOUND HIMSELF grinning as he crossed the hall and left the house, her surprised gurgle of laughter echoing in his ears. He liked the way she laughed and the way her eyes danced behind her spectacles.

He wondered how many people wrote her off as merely eccentric. Fewer than she thought, he suspected. For though she might lack the dazzling beauty of the sister he had met yesterday, Grizelda had her own quieter yet deeper beauty, a fascinating vitality that came from her interest in people and her surroundings, a desire to always know more.

He liked her spirit, her sense of justice that urged her to pursue the killer of a maidservant, whom she must have been brought up to regard as far beneath her. There was guilt, of course, because she hadn't made enough effort to assure Nancy's wellbeing. And simple compassion, which was strong in her.

Even for him. Her unexpected embrace had caught at his breath. He wasn't coxcomb enough to believe she had meant it in any way other than comfort, but it was sweet all the same. And if he had had the urge to sweep her up in his arms in return, well, that was his baser instinct as he was well aware how it would have been greeted. As betrayal.

There may have been a twinge of disappointment in that, but he also felt a surge of happiness that they were friends. He sensed a fellow spirit in her, which was a pleasure, an excitement, even. He hadn't lied when he'd said she brought color to his life.

Tomorrow, after the inquest, of course, he might just take her friend Mrs. Worth up on her invitation to tea.

Not for the first time, he turned his mind to questions of coroners and their medical men and how much influence Dr. Cordell would prove to have with the latter.

⟫⟫⟫⟪⟪⟪

ENOUGH, AS IT turned out. Dragan spent part of Sunday evening in a cold mortuary, examining Nancy's corpse.

"The weapon that was found at the scene," Dragan said, "did not make this wound."

"No," agreed Dr. Smith, a middle-aged man with an impressive shock of white hair and an incongruously cheerful disposition. "God knows what it was doing there. Possibly completely unrelated to this girl's death or left to lead the police in the wrong direction. Though, they don't seem to have made much effort to trace it. Not relevant, I suppose."

"What kind of weapon would you say did this?" Dragan asked. "Clearly not a sword or a bayonet."

"Possibly a small kitchen knife or a pocketknife. The wound isn't ragged or even very deep, but it was well-placed."

"So, either very lucky or very deliberate?"

"Exactly."

Dragan glanced at Dr. Smith. "Could she have done it herself, in your opinion?"

"She could. But I don't think she could have held her own throat at the same time."

Dragan was glad he didn't have to bring up the bruises on her throat. "You think he tried to strangle her first and then gave up and stabbed her?"

"Possible. I'd say it's more likely he held her by the throat, and when she reached up to dislodge his fingers, he stabbed her through the heart. Bastard."

"As you say," Dragan said bleakly. He forced his gaze back to the body. "I see no other injuries on her."

"No, she seems otherwise a healthy young woman. I suppose she would be if she worked for the Duchess of Kelburn. God knows what she was doing in a place like Mudd Lane." Dr. Smith eyed him curiously. "What's your interest in this girl, Doctor?"

"Someone in the duchess's household asked me to help find out what happened."

"Sometimes," Dr. Smith observed, covering the body back up, "one is better not knowing."

"Perhaps. Thank you, sir," he said politely. "I appreciate your time and insight." He moved toward the door, then, on impulse, turned back. "Just as a matter of curiosity, has anyone—someone of power and influence—asked you to keep any of your findings to yourself?"

Dr. Smith looked affronted. "Of course not!"

BIZARRELY ENOUGH, THE inquest was held in a hostelry in Castle Street. According to Cordell, this was the normal custom unless the deceased person had died in a hospital or workhouse.

By the time Dragan arrived there, the jury had, apparently, already viewed the body. They seemed to be largely tradesmen and sat in a group, looking important, anxious, or slightly sick, according to their character.

Taking a seat, he saw Inspector Harris at the other end of the row, glaring at him. Also, at the front, Nancy's one-time suitor, Jack Payne, stony-faced, beside a drooping middle-aged couple, who he guessed were her parents. On their other side sat a lady in an impenetrable veil. Behind them sat Mrs. MacKenna from Kelburn House and one of the maids.

Dragan's gaze drifted back to the veiled lady. He almost imagined she gazed back, though it was impossible to tell. Although she was not ostentatiously dressed, he knew, with a twinge of pleasure, that it was Grizelda. Present from curiosity, of course, but also because she cared.

The coroner, one Mr. Bedford, recited the reason they were here, Nancy's name, and the place of her death. At once, he called on Dr. Smith to give his opinion.

The doctor stood up. "The victim died from a stab wound to the heart," he said bluntly.

"When?" the coroner demanded.

"Thursday last, the same night she was found."

"And in your opinion, could she have done this to herself?"

"Only if someone else then stole the weapon. The stiletto found at the scene was not that which killed her." His eyes flickered to the parents. "I believe she died instantly when the blade entered her heart."

"And the bruising on her throat? Was she strangled?"

"Held against her will would be more accurate. There is another on her left wrist, consistent with a tight grip. But the wound to her heart killed her."

"Had she been otherwise molested?" the coroner asked delicately.

"There were no signs of it."

"Thank you, Doctor." Mr. Bedford scowled at the jury. "The body was found just before ten on Thursday evening. I have a statement to read to you from the person who discovered it first."

He then read out a brief, anonymous statement of how Griz had found the body. This was designed, of course, to keep her person and the Niven name out of proceedings and the press. Dragan wondered what her family would say if they knew she was here anyway.

Mr. Bedford then frowned around the room. "Mr. Tizsa?"

Dragan stood.

"I understand you arrived on the scene only seconds later? Tell the jury what you found, if you please."

"I found the victim's body lying on the ground, exactly as you just described. She was warm still to the touch but dead."

"Are you qualified to be sure of that?"

"I did not sit my final examination," Dragan said patiently. "But I studied medicine and served as an army surgeon for two years. I am certainly qualified to recognize death."

"What did you do when you found the young woman?"

"I looked for signs of breath and took her pulse. There was none. I tried to give her my own breath, but it was too late."

"And then what happened?"

"A policeman came and summoned his colleagues."

"Thank you."

The policeman who first attended the scene was then asked to give his evidence, which he did in an unnatural monotone, enunciating each word with care. He had nothing to add about the victim, but one of the jury suddenly piped up.

"Didn't you arrest someone at the scene, though?"

"Yes," the constable admitted, glaring at Dragan, "but he didn't do it, so we had to let him go. The weapon he was holding wasn't the one that killed her."

That wasn't the reason they had let him go, of course, but no one questioned it. Grizelda's brother did seem to have quite some hold over the police and the workings of the law. No one asked any questions at all about the supposedly absent witness who had been first on the scene. Her name was never even mentioned.

That kind of privilege was not unknown to him. It happened everywhere, but he had hoped better of England, of Great Britain, which had been the model of many of his more moderate compatriots in the late revolution.

He mulled this over for some time, only half-listening to the rest of the evidence, which was Nancy's parents and colleagues stating that she would never under any circumstances have taken her own life. Even though the doctor and the police had ruled suicide out, it was clearly a point worth making, for a suicide could not be buried in hallowed ground. Like the churchyard in Lincoln favored by her parents.

Dragan found it silly superstition and couldn't understand why people put themselves through such nonsense. To him, a suicide was as much to be pitied and respected as any other victim of death.

The jury's verdict was not a surprise, considering the police were already investigating murder. Dragan made his way toward the door and glanced back to see the veiled lady deep in conversation with Nancy's parents. There was no way to tell if she noticed his departure.

From sheer curiosity, he lingered in the street, watching everyone emerge—members of the jury hurrying back to work, the bereaved family saying goodbye to Mrs. MacKenna and the weeping maid, then stepping into a hired coach. Mrs. MacKenna and the maid were clearly waiting for someone, and sure enough, the veiled lady emerged a few moments later, deep in conversation with Inspector Harris.

The inspector eventually tipped his hat to her and strode off, fortunately in the opposite direction to Dragan, who didn't particularly want to be seen by the policeman conferring with Lady Grizelda.

He strolled up to her, and the veil turned toward him.

"Go back without me, Mrs. MacKenna," she told the housekeeper. "I have some things I need to do."

The housekeeper seemed about to argue, then thought better of it. "Come along," she commanded the maid, and the pair walked briskly away.

"I don't think I learned anything new," Grizelda said discontentedly. "Did you?"

On impulse, he offered his arm. "There's a tearoom round the corner where we can discuss it."

Without hesitation, she took his arm and began to walk. He felt oddly protective.

"They did not mention her baby," Griz said, "for which I am glad, for her parents' sake, and Jack's. Only it makes me wonder how thorough the autopsy was."

"Only thorough enough to see how far the blade penetrated. The wound measurements were quite precise."

"I suppose that is why no one is very interested in our dagger," Griz remarked.

"I'm surprised no one has yet connected it to your father's collection..." Dragan tailed off as the veil turned toward him. "Ah. Someone has."

"It's back in its place in the cabinet," Griz admitted. "No one has even mentioned it. I asked my father when it reappeared, and he just looked at me as though I'd grown horns."

"Did you ask your brother?"

"Horace? Yes." She hesitated, then blurted, "He told me to mind my own business. And claims to know nothing of Art Dooley."

"Hmm. Your family is powerful. Your name was never mentioned, and you were never summoned to give personal evidence. Nancy's employer was never once mentioned."

"It keeps the press away," she said, almost desperately.

He halted and impatiently dragged up her veil, casting it over the top of her hat. Though she looked stunned by his unconventional behavior, he ignored that, demanding, "You don't really think one of them did it, do you?"

"I can't think why or how, or what on earth would be worth the risk of such scandal." She adjusted the veil and walked on.

"Then you *have* thought about it," he observed.

"So have you," she retorted, walking faster. She drew in a breath.

"Yes, I thought about it and discarded them all. My father and Forsythe were in the opera house. And Horace...look, he might be ruthless in his own way, but he respects the law, and murdering a maid would be *beneath* him. Does that make sense? Nor would he be stupid enough to take a weapon from his own home."

"No, I still think Nancy took it." When he became aware she was frowning up at him, he added quickly, "I think she was frightened and took it for protection. I think she wanted my help, and before she got it, someone chased her into that alley. Cornered, I think she threatened her attacker with the stiletto. He seized her by the left wrist—did you notice she was left-handed?—and squeezed to make her drop the weapon, which she did. She tried to flee, but he caught her by the throat, killed her, and ran off to the far end of the alley, vanishing, probably, just as you arrived at the other end."

She shivered, and he squeezed her hand in the crook of his arm. "I'm sorry," he said gruffly. "I think it was brutal and quick. I just don't know who or why. How is Nick? Did he stay in the house?"

"He was there this morning, and so is the silver. He seems dazed and wide-eyed."

"What do you mean to do with him?" Dragan released her to open the tearoom door, and she stepped inside.

"I don't know yet. He can help keep the kitchen fire stoked just now. He might want to learn some trade or other, or... Good morning," she greeted the smiling waitress, who showed them to a table and took their order for coffee. "And cakes," Griz added as an afterthought.

She was frowning as the waitress scuttled off. "He feels Art's betrayal very deeply. I don't think he's going to trust anyone else very easily."

"No, but he might tell us a bit more about Art's rival."

"Those who were arrested... I shall ask Horace about that. In a very round-about way, or he'll tell me to mind my own business again."

"What did you get out of Inspector Harris?"

"That they've searched for the murder weapon and witnesses and found no sign of either."

"And yet there were people around. I heard footsteps, more than just yours. And there were moving shadows. Someone saw who chased her into that alley and who left again. They're just not saying."

"Loyalty again?"

"Or fear."

Her smile was cynical. "Does it not amount to the same thing? In that world at least."

"And in others," he allowed.

Their coffee and cake approached, and she changed the subject, asking politely after the Cordells.

Even after they had their coffee and she cut into a very elegant pastry, and no one else was close enough to overhear, she carried on the conversation. "How did you come to meet the Cordells?"

"I knew the doctor's younger brother in Vienna, years ago when he was traveling. He had graduated by then, but we shared many an argument about medicine and politics. And many a bottle. We kept up correspondence once he left, and when I ended up here, he was the only Englishman I knew."

"Is he in London, too?"

"No, in Berkshire. But there is more work for me in London, and his brother had both need of an assistant and a spare room to lodge me." Her eyes, interested but unpitying, were really rather beautiful— a unique shade of hazel he had no name for, with odd, fascinating flecks of amber. Although, that might have been a trick of the sunlight through the window. "It's not how I imagined my life would be. Exiled. Poor. Useless."

He hadn't meant to say such words, ever, least of all to her, but somehow, they slipped out. He didn't even have time to wave them away with a joke, for she said seriously, "I will allow you the first two, but you do not appear to be remotely useless. What would you have been doing if the revolution had succeeded?"

He shrugged. "I would be practicing as a physician, probably in Pest."

"As some more experienced doctor's assistant, perhaps?" she suggested innocently.

He smiled faintly. "Perhaps."

"At least partly among the poorest and sickest?"

"You are right, of course. I complain about nothing when I am lucky to be alive."

"I don't underestimate exile and poverty," she said carefully, "although I have known neither. And I know you wanted to change the world."

"I thought we could all have a say," he offered. "Eliminate injustice and poverty. Instead, we made it all worse."

She seemed to think about that. "I doubt it," she said at last. "I think change is only ever gradual. Two steps forward and only one back. It just won't be as quick as you might like."

"Where did you learn such wisdom?" he asked lightly. "From your aristocratic ancestors?"

"Books," she said in surprise, and he laughed.

"I like you, Griz. You are a breath of fresh air."

She blushed and smiled at the same time, and the world seemed to fade, leaving only her. And he smiled, too, spontaneously, wanting her to like him back, even while the sane and sensible part of his brain flashed warnings at him.

Oh no, draw back from this now. She is not for you.

"Why are you not married long ago to some rich and honorable young nobleman?" he asked mildly.

"The best of them married my sisters, and I can't be expected to look lower." It was light and practiced, and Dragan didn't believe a word.

"You wanted a different life," he guessed. "You see? You are as revolutionary as I am."

There was a speculative look in her eyes. "You mean you believe women should be able to do more than marry and have children?"

"Women do."

"Lower class women without husbands,"

"I don't recognize class," he said promptly.

"Yes, you do. You just don't like it."

"Perhaps not, but I do agree with you that women's minds are as capable as men's."

"Then you would be happy to see your sister or your wife at university? To work alongside her in your medical practice? As your fellow doctor?"

"Yes," he said at once. "Though I should point out I have neither a sister nor a wife."

"But no one will ask *you* why you are not married," she pointed out. "They don't think you are eccentric or lacking in some way."

He blinked, startled. "Surely people do not think that of you?"

"Well," she said reasonably, "I suppose I *am* eccentric, but the point is, marriage is the only profession, the only trade open to women of my class. Unless I wish to be a governess, which I can't help thinking would be tedious and thankless."

Distractedly, he helped himself to a cake. "You have considered all this very carefully."

"Well, I have nothing better to do," she said, her eyes dancing. "Being unmarried and without purpose or use."

"I might allow you the first two," he said, referring back to her remark about him. "But you do not appear to be remotely useless."

She laughed. "*Touché.* In truth, now that I have managed to shrug off everyone's expectations, I enjoy my life very well."

He found it hard to look away. "That is a rare gift," he said slowly.

"Treasure it."

IT WAS NO hardship to walk with her back to Park Lane. She moved briskly, clearly used to exercise, while they talked mostly of Nancy, though occasionally got distracted onto other subjects. The incongruity of the situation was not lost on him—walking in the spring sunshine with a beautiful, blue-blooded girl and talking of murder.

The other incongruity didn't actually strike him until they reached the more rarified streets of Mayfair and passers-by who exchanged bows with her and eyed him askance.

"Will it hurt you to be seen with me?" he asked abruptly.

Griz, who had been frowning over the puzzle of what could have persuaded Nancy into an insalubrious back street in the dark, took a moment to refocus on his words.

She waved one dismissive hand. "Lord, no. Most of them won't remember my name any more than I recall theirs. Besides, it's not as if I'm hanging on your arm and gazing up at you adoringly."

For an instant, he imagined her doing just that, though not on the public street, and was obliged to fight down the inconvenient surge of desire. All the same, as they drew closer to Grosvenor Square, he was reluctant to leave her. He wondered what she was like to talk to about subjects other than murder, to dance with, to merely enjoy the moment. Fun, he suspected, remembering the mad chase on Sunday.

His breath caught. "Griz, would you…?"

"Would I what?" she prompted.

Come with me to a charitable event raising money for my countrymen. Dance with me, laugh with me, no barriers between us. It wouldn't just make the dreaded evening bearable. It would be intoxicating…. And impossible.

"Keep me informed of anything else you discover," he said hastily.

He tipped his hat and bowed before she could even answer. "I won't cause talk by accompanying you all the way home. Goodbye." And he strode away, turning the corner into Mount Street without considering where he was going.

He really did not need this complication in his life. He would help her find the truth of the murder because they both seemed to owe Nancy that, but pursuing anything else between them was madness.

Wasn't it?

"Mr. Tizsa!" The female voice calling his name did so with the kind of half-amused frustration that told him it was not the first time she had addressed him.

He halted, blinking at the fashionably dressed lady in front of him. Lady Trench, otherwise, Grizelda's beautiful sister Azalea. She had clearly just stepped down from a carriage emblazoned with an impressive coat of arms, in which sat another, curious lady, her eyes out like organ stocks.

"Lady Trench." He bowed politely.

"How charming to run into you. Come and take tea with us. Or luncheon, perhaps." To his surprise, she actually took his arm, as though they were much closer acquaintances. The carriage began to move forward with its solitary occupant, and Lady Trench murmured in some amusement, "Don't look so appalled. I won't eat you. I merely wish to give my sister-in-law something to gossip about."

He regarded her in some amusement. "That's a dangerous temptation to throw in a man's way."

"Not really, if you are at my little sister's feet."

He was too startled to do more than follow her into what was, presumably, her own house. "What makes you say that?"

She cast him a brilliant smile reminiscent of Grizelda's at Great Scotland Yard. "You mean you are not? Tea in the drawing room, if you please, Turner," she added to the waiting butler, to whom she gave her gloves, hat, and coat. "Is his lordship at home to join us?"

The butler took Dragan's hat with a bow. "No, my lady. I believe he stepped round to his club."

"Thank you, Turner." She crossed the hall, leading the way up-stairs. "What do gentlemen find to do in these wretched clubs all day? Do you have a club, Mr. Tizsa?"

"No," Dragan said, baldly.

"Good. I shall tell my husband it is perfectly possible to live with-out one." She led him into a light, elegant drawing room, and invited him to sit, after which, removing all doubt about possible seduction, she chose a chair at a very respectable distance.

"Why do you want to annoy your sister-in-law?" he asked.

"Because I have just sustained a somewhat impudent lecture from her on the subject of correct appearances and what is due to my husband, as well as the Niven name. I did not point out that I had been born with the name and had carried it longer than she."

"Instead, you plucked a stranger off the street and invited him into your house without a care for even the appearance of a chaperone."

Lady Trench allowed herself a small smile, which was not entirely indignation free. "I believe the point was well made. Thank God my husband is not half as stuffy—or foolish—as my brother and his wife. Have you met my brother, Mr. Tizsa?"

"I have met Lord Forsythe," he replied as the servants entered with a tea tray and placed it on a low table before Lady Trench.

"Oh, Forsythe is a completely different kettle of fish to my eldest brother, Lord Monkton. Thank you," she added to the servants, which appeared to be their dismissal.

One could learn a good deal about wealthy people by the way they treated their servants. Lady Trench seemed to have the same light, civil touch as Griz. So far, at least.

"Monkton will be the duke one day, and Augusta—his wife—lets it go to her head. What are you up to with Grizelda?"

Perhaps the sudden question was designed to take him by surprise, but he held her gaze and even smiled. "Oh, the usual. Seduction, fortune-hunting, that kind of thing."

She smiled back, her eyes icy. "Mr. Tizsa, if I truly thought that—if I ever think that—you would not be sitting there. Sugar?"

"Please. No milk." He stood to accept the tea and made a quick decision. This woman cared for her sister, perhaps even understood her. He sat back down. "Grizelda asked me to help her discover who killed Nancy Barrow. Your mother's housemaid."

"Oh, I know who she is. Was." She sighed. "I suppose I should have known, too, that Griz would not leave it to the police. She says you didn't do it."

"I didn't," he said mildly.

Her eyes lost that faintly challenging look. "Did she really charge into the police commissioners' office to rescue you?"

"Like a one-woman cavalry charge. With a dog. The police never stood a chance."

Lady Trench laughed, an infectious, full-throated chuckle. "I wish I had been there!"

"Would you have gone with her if she had asked you?"

"Probably not. I would have tried to talk her out of it. And she would have gone anyway. Is that what you do? You go with her?"

"Or she goes with me. It seems to be a…partnership."

Her eyes searched his over her teacup. Dragan had the feeling she was weighing her words. "My little sister is kind and brave and excessively curious. She treats everyone as a friend. But she is not…worldly."

"She seems extremely sharp to me."

"Oh, sharp, yes. She is clever. But she has little experience with men. If you take advantage of her, I will know."

She was quite impressive in her own way. He considered her in silence, until she said sharply. "You have nothing to say?"

He stirred. "Forgive me. I was wondering whether or not to be offended. And then I wondered if there was a reason for this lack of worldly experience. Beyond her desire to travel her own path, which I applaud, by the way."

Lady Trench frowned, only half-amused as she searched his face. "I had a feeling you might. I suppose that is why she likes you."

"Does she?" he asked too quickly.

Lady Trench sighed. "I should not have begun this conversation. It is too fraught with offense and small betrayals. You may think we do not care for her, but we do." She lifted her chin. "You may not think she cares for *us*, but she does."

"I know. That was clear from the beginning when she kept quiet about your father's dagger being found at the scene of Nancy's murder."

Her eyes flew to his, widening in clear alarm. Her flawless skin paled. Her shock was abundantly clear. "Dear God, that is what killed Nancy? And Griz thinks—"

"No, another weapon was used to kill her. We think Nancy borrowed the dagger for her own protection and dropped it at the scene."

"And Griz did not tell." She seemed appalled by her sister's burden. Her eyes refocused on Dragan's face. "But she told you."

He shrugged. "Eventually."

But Lady Trench had moved on. "I wonder which of us she thought..." She broke off, drinking her tea as an excuse, he suspected, to lose the rest of the thought. "Is that why she was so sure you did not do it?"

"Oh no. She worked that out for herself with logic and science."

Lady Trench looked unsure whether to be proud of her sister or appalled by her involvement. She asked more questions about what they had learned in their investigations, and Dragan saw no reason not to tell her about their adventures in St. Giles, although he left out the murderous part at the end. Lady Trench laughed as he described their mad flight through the back streets.

"I should be utterly appalled by this," she commented, at last. "But in fact, I find myself merely glad that you were with her. Was that your intent?"

"More of an additional benefit."

"Because you don't want me to try and end your…alliance?"

"Because I don't want her put in that position," he said frankly. "I value her friendship."

Again, her surprisingly piercing gaze reminded him of Griz. "I believe you do," she said at last. "Very well, I shall invite you to my soiree on Thursday evening."

He blinked. "Why?"

"Sir, that is not a gracious way to accept—or decline—an invitation."

"I beg your pardon."

She regarded him. "I want Griz to be happy."

"Has she been unhappy?"

"No, not recently." She held his gaze. "I believe a man broke her heart once. Years ago, but it has made her wary to trust."

"Are we back to warnings?" he asked mildly.

"No, Mr. Tizsa. Promises. More tea?"

CHAPTER ELEVEN

GRIZ WAS GLAD when she finally returned from the inquest to discover Nick still in the kitchen, playing with the dog and getting under Cook's feet. When Vicky licked his face before galloping up to greet Griz with excitement, Griz decided she had done the right thing. Vicky, after all, did not actively like many people.

While Vicky hurled herself into Grizelda's arms, Nick's demeanor changed to one of wary watchfulness. Griz pretended not to notice.

"Would you like to take Vicky for a walk?" she suggested.

"Where to?" he asked suspiciously.

"Just to the park. Come, fetch your cap and jacket, and we'll go now."

He was wearing a slightly worn but respectable suit of clothes that had probably been collected from Azalea's son for charity. However, with a hint of defiance, he clapped his bright red cap on his head. It had been cleaned since Griz had seen it last, so she didn't mind in the slightest.

Since it was more convenient, and she wasn't yet ready to explain Nick's presence to her family, they left the house by the area steps, Vicky dancing on the end of her leash.

"What's that for?" Nick asked, indicating the leash. "To stop her running away?"

"Well, to stop her running under horses' hooves and carriage wheels. And she can growl at strangers."

"Oh, can we let her do that in the park?" Nick asked eagerly.

"No, she might frighten someone. And someone might hurt her."

Nick looked dubious but pushed no further. For her part, Griz did not question him about his past or his future, or even about anything to do with Nancy. She wanted him to be comfortable, to have no reason to bolt back to his old life. He chattered easily enough about the size of his dinner and his breakfast, how Mr. Butler looked down his nose, and how Cook gave him an extra slice of custard pie. He asked questions about Vicky and asked if the Green Park was Grizelda's garden.

"Oh, no, it's a public park," she assured him.

"Just wondered," he said defensively. "Because of your huge house and all them servants and rooms and pretty things."

"They're not really mine," she explained. "They are my parents'."
And then she wondered if his peculiar honor would allow him to steal from her parents but not from her. Still, she couldn't take it back.

"And the soldier-doctor?" he asked casually. "Is he rich, too?"

"No, I don't believe so. He lost everything when he had to leave his own country."

"Why'd he have to leave?" Nick asked, bouncing in time to the dog.

"I believe they would have executed him," she said unwisely.

Nick's eyes widened. "Really? I never guessed! What'd he do?"

"Fought for what he thought was right. Against his government."

"And they won?"

"Yes."

"Never mind," Nick said cheerfully. "He can go back and kill them all later."

Which, Griz supposed, at least meant he was on Dragan's side and was no longer afraid of him.

Should one be afraid of Dragan? Whenever she thought of him, which was probably more than she should, she was conscious of a little knot in her stomach. She wasn't quite sure what this knot was made of. She didn't think it was fear, for she liked him too much for that, but there was certainly some tension and a lot of excitement. Although novel, she rather liked the feeling, which seemed to spread and intensify whenever she saw him. Especially when he had lifted her veil in the street, when he had smiled at her in the tearoom.

Of course, he was quite ridiculously handsome, and she couldn't ever recall any other handsome faces having quite such an effect on her, not even at sixteen when she had met Captain Galbraith at Azalea's wedding. No, it was more his inner workings that intrigued her, his beliefs, his compassion and sensitivity, even his odd moment of weakness yesterday when he had saved them from the falling masonry.

And his interest in her, which she knew had nothing to do with her family. Nor was it the kind of superior, tolerant amusement occasionally displayed by gentlemen toward her. It was as if he *saw* her...

She became aware, suddenly, that Nick was no longer beside her. He had bounded ahead with the dog and seemed to be in some kind of altercation with an elderly gentleman whose walking stick Vicky had taken a shine to.

Hurrying after them, she heard Nick saying, "Well, what do you expect? It's just a stick like any other to her." He made no effort to pull Vicky off as she tugged at the end of the stick, even though the old gentleman was in danger of being dragged over. In fact, Nick seemed more entertained than anything.

"Vicky, drop!" Griz commanded.

Immediately, the dog lifted her head, giving Griz the instant she needed to seize the leash from Nick and pull her into her side.

"I am so sorry, sir. She thinks it's a game."

Now that he was no longer in danger of overbalancing, the old gentleman seemed to see the funny side. "Ha! I'd throw it for her if I could be sure she'd bring it back." He tipped his hat and toddled onward.

"Can't I take her again?" Nick asked, disappointed.

"Yes." Griz handed back the leash. "But you mustn't let her annoy people. Shorten the lead and pull her in when you're close to people. Otherwise, you can let her sniff wherever she likes."

They returned to Kelburn House quite in charity with each other. Griz sent Nick back to the kitchen to see if Cook or Mrs. MacKenna needed him, and she repaired to her chamber to change.

She was going to Annabelle's for tea, which she usually enjoyed. But this time, she was slightly ashamed because the excited little knot in her stomach was growing. It was Dragan rather than Annabelle, whom she most wanted to see. Even though they had parted only a few hours previously.

Deliberately, she did not fuss over her dress but let Emmie, who had replaced Nancy in helping her, choose the gown and pin her hair. She was better at it than Nancy had been.

On the stairs, she encountered Forsythe on his way up.

"Where are you off to?"

"Tea at Annabelle's. Do you want to come?"

He thought about it. "No," he said at last. "I'm sure Letty Watters is going to be there."

Since it was not far to Brook Street, Griz walked, and as was her habit, took no maid or footman to accompany her. Her family had largely given up telling her off for this, in part because they were unaware how often she did it or how far she went.

A frequent visitor to the Worth house, she was shown directly up to the drawing room, where she was surprised to find a large number of people, all eagerly turning their faces toward her. They seemed disappointed.

Annabelle jumped up from the sofa and came to meet her. "I hope your Mr. Tizsa is going to come," she murmured as they embraced. "I promised them a hero from the late Hungarian war."

Annabelle's husband, Timothy, cast her a tolerant smile and greeted Griz with casual friendliness.

As the Duke of Kelburn's daughter, she was never unwelcome at any society gathering. Every gentleman offered her his chair. Flustered by the attention, she went straight toward the man she knew, Mr. Watters, before she realized it placed her beside Miss Watters, whom her mother wished to marry Forsythe.

"Thank you, sir," she said civilly, seating herself since she could not now change her mind. "How are you, Miss Watters?"

"A little fatigued from the season," Miss Watters replied very properly. "Such a constant round of pleasure! And you, Lady Grizelda? I believe I did not see you at Lady Tamar's ball on Saturday night?"

"Oh, no," Griz agreed. "I had a previous engagement. I imagine it was a very smart affair."

"Indeed. So many people one could not move!" She glanced toward the door again. "Did Lord Forsythe accompany you today? Or one of your other brothers?"

"Goodness, no, they are all busy about their own business. Or so I imagine."

Miss Watters's eyes widened. "You came alone?"

"I frequently do. Annabelle and I have been friends forever, and it is only a step, you know."

The drawing room door opened again to reveal only Annabelle's butler, who walked sedately across the floor to murmur in his mistress's ear.

"Oh, yes, of course, show him up, Stevens!" Annabelle smiled around the room as her butler departed. "Mr. Tizsa," she confided in tones of one supplying a long-awaited treat.

Griz awaited his arrival with a mixture of amusement and unease, unsure how he would take to being the chief attraction of the event. In fact, he did not appear to notice, striding straight in and bowing civilly over Annabelle's outstretched hand.

Annabelle beamed. "How lovely to see you again. Timothy, this is Mr. Tizsa, whom I was telling you about. Mr. Tizsa, my husband."

Timothy shook hands with his usual good nature before Annabelle whipped her guest of honor away to introduce him to everyone else. As he passed Griz, his gaze met hers for an instant, and his eyebrows shot up.

It wasn't quite the quiet meeting and further conversation that Griz had hoped for. Dragan was feted and avidly questioned about the late campaigns in Hungary and how his people had held out so long against the emperor. He bore it with good nature and without flinching, and the women gazed at him with awed appreciation, while their menfolk stuck to military and political questions.

"Why are they making such a fuss of him?" Mr. Watters murmured. "Just because he is Hungarian?"

"Well, it *is* fashionable," Miss Watters replied with a hint of humor. "I believe Mr. Kossuth himself is expected in London later in the year."

It became clear that there would be no private discussion with Dragan this afternoon, and, indeed, since she had discovered nothing new since the morning, there was no real need. Still, she could not help being a trifle disappointed when she went over to Annabelle to say goodbye.

"What a successful tea party," she teased.

"I suspect it would have been the opposite if he hadn't turned up. Are you leaving already?"

"I have taken up my allotted half-hour of your time. Although I thought I might step up and see Timmie before I go?"

"I'll come up with you..."

Timmie, a lively young gentleman of three, appeared delighted to see Griz, galloping across the nursery on his hobby horse and casting his wooden sword aside to jump on her. Griz laughed, hugging him and spinning him around and back onto the horse.

She had always been fond of Timmie as an extension of Annabelle, but she realized now the child was his own lovable little person. For the first time, she wondered if she would ever have children of her own.

Veering hastily away from that thought, she told Annabelle she would have to hurry home and waved goodbye to the exuberant Timmie. As they descended the stairs, Timothy and Dragan emerged from the drawing room, the latter clearly being shown out by his host.

"You are not going already, Mr. Tizsa?" Annabelle called, hurrying after them.

"I have a patient to see on my way home, but I have had a most agreeable break from work. Thank you for the tea and company." He hesitated, then said, "I would like to invite you to a Hungarian evening at the Blue Horse in Kensington. It is no grand affair, merely a fund-raising event to help those refugees from the war who have landed here with nothing."

"What a noble cause," Annabelle said warmly.

"It's tomorrow evening, and I shan't be remotely offended if you cannot come, but I shall send you cards."

"For Griz also?" Annabelle said.

"Of course," he said without hesitation.

They left the house together and turned as one toward Park Lane.

"Will you come?" he asked abruptly.

"If I can escape."

"I thought attending with your friends would make it easier," he murmured.

She glanced at him, startled. Had he really asked Annabelle and Timothy just so that she could be there with propriety? A flush of pleasure surged up from her toes.

"I met your sister Lady Trench earlier," he said casually. "She invited me in to annoy Lady Monkton. Or so she said."

"Did she flirt with you instead?" Griz asked as lightly as she could.

"Quite the opposite. I think she was telling me off. Or at least examining me to be sure I was not a danger to you."

"She still thinks I am fourteen," Griz said irritably. "I apologize if she was rude or prying."

"There is no need."

"Hmm." She glanced at him sideways, dragging her feet as they approached Kelburn House. "What else did she say?"

"That someone broke your heart."

Griz laughed. "I wonder who she imagines did that?"

"Then it isn't true?"

"I was very fond of the stable boy at Kelburn when I was twelve."

His dark, deep gaze lingered a moment too long. His lips quirked. "Then I look forward to seeing you tomorrow evening."

Because her heart was whole? Was he really connecting the two? The implications disturbed her, excited her. She didn't know whether or not she was glad he was already tipping his hat and striding off.

Only as she walked up the steps did she remember that she was the daughter of a wealthy duke with a generous allowance. Her presence tomorrow night would be good for the cause. The rest was just...conversation.

⤜⤜⤜⤙⤙⤙

HER INVITATION FROM the "Society for Hungarian Refugees" arrived with the mid-morning post, just before she set out for her charitable work at the soup kitchen. She stuffed it in her pocket, hoping Annabelle would not back out. She wondered if she had the nerve to go alone, for she was curious to meet his friends and fellow refugees.

But that was for later.

Now, she donned her old cloak and bonnet, and on impulse, summoned Nick, still present in the kitchen. If he had his eyes on the silver, he was clearly biding his time.

He came leaping across the hall, his gaze darting around. "Are we not taking Vicky?"

"Not today. I wanted your help somewhere else."

"Where?" he asked, bowing her elaborately through the door. The footman's lips twitched, and then his face straightened immediately as he caught Grizelda's gaze. She nodded pleasantly and sailed through to the street where the hired hackney awaited them.

"A soup kitchen in St. Giles," she informed Nick. "I help people there, thought you might like to, also."

"What do you do that for?" he asked, clearly amazed as he clambered into the carriage after her. He waved his hand toward the house. "You got all *this!*"

"Exactly. When one has all this and time, it seems only right to give at least something to those who have nothing."

"Yes?" He was still astounded by the idea, mulling it over until he said abruptly, "Like me?"

"Perhaps," she said lightly.

After a few moments' mulling, he began to chatter away, telling her funny stories about happenings below stairs, scattered with bits and pieces about his life on the streets. Once or twice, he broke off on someone's name—Art's, she suspected—and veered off in another direction, making observations about people and buildings and horses passed on the way.

She gave him money to pay the driver, which clearly made him feel very grown-up, and then took him inside to meet Mr. Wells and the other helpers. They greeted him kindly, although there were one or two suspicious looks in his direction.

"Where did he come from?" asked Mrs. Verney, a banker's wife, as they tied on their aprons.

"He's a homeless waif who came to our aid one day," Griz replied, deliberately vague. It seemed best not to mention he'd also tried to lead them to their deaths.

"You mean you have him in your *house*?"

Fortunately, they were distracted by the entry of their hungry clients and had to turn their attention to cooking and serving.

Nick, who seemed to have suddenly realized that in this place he was closer to Grizelda's position than the homeless poor surrounding him, ran happily about with plates and spoons and cups, washed dishes, and swept up. Griz was rather proud of him.

They were almost finished when a toothless man at the middle table stopped slurping soup to say, "What you doing here, young Nick?"

"Helpin'," Nick replied proudly, which seemed to amuse his acquaintance in a sour sort of way.

While Nick carried on sweeping, Griz made her way across the room and took the vacant place beside the toothless man.

"I wonder if you can help me?" she murmured.

He eyed her suspiciously over his spoon. "Shouldn't think so."

"You seem to know Nick."

He showed her his gums. "Seen him around."

"Where are his parents?"

He shrugged. "Dead, or good as. His mother vanished. His dad— Old Nick, evil, old bastard he was—died in a tavern brawl."

"Who looks after him now?"

"Seems to me he looks after himself." The toothless man set down his spoon. "Got any more of that?"

"I'll have a look in a minute," she promised, as he devoured the last of his bread. "Do you know Art?"

The bloodshot, muddy gaze flew to hers. "Everyone knows Art. Nick was hanging around him last I saw."

"Bit of a criminal?" Griz guessed.

"Ha! Arch criminal. Guv'nor of criminals." He looked furtively about him. "Though you didn't hear that from me."

"Of course not," Griz agreed. "Ambitious, is he? Art?"

"Yes, got his finger in pretty much everything on his manor. And spreading into others. Especially since they hauled Goddard off to the clink."

"Goddard?" she said quickly. "He, who was just arrested for seditious leaflets?"

It was a shot in the dark, and it certainly caused her informant to snort. "Goddy can't read. What's he doing with such things?"

Griz frowned at him. "You think he was set up?"

He polished up his empty bowl with a very small crust. "Art can read. And write."

"I see... And this Goddard, apart from not being able to read, would you say he had a gentlemanly appearance?"

The toothless man gave a shout of laughter. "Gentleman God, they call him. On account of being a bit of a dandy. But ain't anything gentle about him."

"Do you know his full name?" Griz asked eagerly.

"Nah," said her companion, and Griz realized Nick was leaning on his broom, staring at her.

"Thank you," she said, picking up the empty bowl. "Nick, is there any soup left?"

Nick stalked away, leaving someone else to answer. Griz took her helpful informant another ladleful with a crust of bread and then tracked Nick down to the standpipe in the street, where he was furiously pumping water into a bucket.

"What's the matter?" she asked bluntly.

"Nothin'."

"The man I was talking to...has he ever hurt you?"

Nick cast her a scornful glance. "'Course not."

She waited in silence until the bucket was full.

Nick wrapped his fingers around the handle, then glared at her. "You leaving me here?"

"Leaving you here?" she repeated, startled. "Of course not! Well, not unless you were desperate, and even then, I would have to know whoever you went with was going to... Why would you imagine I meant to leave you?"

"Sending me back with *him*." He nodded at the toothless man, who was just leaving the kitchen, slapping his lips with satisfaction.

"Dear God, no," Griz said fervently. "I'm afraid I was picking his brains. I want to find out what happened to my friend, the one I asked you about."

The boy looked down at his bucket and sniffed. He dashed his sleeve across his eyes, and although touched, she pretended not to notice.

"Come on. Bring the bucket, and we'll finish up here. Vicky will want her afternoon walk."

CHAPTER TWELVE

"A REN'T YOU DINING with us?" the duchess said in surprise as Griz passed her on the landing, evening cloak over her arm. "I was hoping you would come to the theater with us."

"Sorry, Mama, I'm promised to a charitable event with the Worths."

"Oh," said her mother, almost mollified. "Which charity?"

"It's for the Hungarian refugees."

"Hmm." The duchess considered. "You may invite them to write to me."

Griz smiled. "Thank you, Mama."

"It is shocking, the way they've been treated," she pronounced, already sailing off toward the library.

Griz breathed a sigh of relief and ran down the rest of the stairs to the front hall. Annabelle's carriage was waiting for her outside, and in moments, they set off for the Blue Horse.

"What is a 'Hungarian evening,' do you suppose?" Annabelle wondered.

"Hungarian food and wine and dancing," Timothy replied unexpectedly. "According to Tizsa," he added as they both looked at him. "Basically, a party, with a few Hungarian elements. There will be wealthy British people there, too, but we mustn't expect only the upper ranks of society."

"Well, one wouldn't at an inn, would one?" Annabelle said reasonably. "I'm surprised you agreed to go."

"Decent bloke, Tizsa," Timothy said vaguely.

Certainly, the thought of the rumpled, careless Dragan in evening dress was one that both amused Griz and tightened that knot in her stomach. She might tell herself it was all about discussing with him what she had learned that day, but in truth, he had a peculiar effect on her. She wanted to see him enjoying himself. She wanted the haunted expression gone from his eyes, even if just for a few hours.

The event was held upstairs at the inn. Entry was by an outside staircase. Inside, they were greeted by the evening's hostess, a Mrs. Cartwright, representing the Society, and an ancient, faded but extremely proud looking Hungarian countess.

Mrs. Cartwright, smiling archly beneath her feathered headdress, waved a bulging string bag beneath their noses. Obligingly, Griz and Timothy each dropped in a substantial banknote.

"My mother's card is there, too," Grizelda told Mrs. Cartwright. "If you write to her, she will be happy to donate."

"Thank you for your kind contribution," Mrs. Cartwright beamed and glanced down at the invitation cards Timothy had passed to her. "Mrs..." Her eyes widened and flickered to the Worths and back. "Lady Grizelda?"

Griz smiled encouragingly, and the woman turned, flustered to the haughty noblewoman beside her.

"Lady Grizelda Niven, ma'am! Who, if I am not mistaken, is the Duke of Kelburn's daughter! And Mr. and Mrs. Worth." She smiled as they all bowed. "Our patroness and guest of honor, Countess Miran-yi."

The countess shook hands, using only two deceptively frail fingers. Griz imagined them wringing the necks of chickens. Or of peasants with egalitarian pretensions.

Grizelda accompanied the Worths further into the room to make way for a family behind. While Timothy was dispatched to fetch wine,

Griz looked around the guests already assembled and eagerly chatting. Dragan did not appear to be among them.

Two violinists were scraping gently away in a corner, supplying background music with a vaguely eastern sound. Catching sight of the Cordells, Griz took Annabelle's arm and led her across to meet them.

"Miss Niven!" Mrs. Cordell exclaimed. "What a pleasant surprise." Her elder daughter nudged her, and she blushed as she took Grizelda's outstretched hand. "It isn't Miss Niven, though, is it? Excuse me. Lady Grizelda."

"Excuse *me*," Griz replied ruefully. "It seemed silly to correct a reasonable assumption. I never stand on ceremony. Annabelle, this is Mrs. Cordell, Dr. Cordell, and the Misses Cordell. My friend, Mrs. Worth."

"And Mr. Worth with the wine," Annabelle said gaily as her husband joined them, ably distributing wine glasses.

After the introductions, Timothy proposed a toast "to the confusion of tyranny," and everyone drank.

"Mr. Tizsa is not here yet?" Annabelle asked, saving Griz the trouble.

"He's brushing the cobwebs off his evening coat," confided the youngest Cordell.

Her sister curled her lip. "He doesn't want to come. He's only doing it because they're his people."

"Hush, Annie," her mother scolded. "It's not quite as simple as that. But I do think he doesn't always like being reminded of what he has lost."

The reason for his invitation became a little clearer to Griz. She sipped her wine, spotting a couple in colorfully embroidered dress seated beside the violinists. She supposed it was national Hungarian costume and let her gaze drift on to a crowd of young people eagerly clustered around a couple, as though hanging on their every word. The man, young, thin with dark blond hair, did not look well, but kept a faint smile on his lips. The young lady with him, modestly dressed, was the only other female in the room to be wearing spectacles.

"Is there an order of events for the evening?" Annabelle asked Dr. Cordell.

Dr. Cordell smiled placidly. "I believe there will be a poetry reading, a dancing demonstration, supper, and more dancing, but in what order, I have no idea. Ah, there is Dragan at last."

Grizelda's heart gave the funny little leap she was growing used to. Dragan strolled in, bowing to both the countess and Mrs. Cartwright. As always, he looked almost ridiculously handsome, but in his dark green and gold military uniform, he snatched at her breath.

Several faces turned in his direction as his gaze swept the room, coming to rest on Griz. For the barest instant, she was sure he smiled, and then, abruptly, his gaze flew back over people he had already scanned—the lady with the spectacles and her partner.

His eyes widened, and then he strode up to the blond man.

"Lajos! Thank God!" he said in an odd, muffled voice, as the two men embraced. The chatter around them increased, and Griz tried not to stare. Vaguely, she was aware of him taking the lady's hand.

"Who are they?" Anne Cordell wondered resentfully.

"Old friends, I imagine," said her father, "newly arrived in London."

After a few moments, the three of them began to walk, still exchanging low-voiced comments. Griz forced herself to look away, but moments later, she sensed Dragan's powerful presence behind her and turned.

He encompassed everyone in his bow. "This is an unexpected pleasure," he said warmly, "to be able to introduce my old friends, Mr. and Mrs. Lazar, who have only just arrived in England. Lady Grizelda Niven, Mr. and Mrs. Worth, Dr. and Mrs. Cordell, who so kindly took me into their family."

Everyone murmured civil greetings, and Mr. Lazar shook hands with Dr. Cordell and said in almost accentless English. "I met your brother in Vienna, I believe. I hope he still thrives?"

"Indeed yes, although he is a lot quieter these days! Are you also a doctor, sir?"

"No, I was a lawyer."

"And a soldier," Dragan added, "though you are out of uniform, Captain!"

"I thought you could strut for both of us."

Dragan sighed. "My other coat just would not do, in the end. But I feel a fraud in this. I was not a good soldier."

"Yes, you were," Lazar said quietly with the flicker of a smile. He turned at some question of his wife's to join in the larger conversation, and Griz and Dragan were left momentarily as good as alone.

To her surprise, he was smiling down at her, his eyes unnervingly warm. "You look very beautiful."

"So do you," she retorted before she could help it. Mostly, she spoke from disappointment because the men who said such things to her were trying to please her parents or her sister.

His eyes gleamed. "You think it base flattery and fortune-hunting?"

"I don't have a fortune," she said bluntly.

"Whatever little you have is a fortune to me."

"It won't be when you are a fashionable physician, charging outra-geous fees to cure the imaginary ailments of the rich."

"Ah, so that is why *you* flatter *me*? I have never been pursued for my wealth before."

"I don't imagine you have," she murmured, considering his ex-traordinarily good looks. Then she blushed and added hastily, "I have never pursued anyone in my life."

His lips quirked. "I don't imagine you have."

She eyed him uncertainly, looking for the joke. Somehow, they had moved as far as the wine table and, recklessly, she allowed him to fill her glass.

Mrs. Cartwright tinkled a spoon against a glass for silence, welcomed everyone to the event, and introduced a man whose name she didn't catch.

He appeared to be an aristocratic gentleman, although by his wild hair and careless necktie, he seemed to be cultivating the look that came naturally to Dragan—who groaned in her ear. "Oh, no, I'd hoped to avoid this part of the evening! His verse is—"

"Hush," Griz hissed, and he subsided while the poet declaimed in Hungarian.

Dragan supplied a running and irreverent translation. And yet, when the nobleman bowed and retired to polite applause, Dragan suddenly tensed.

His friend Lazar had stepped up.

Mrs. Cartright said, "Mr. Lazar will recite one of the poems of the late Mr. Sandor Petofi, the great poet of the Hungarian cause, who, sadly, died in that same cause."

This time there was no groaning from Dragan, no translating, facetious or otherwise. He gazed at Lazar, unblinking. His eyes were as haunted as ever, and he held himself so tensely that he seemed about to break.

Worried, she glanced from him to Mrs. Lazar, who wiped surreptitiously at her eyes and pretended to polish her spectacles. Her husband spoke with animation, words Griz could not understand, though the emotion was palpable.

"You knew him," she said slowly as Lazar stepped away, receiving many comradely pats on the shoulder as he passed.

By way of answer, Dragan caught her fingers, squeezed them once, and released her, already walking away.

But she could not let him go alone, not when he was distressed. On impulse, she started after him, following him out of the room in time to see the door to the outside staircase bang closed.

She slipped outside into the darkness, wondering if he had gone home. But a dark figure leaned his shoulder against the wall by the stairs, and by the light of the dim outside lamp, she knew it was him. Without a word, she moved and touched his elbow.

His face turned toward her, half-hidden in shadow. "He personified the revolution, from the beginning to the last battle. Passionate and irreverent, and determined. Always ready to die for his beliefs. He was Lazar's best friend. It's *his* grief I cannot bear because it reminds me... because everything rushes—"

He broke off with an almost angry shake of his head. With quick sympathy, she stepped closer and threw her arms around his neck, drawing his head down and pressing her cheek against his.

He shuddered once and stood perfectly still. Only when she began to draw back did he bring his arms up to hold her. A rush of awareness flooded her. Suddenly, he was too large, too...physical. His arms were strong and firm, his body lean and hard against hers, forcing her to recognize the powerful attraction that had always been there.

His cheek, warm and slightly rough, moved against hers. His lips trailed across her jaw, setting every nerve tingling in wonder. To be kissed by such a man, *this* man with the haunted, beautiful face and the strong, urgent body of a soldier...

He dragged his parted lips over hers, making her gasp, and then his mouth fastened on hers and her world exploded.

In her past, a couple of desperate suitors had attempted to persuade her with kisses that had left her quite unmoved. She had never experienced, never truly imagined passion like this—searing, raw, powerful. His mouth moved hungrily on hers, strong and invasive and entirely wonderful. Without conscious thought, she kissed him back, pressing herself against him, seizing and caressing the soft, thick hair at the back of his neck. Desire, sheer emotion, battered at her, blotting out everything else. There was only Dragan.

He swung her around, trapping her between the cold, stone wall and his warm body. A soft moan of pleasure and need escaped her. He cupped her face with his hands, gentle now, softly caressing as he slowly detached his mouth from hers.

Stricken, she opened her dazed eyes to meet his, hot and clouded, devouring her.

"Why are you so kind to me?" he whispered.

She drew a shaky breath. "I'm kind to everyone." She paused, then added, in the interests of honesty, "Nearly everyone."

A breath of laughter shook him. His gaze dropped to her lips, and her stomach plunged once more in a way that was curiously exciting. Her desire and the recognition of his still overwhelmed her.

"Will you dance with me?" he asked huskily.

For an instant, she was confused before she picked up the strains of violin music inside. Even so, she frowned with incomprehension. "Why?"

"Because I don't trust myself alone with you out here any longer." Very slowly, he peeled himself back from her, and her hands fell back to her sides. Her body seemed to scream with loss, but at the same time, the real world and sanity began to seep back.

She swallowed. "I suppose this is hardly discreet." Her hands trembled as she ran them over her miraculously still pinned hair.

"Sorry," he murmured, brushing stray dirt from the wall off her back. She shivered at his touch. Every nerve was wildly sensitive.

He opened the door and bowed her inside before him. When he placed her hand on his arm, everything in her leapt once more.

With a hint of desperation, she blurted, "I wanted to tell you what I learned this afternoon."

She was still talking about her discoveries at the soup kitchen as they reentered the hall, his head inclined toward her as he refocused his attention. Was she relieved or piqued that it seemed to be so easy for him? For her, the subject felt curiously like a lifeline to a drowning victim.

"Apparently," she finished, "this Goddard who was arrested was a bit of a dandy, so perhaps he really did fool Nancy into believing he was a gentleman, especially if he was inclined toward her cause."

"Yes, but why would he kill her?" Dragan demanded.

Griz, distracted by the music, took a moment to answer. The fiddler was playing a slow, beguiling tune, and the couple in Hungarian costume were dancing, sedately turning together, separating, advancing and retreating, and turning once more. Then, suddenly, the music's rhythm sped up, and the dancers were spinning, almost flying through the steps.

Griz blinked, forcing herself back to the reasons why Goddard might have killed Nancy. "Because she had found out about him and told the police? After all, he and his people were all arrested the next day. Is that the famous czardas?"

"Yes," he answered, sparing the dancers a mere glance. "But none of them were charged with murdering Nancy."

"I did mean to talk to Horace about it, but I didn't see him today. Tomorrow, I'll make a point of it."

"And I will try and see this Goddard."

She blinked. "In prison?"

"Since that is where he is. Come and dance with me, Griz."

The music had slowed again, and the couples, including the Lazars, were taking to the dance floor, too.

"I don't know the steps," Griz warned.

"You'll learn quickly." He took her hand, tugging her with him. He smiled. "And it is fun."

He was right. This was no formal ball, and no one stood on their dignity. The British joined in, clumsy and late at first but quickly improving. Griz stumbled, laughing when she danced forward instead of back, and curiously breathless when he caught her and spun her, his body touching hers like a tantalizing caress. And when the dance sped up once more, her guilty embarrassment at their outside encounter melted away. She gloried in her secret new pleasure, euphoric in the knowledge that she was doing nothing wrong, nothing different from every other woman on the dance floor. And she, the plain, overlooked youngest sister, was dancing with the handsomest man in the room. Even that amused her, for even without that sudden flare of passion, they were friends with an unlikely but undeniable bond. She did not care what he looked like.

Well, not much. It was the man beneath who truly intrigued her. Especially now.

Breathless and laughing, she was happy to take his arm when the dance finally ended and to move into the supper room which opened off the main hall.

They sat informally with the Lazars and a few other of his Hungarian friends. Although he named and explained all the dishes to her, none of the talk around the table was of Hungary or revolution. Occasionally, they compared aspects of their lives in London, but mostly they bantered in excellent English and covered a wild array of subjects, jumping like quicksilver from philosophy to history, theology to literature. They were all delightfully well-read and Griz, who rarely found a fellow spirit for such discussions, thoroughly enjoyed herself.

If she was conscious of Dragan's gaze on her, well, she rather liked that, too.

Once, she caught Annabelle's eye in the distance. And once, she noticed Anne Cordell watching her with resentment and dislike. Which she understood, although she thought Dragan himself was blissfully unaware of the stir he caused in young girls' hearts.

And not just young girls either…

"You are quite the bluestocking, are you not?" Dragan murmured as they rose from the table.

"You have guessed my guilty secret. No wonder I am not married."

His eyebrows flew up. "Do Englishmen prefer ignorant wives?"

"I believe it's a truth universally acknowledged that a man wants a wife who doesn't make *him* feel ignorant."

"*I* don't acknowledge it," he exclaimed. "Sounds like a dull marriage."

"Talking of such matters," Griz said delicately, "are you aware that Anne Cordell is in love with you?"

"Don't be silly," he replied. "She's a child."

"No, she isn't."

He glanced at her, frowning. "She does not think of me in that way. I have given her no cause to."

"Dragan, do you never *look* in the mirror?"

He blinked, and then a warm smile began to grow in his eyes. "You mean, you think I am handsome? In that case, I shall ask you to dance again."

In fact, the violinist had begun to play a waltz, and Griz had no objection to dancing it with Dragan. At least this time, she knew the dance.

That is, she thought she did. Dragan and his countrymen were accustomed to the wilder Viennese waltz. As soon as he took her in his arms, she was spun around and around until she was dizzy. Her startled feet took a few moments to catch up before the exhilaration took over, and she simply enjoyed it.

As they danced, she was only vaguely aware of him guiding them skillfully between other whirling couples. For the most part, the rest of the world receded, and there was only Dragan, joyous and untroubled, as she had longed to see him, set only on the fun of the dance and their quick, bantering conversation.

She barely knew what she said or what he did. Her other senses seemed to have taken over. She inhaled his distinctive scent of fresh male and faint herbs, relishing the strength of his arms and the clasp of his long fingers. The touch of his body, the way he moved, the smile in his eyes, all beguiled her, reminding her of his wild, stunning kiss.

"I like being with you, Grizelda Niven," he murmured. "Too

much, if the truth be told."

Suddenly, there was something more serious to her happiness, something she was afraid to read too much into. She liked his company, too, more than that of anyone else she had ever known. And as the music came to a close, she found she could not look away, could not breathe…

Somehow, her hand was on his arm. She seemed to be walking on air as a wonderful and terrifying truth began to form in her head.

"Good evening, Griz."

Bewildered, she looked up into the face of her brother and blinked. *"Horace?"*

CHAPTER THIRTEEN

"WHAT ARE YOU doing here?" she blurted.

"I was about to ask you the same question," Horace drawled. "I am assuming you did not come alone."

"Of course not," she replied with dignity. "I came with Annabelle Worth."

Horace's gaze shifted at last to Dragan. "Won't you introduce your companion?"

It was, she supposed, inevitable. After all, Azalea had already met him. "Mr. Tizsa," she said resignedly. "My brother, Lord Horace Niven. Oh, and Mr. Gabriel," she added, catching sight of Horace's underling, hovering discreetly nearby.

Dragan, who was clearly never overwhelmed by rank or supercilious looks, bowed as distantly as Horace. "You don't have wine, gentlemen," he noted.

It might have been a hospitable offer or a request to go away.

Mr. Gabriel chose to take it as the former. "You will join me in a glass, Mr. Tizsa?"

After a quick interrogative glance at her, which Griz found rather touching, Dragan walked reluctantly away with Mr. Gabriel.

"What are you about, Griz?" Horace demanded, urging her to walk with him around the room. "I suppose this Tizsa is the same man you insisted on springing from police headquarters. What is he to you?"

"A friend." She regarded him uneasily. "What is he to you?"

"Nothing, yet."

"But you are working, aren't you? This is a charitable event, Horace. Even Her Grace is happy to donate."

He looked amused. "I donated, too. You don't need to protect them from me, you know. Just keeping my ear to the ground, you might say. These people began a revolution, remember, one that very nearly succeeded. I wouldn't like our people to be learning from them."

"Our people already have what *they* were fighting for. A constitutional monarchy with an elected parliament."

"A worthy aim," Horace agreed. "But I think you already know some of them wanted a great deal more."

Following his gaze, she saw he was looking at Lazar.

"I think you are being over careful," she said quickly.

Horace smiled faintly. "So I believe. But at least I discovered one of your hideaways."

"I'm not exactly hiding! Horace, that thief you arrested last week—Goddard."

"What about him?" Horace asked distractedly.

Griz bit back her grin of triumph. "Are you *sure* he didn't know Nancy?"

"Nancy?" His frowning gaze came back to her. "Of course not. Nancy was a respectable girl."

"Then what was she doing in a back street at Covent Garden, with His Grace's dagger?"

"That is a problem for the police," Horace said severely. "It is not my area of expertise. Or yours."

"You know Goddard can't read, don't you?" she threw at him.

His scowl deepened. "No, but it wouldn't surprise me. Trust me, the documents he was distributing were barely literate." His gaze moved suddenly from Gabriel and Dragan back to Griz. "Why do you even know that?"

"I heard from someone who knows him," she said vaguely. "On one of my good works."

"Is that fellow, Tizsa, also one of your good works?"

"I told you, Mr. Tizsa is a friend. What are you going to do here, Horace?"

His eyebrows shot up. "Nothing. Just donating and observing."

"I'm sure Mrs. Cartwright is thrilled to have two of the duke's children here."

"Quite a coup," he agreed blandly.

"How did you hear about it?" She expected him to make some lofty, if vague statement about knowing everything that went on in London, but again he surprised her.

"Countess Miranyi invited me. We shall be leaving again in ten minutes. I trust you will accompany me."

"Oh, no," she said. "Annabelle will bring me home."

Irritation flashed in his eyes, though he only murmured, "Then do yourself a favor and don't dance again with that fellow, Tizsa. You looked like a moonling."

She glared at him, although the tell-tale blush must have been visible to everyone. What if he had seen them at the top of the stairs outside, only an hour before? What if he had witnessed that soul-shattering kiss?

"You are ridiculous," she said grandly and walked deliberately away to join Dragan and Mr. Gabriel.

DRAGAN DID NOT trust anyone with eyes as cold as Gabriel's. On the other hand, the man seemed disposed to be polite, making civil conversation about the event and about Dragan's route from Hungary to England.

"How long have you been acquainted with Lady Grizelda?" Gabriel asked at last, apparently casually, although Dragan was not fooled.

"A few days, only," Dragan replied. Over his companion's head, he could still see Griz and Lord Horace talking animatedly, though not with obvious anger. They were a handsome, aristocratic pair, like fine porcelain among coarse earthenware. And yet, she had no idea how beautiful she looked in her rose silk evening gown with its low, sloping neckline, revealing the warm, creamy skin of her shoulders. The sweetness of holding her in his arms so recently made his heart ache, because her beauty seemed to shine from within. With an effort, he brought his gaze back to Gabriel's. "Are you a friend of the family?"

"I hope so."

"Ah yes. Are you not the colleague of Lord Horace who dined at Kelburn House last Thursday?"

Gabriel's eyes narrowed very slightly. "You are very well informed."

"I made it my business to be, after I was arrested for the murder of a Kelburn maid."

This time, there wasn't the faintest change in Gabriel's expression. He knew exactly who Dragan was. "You must have been grateful for your fair savior."

"You must be grateful you missed the opera," Dragan returned.

"On the contrary, I am fond of opera. But both his lordship and I had matters to attend to."

"Together?"

"In part." A hint of amusement entered the cool, grey eyes. "Mr. Tizsa, are you interrogating me?"

"I cannot help being interested in every aspect of that evening."

"And, perhaps, turning interest away from yourself?"

"I am no longer of interest in that particular crime," Dragan pointed out. Griz was walking away from Lord Horace, directly toward him. Her brother's expression was amiable as he sipped his wine, though Dragan didn't quite believe in that apparent benevolence.

"And yet," Gabriel said gently, "you knew the victim. You left the opera to meet her. And were discovered leaning over the body with a dagger in your hand."

"A dagger that did not kill her. That came from the Duke of Kelburn's collection."

Gabriel smiled incredulously. "Are you accusing His Grace of this crime?"

"I am not an imbecile, sir. Nor are you. Lady Griz," he acknowledged as she joined them.

Gabriel smiled at her before glancing toward Lord Horace and setting down his glass. "I believe his lordship is ready to depart. I imagine you will accompany us, Lady Grizelda?"

"Oh, no," Griz said blithely. "I'm sure there is another dance to come. Good night, Mr. Gabriel."

The man bowed and walked toward Mrs. Cartwright, where he met up with Lord Horace.

"What were you talking about?" Griz asked him.

"The night of Nancy's murder. He knows an awful lot about it."

"He works very closely with Horace."

It was too easy to blurt out his thoughts to this girl. This girl he had kissed with an emotion approaching release. He hadn't expected her to respond, and when she did…the explosion of joy in his heart—and his loins—had nearly obliterated the last of his common sense.

This girl who had lied to the police in case she needed to protect her family. She didn't need to, in the end, since the stiletto had not been used. Nevertheless, that lie betrayed what she considered members of her family capable of.

What reason could Lord Horace possibly have for killing his mother's housemaid? Had he made her pregnant and solved the problem?

But then, there was no real problem for a man of his birth and influence. A pay off absolved him of responsibility. If the duchess found out, she would blame the girl, not her son.

He could see no motive for Horace. And yet the suspicion lingered. Swallowing back his instinct to share it with her, he said instead, "There *is* another waltz. Would it shock the world if you danced with me again?"

An adorable flush seeped into her face. "I can't imagine anyone is counting."

She had a way, he acknowledged, of wiping everything but her from his mind. It might not be safe, but she was so enchanting, he allowed it to happen and simply enjoyed holding her. As if it was the last chance he would have.

◆◆◆❖◆◆◆

IF GRIZ LAY awake a long time that night, her mind dwelling on Dragan Tizsa rather than Nancy Barrow; if she finally fell asleep touching her smiling lips... Well, by morning, she had returned to practicalities.

Dressing in her soup kitchen clothes, she went to enjoy breakfast with Horace, who greeted her with a scowl.

"I was home before midnight," she said mildly, "escorted to the door by both Worths."

He grunted.

"What will happen to Goddard?" she asked after a few bites of toast.

Horace rustled his newspaper. "Transportation, I expect."

"Will he be tried for sedition?" she asked curiously.

"No need. The police found evidence of enough straightforward crime to hang him."

She set down her toast. "Then the leaflets that were found in the rookery won't be used as evidence?" Was that why they were being dumped in a St. Giles alehouse for destruction? "Did the police not take them?"

"How the devil should I know? I'm not a policeman! Griz, I can understand, if not approve, your interest in Nancy's untimely death. But not in Goddard!" He threw down his paper. "You haven't got involved with radicals, have you?"

"Oh, no."

"Then leave Goddard rotting in Newgate! He'll be on his way to New South Wales, or the prison hulks, soon enough."

Having discovered what she needed from Horace, she drank the last of her coffee and bade him enjoy a good morning.

Five minutes later, she stepped into her mother's carriage and gave John, the coachman, instructions to take her to Kensington. Time enough to add Newgate to the itinerary when the house servants had no chance of hearing.

She was lucky enough to catch Dragan striding along Caroline Place and looking quite startled to see her hanging out of the carriage window as the vehicles slowed. "Quick, get in!" she instructed, throwing the door wide.

She thought laughter hissed between his teeth, but he didn't hesitate. While he climbed in, she spoke into the tube to the coachman. "Newgate Prison, please, John."

"Is that where Goddard is?" Dragan asked, sitting down beside her. "I suppose it saves me a lot of shoe leather going from prison to prison, but you don't really intend coming with me, do you?"

"Of course. You might not ask the right questions."

He arched one eyebrow. "Might I not?"

"No. Do you know, they're not bothering with charges of sedition? I think Art somehow planted those leaflets and persuaded the police to raid the rookery because of them. Only Art benefits from Goddard and his people being transported."

"Not law and order?" Dragan asked mildly.

"Not if Art just takes over everything Goddard was doing."

Dragan shifted position, causing a flutter of awareness down her spine. How close he was. How long his legs.

"Why bother with the leaflets?" he demanded. "Why not just inform against him for the things he *did* do?"

"Because the police already know what goes on in the rookeries. There's a sort of stability in that knowledge, and they won't risk their officers in raiding them without a very good reason and a big push from behind."

Dragan gazed at her as though wondering if she saw where that push must have come from. But he said only, "We still can't tie any of that to Nancy."

"Except the note of the alehouse among her letters."

"I certainly can't imagine any gentleman suitor taking her there," Dragan said. "But to the more immediate point, prisons are hardly salubrious places for ladies to visit either."

"Well, the Kelburn coach and the Niven name worked like a charm at Great Scotland Yard," she said blithely.

"I would rather go alone," he said firmly.

"I would rather be there, too."

"Has anyone ever told you that you're annoyingly stubborn?"

"Of course!"

There was no denying that the ancient prison was much grimmer the closer she got to it. And when the door closed behind them, she was conscious of a sense of panic. She couldn't help shivering. The very air seemed redolent with the misery of hundreds of years, with the captive souls of those who had died in their cells or on the scaffold.

Griz, prepared to adopt her mother's dignity and Augusta's disapproval to gain access to Goddard, found herself instead, standing back and admiring.

Having read Mr. Dickens's *Sketches by Boz*, she knew to enter the prison by the governor's house, where a servant, having admitted them, scratched his head in consternation over their lack of an appointment.

"We need to see one Goddard," Dragan pronounced. "Without delay, if you please. His Grace's carriage is waiting."

Dragan's new manner was a revelation. Gone was the amiable, easy-going refugee. This was the army officer, the commander of men. Even his speech was clipped, his accent almost entirely gone. More than that, he had told no lies. By his very presence, it seemed, he had the servant falling over himself to show them into the governor's office to wait, while he scuttled off in search of someone to take them to Goddard.

Griz and Dragan exchanged speaking glances, but they did not have long to wait.

A serious but not unamiable turnkey, dressed all in black, arrived and led them to a room where they signed the visitors' book, and then through a series of dismal stone passages and heavy, locked doors. This, the turnkey informed them, was a ward for the better-off class of prisoner—those who could, presumably, afford better food and drink.

A huge key unlocked another door with an echoing crash. And Griz found herself facing a pair of gratings, through which she could see listless men pacing or sitting around. Few were talking. The smell was not pleasant. God knew what it was like in the more crowded wards.

"Visitors for you, Goddard," shouted the turnkey. "You mind your manners in front of the lady."

The light from a small, barred window in the room was dim. The first thing Griz made out clearly was a tall top hat that had seen better days. It resided on a rickety desk, while its owner sprawled on the chair beside it. To her relief, the man was not chained, although he did not immediately rise to greet his visitors. Instead, he looked them over.

Their guide stepped back, allowing at least some privacy.

"Well, well," rumbled the prisoner, unwinding himself and rising slowly to his feet. He ambled toward the grate with an unsubdued swagger. "What have we here? A lawyer, perhaps? I already have one, you know. And you, though you may be a lady, certainly ain't one of mine."

"Correct," Dragan said coldly. "In any case, I heard Art Dooley had all of your *ladies*, now. Be still," he added peremptorily as Goddard jerked his hand futilely between the bars, an ugly look on his thick, heavy-jawed face.

His eyes were small and mean, his nose a little bulbous. His clothing, however, looked very fine, including a very natty, green silk waistcoat. He looked as if he would rather punch Dragan than obey him, but after the briefest struggle, curiosity won.

"Nor you ain't a plainclothes Peeler," Goddard observed. "Damned if I can place you or her ladyship there."

The *ladyship* was intended as a sneer. Griz, however, smiled at him approvingly, and he blinked several times in clear confusion.

"I understand you were set up, Mr. Goddard," Dragan said.

Clearly this was the way to the villain's heart, for Goddard immediately exploded, "Damn right, I was! And I know who by! Bloody Art Dooley!"

"Why would he do such a thing?" Dragan asked. "Weren't you friends?"

"'Course not, but we had an understanding, and he broke it."

"Do you have proof of that?" Griz asked.

He blinked as though surprised she had spoken. "I'm here, ain't I? And like your man says, Dooley has taken over everything."

"Then the stolen goods, the proceeds of extortion, the women, the bodies, were all brought to that building by Dooley?" Dragan said mildly.

Goddard eyed him with dislike. "Why not? He sent a load of bloody pamphlets. That's what brought the rozzers down on me. And it ain't the first time."

"He's done this to you before?" Griz asked, surprised.

"Not to me," Goddard said impatiently. "But Titch over in Seven Dials got put away last winter by some damned informer—and guess who stepped into *that* breech? Bloody Dooley."

"Beat you to it, did he?" Dragan said with patently false sympathy.

"That time, he did. Not saying he didn't learn it from me when the Peelers took Hairy Harry, and I inherited his business." There appeared to be bitterness in that thought.

"Did you have warning of that arrest?" Griz asked.

Goddard grinned ferociously.

Dragan leaned closer to watch his face. "Did you...ally with anyone else to bring it about?"

"Like who?" Goddard demanded.

"Like a policeman," Dragan suggested.

Griz stared at him.

Goddard spat on the floor. "What sort of stupid question is that?" His gaze flickered to the door, clearly unwilling to say more in earshot of the turnkeys. Or without knowing exactly who he was talking to. But he had already said enough to send Grizelda's mind reeling.

Dragan murmured. "I would like to know your ally's name."

Goddard showed his teeth. "I'll bet you would."

"Do you think Art Dooley had the same ally?"

Goddard just stared at him, hands clenched.

"Wouldn't you like to see this perfidious ally fall as you have fallen?" Dragan suggested.

Goddard's eyes were frightening. "Oh, I'll see him fall. But it won't be you cuts his throat."

"Nor you, from Australia. Or the hangman's noose."

"That's my business."

Dragan searched his face, then stood back with a shrug. "Fair enough." From his pocket, he took out his notebook, which was already open at Nancy's portrait. "A different question. Have you ever seen this young woman?"

Goddard stuck his forehead against the bars and peered at the sketch with interest. "Nah. Can't say I have. She ain't one of mine." His lip curled. "Or Art's."

Though she observed closely, Griz could see no sign of recognition in his face.

"Who is she?" Goddard asked.

"Nancy Barrow," Dragan said. "Ever hear the name?"

Goddard shook his head.

"She was murdered," Griz said. "In Mudd Lane behind Covent Garden. The night before you were arrested."

"Well, you can't pin it on me," Goddard said at once. "Got no reason to go near Covent Garden. Who *are* you people?"

"Did she set you up?" Dragan asked. "Or this Titch or Harry you mentioned?"

Goddard stared at him. "You got bats in your belfry. No woman would set me up. No woman could. What do you think I am?"

"I don't really think you want to know the answer to that," Dragan said mildly. "Thank you for your time, Mr. Goddard. Good day."

⇛⇚

ON EDGE AND furiously thinking, Griz could only be glad when they finally stepped out of the infamous goal into fresh, free air. She was never so glad to see John, the coachman, or her mother's carriage. She hurled herself in without a word.

"Ask him to drop us at Covent Garden," Dragan said.

Since she had meant to go there anyway, she did as he asked, then burst out, "What is it you suspect, Dragan? That the police or Nancy or both together were informing on a succession of villains?"

"It crossed my mind."

"But why would the police do such a thing?"

Dragan rubbed his forefinger and thumb together in the universal gesture for money.

"But Nancy—" She broke off, remembering the silk hat and gown in Nancy's room, the money she had not earned from her employment by the duchess. "No," she said determinedly, "she wouldn't. She couldn't!"

"Probably not," Dragan agreed. "I don't believe Goddard *did* know her. But there could be some connection to the police."

Griz rubbed her forehead. "How on earth do we investigate that?"

"Do we even need to? We don't know that these criminal wars are related to Nancy at all."

"Except for the note of that alehouse in St. Giles." She sighed. "Are we going in circles?"

"Perhaps," Dragan admitted. He hesitated, then, "I was throwing ideas at him to get a reaction."

"And people are never *only* what they show you... Still, Nancy would never have called Goddard a gentleman. And I cannot imagine either of them going within ten feet of the other."

"Neither can I," Dragan admitted. "Whatever connection is there, we cannot yet see it. Let's go back to where she died and see if we can find any witnesses."

"The police have already looked."

"It does no harm to look again. We might even remember something important once we are there."

CHAPTER FOURTEEN

THEY ALIGHTED CLOSE to the Covent Garden flower market, and Griz sent the carriage home. In no hurry to return to the back street where she had found Nancy's lifeless body, she was happy to linger in the market, admiring the bright flowers from the exotic to the common.

"Posy for your lady, sir," offered a thin, shabby-looking girl with a pot of anemones at her feet. The flowers were bright and vibrant in contrast to their seller, and Griz reached into her cloak pocket for a coin.

"Thank you, sir," the girl said gratefully, and Griz realized Dragan had beaten her to the purchase. The girl's smile was as bright as her flowers, now.

"May I?" Dragan stepped closer to Griz, threading the stems of the posy through the loops of her cloak. His knuckles brushed against her neck, her jaw. She inhaled his familiar scent, trying not to remember his embrace, his kiss.

"Thank you," she managed with a shy smile. "They brighten up this drab cloak."

"No, you do that." He stepped back, drawing her arm through his. "Now, let's face our demons."

Together, they walked through the market, toward the opera house. And there, leaning against a pillar, lurked Jack Payne.

"Jack?" Griz stopped in front of him, and he straightened with a jump that looked almost guilty.

"My lady!"

"Why are you still here? I thought you were going to Lincoln."

"No point, is there?" Jack said gloomily. "Won't bring her back. I'd hoped to marry her there, bring her back to Sussex."

"I know," Griz said gently. "But you should not linger around here where she died."

"I know. Just can't bring myself to go home."

"Where is your room?" Dragan asked.

Jack glared at him. "Above a public house. I can't take *her* there."

"Just from the outside," Dragan said firmly. "I'd like to know which windows look where. And we'd probably quite like to speak to the patrons of the public house."

Jack's gaze flickered to Griz, then, muttering something unintelligible under his breath, he strode off to the right of the theatre, not left in the direction Griz had followed Nancy on the night she died. In fact, he led them away from the theatre altogether.

"Do you know who did it?" he burst out. "Do you suspect?"

"No. We have several suspicions but no proof. No theories that even make sense. Do you?"

He shook his head. "I hadn't seen her for so long. She kept my letter, though. Mrs. Barrow gave me it. I'm glad she kept it."

Griz nodded. There was nothing more to say.

The window of Jack's rented room faced away from the theatre. Even from the front of the building, no one could have witnessed Nancy's murder.

"You should go home, Jack," Griz advised. "To Sussex."

"I know. I'm doing no one any good here." His bowed head lifted. He glanced from Griz to Dragan. "But if you like, I can listen, even ask questions in the alehouses round about. I've heard mention of the murder before, but I couldn't listen."

"You shouldn't have to," Griz said stoutly.

"If you can, I can."

"Jack—"

Her protest was cut short by Dragan. "That would be very helpful. Thank you."

Griz closed her mouth, frowning at him. If he saw her disapproval, he gave no sign, merely adding, "Let us know what you learn."

"I will," Jack said, almost eagerly.

Dragan offered his hand, which seemed to stun Jack into shaking it. Then Jack bowed jerkily to Griz, and Dragan urged her away.

"He would be better at home," she said at last as they made their way through the market once more.

"Probably."

She frowned at him. "I didn't think you would even trust him."

"I don't. If he brings us information, well and good. Either way, it's a test. If he actually asks the questions, he's less likely to be guilty."

"He is not guilty," Griz insisted. "I have known him all my life, and he would not hurt a fly, let alone the girl he loved."

"Love does strange things to people."

"I suppose you speak from experience!"

"I suppose I do, though, in all honesty, it has never inspired me to murder."

They were walking up the side of the theatre, where carriages had lined the street on the night Nancy died.

"He didn't do it," Griz said firmly.

He cast her a quizzical glance. "He was not your stable boy, was he?"

"He is a farmer," she replied with dignity.

Her stomach was beginning to roil now that she turned up the back street, even though it looked different in the daylight. Two women with baskets walked toward them, deep in gossip. A boy with an empty barrow was hurrying toward the market. Two of the windows in the building opposite were open to allow a man and a woman to make conversation.

Griz said, "There never was a stable boy. I made him up."

"I know."

She didn't know why, perhaps to distract herself from the memory of what she had found the last time she had turned into Mudd Lane, but the words tumbled out. "There was an army officer. He teased me and flattered me. He made me laugh. I liked him until he…frightened me."

Dragan halted, frowning down at her. "How did he do that?"

"He pulled me into a dark room and tried to kiss me. When I pushed him away, he wouldn't go."

Dragan's lips tightened, although his eyes gave nothing away. "Did he do anything else?"

"No. That is, he might have, but I hit him with a candlestick."

His eyes lightened with what might have been admiration. "Good for you. Did you make good your escape?"

"I did, and I never spoke to him again." She considered. "To be fair, he never spoke to me either. He must have spent the rest of the evening with a shocking headache."

She began to walk on, but he caught her arm. "I kissed you, too."

Blood surged up into her face. "I let you." She had more than let him. She had kissed him back. Until now, she had never even thought of their kiss as the same act.

His lips quirked as his hand slid down her arm to her fingers, which he quickly raised to his mouth and kissed. "Thank you."

Her lips were trying to smile back, but suddenly shy, she hurried on. "This must be about where I kicked the dagger," she said, just a little breathlessly.

He walked past her and halted. "And this is where Nancy lay." He looked around at the surrounding gates and buildings. "These are the backdoors to shops that no one would have been using at that time of night. A warehouse of some kind, a carpenter's workshop."

"No wonder the police could find no witnesses," Griz said. "He must have chosen this spot deliberately. Which rules Jack out because he couldn't have known the area well enough."

"I don't understand why she came here. If she was afraid of this man, as we presume she was since she carried the dagger, why move away from the lights by the theatre and the waiting carriages?"

"If he was chasing her, she must have been too flustered to think properly, just acted on instinct." She shivered at the very idea of such fear, then frowned. "But I thought I saw her skirt vanishing around the side of the theatre. That was why I followed her. And there was no one behind me. I looked and listened all the time." Her eyes refocused on Dragan with growing horror. "Do you suppose she was running from *me*? That I drove her into the arms of her killer?"

"From what you said before, she wasn't frightened enough of you to run into danger. I don't think she even saw you. She wasn't chased along here. She was *enticed* by someone who knew exactly where he was going."

"By why did Nancy go?" Griz demanded. "If she was frightened of him, she would never have followed him."

"Then someone else enticed her, and our killer took advantage? Or the killer was someone she did not fear, but who had actually been sent by the man who frightened her."

"Or she didn't take the dagger because she was frightened, but because she meant to sell it to Art or one of his fences."

"Who then left it behind? And where do I come in? Why did she want to speak to me?"

Griz swallowed. "Perhaps she wanted to be rid of her baby. She stole the dagger to pay for it, and she wanted you to advise her, or even to—"

"This is all speculation," he said impatiently, striding back the way they had come. "And none of it makes sense. We have no evidence of any of it. Come on, let's make the journey again, concentrating, this time."

They returned to the front of the theatre, and as they walked, each described to the other what they had seen and heard. There had been no lights, no sounds of anyone working late, only occasional, distant footfalls.

"There might have been two sets in front of me," Griz said doubtfully. "Or it might have been Nancy's echoing."

Dragan stopped at the corner of Mudd Lane. "What did you do here?"

"I hesitated. I looked ahead and behind and peered into the lane."

"Did you hear anything?"

She frowned, trying to relive the moment before the terrible discovery had buried everything else. "Footsteps, but very distant. A scraping sound...like something moving on stone, a heavy foot, perhaps? Someone laughed, even further away. None of it seemed threatening."

"From which direction?"

She turned slowly into the lane and raised her hand, pointing vaguely ahead. "Somewhere over there. It was hard to tell."

"And the footsteps, were they quick? Slow? Heavy or light?"

"Quick. Like someone walking fast but not running. Neither heavy nor light. I suppose they were too distant to tell."

"And what could you see? In the lane?"

"Nothing at first, and then the bundle that was Nancy."

"And as you approached this bundle," Dragan said as they walked toward the same place, "did you still hear these footsteps?"

"I don't rememb... Yes, yes, I did, very slightly, but they were fading away."

"Wait there," Dragan said. "And listen to my footsteps. Close your eyes if it helps."

He strode off to the end of the lane, his steps brisk, hurried without running. She closed her eyes, listening, remembering. The sound faded fast into the distance, and yet when she opened her eyes, she could still see him.

Some peculiarity of the surrounding buildings seemed to disguise the sound, not muffling it so much as sending it rapidly ahead of where Dragan was walking.

She ran after him, the triumph of realization warring with fresh horror. "He must have been there still, hurrying away even as I tripped over the knife. Dear God, if I had been only seconds faster—but she made no sound, no scream of fear or pain."

"He had her by the throat," Dragan said grimly. "Even if she had not been too frightened to call out, it would have been difficult. And the wound was well-placed. She would have died instantly."

"I didn't hear her fall," Griz whispered.

"He lowered her to the ground. She lay too straight to have fallen. And then hurried off into the darkness." Dragan turned and grasped her shoulder. "There was nothing you could have done. Nor I, since I looked for her first in the wrong direction. We can't change what happened, Griz, only find out the truth."

She nodded, glad of his presence, his grip on her shoulder seeming to hold her together and lend her strength. He was used to death and injury. She was not.

"Perhaps," she said, trying to think in a different direction, "Nancy came this way because she was used to meeting her gentleman here."

"It's not a very romantic spot for a tryst," Dragan said doubtfully.

"But it is quite close to St. Giles and people like Art and Goddard."

"True, if you can imagine her with either. But whoever she was with, if you're right, then hopefully someone will have seen them together, and we can finally get a description of her lover."

Accordingly, they spent the next hour talking to a drunken warehouseman, a surly carpenter, a jolly baker, and a harassed looking butcher. They took it in turns who spoke to the principal and who to any servants, apprentices, and messenger boys. None of them, unsurprisingly, had been on the premises the night Nancy had died, and none of them recognized her picture. The butcher's boy snickered when Griz asked him about people using the back lane to tryst but supplied no useful information.

They moved out of the lane, following winding passages that led behind the opera house.

"People live here," Griz remarked. "Though I doubt the windows overlook the lane."

"No, but someone might have seen the killer hurrying away. He might even have hidden in a doorway because the police arrived from both ends of the lane, didn't they? We should come back tomorrow. I need to go to the clinic now to relieve Cordell."

Griz nodded. "I'll go home and write down everything we've learned, or speculated, try to put it into some kind of order that makes sense."

"Good plan. I'll walk with you to the hackney stand."

They walked in companionable silence until, just before the market, they came to a lane where raucous female laughter drew their attention. Hadn't she heard that, too, the night Nancy died?

Three women, gaudily dressed and painted, all laughing together. One of them glanced up at Dragan and Griz and nudged her companions.

Dragan halted. "Wait here," he said and strode purposefully toward the women. Griz, who had no intention of staying put, followed.

"'Ello, 'andsome," one of the women said boldly to Dragan, placing her hand on her hip. "Got a bit of a nerve, ain't you?"

"They're reformers, Nell, watch yourself," said another, clearly preparing for flight.

"No, we're not," Dragan said, scowling as Griz joined him. "Just looking for someone, thought you might have seen her." He pulled the sketch of Nancy from his pocket once more.

The women, although poised for flight, paused to peer curiously at the drawing.

"She ain't one of us," said Nell, the first woman.

"No, but if you were around here last Thursday evening," Dragan said, "you might have seen her near the theatre. About half-past nine. She might have been looking around here a lot, as though frightened of someone."

"Nah," said the first woman, winking at Dragan. "I were busy, weren't I?"

He glanced at the other women, who both shook their heads.

"You a Peeler?" one asked suspiciously.

"Don't be daft, girl," Nell scoffed. "Peelers don't bring their lady friends to tea with us. All the same, what d'you want with *her*?" She flicked one finger over the sketch in Dragan's hand.

Griz, who, by now, had a very good idea of the women's profession, was more curious than shocked. "She was my maid," she said before Dragan could speak. "Someone killed her, and we want to know who."

Nell exchanged uneasy glances with her companions. "She's the one the Peelers were asking about." She looked Dragan up and down. "They were asking about a dark, young foreign gent, too. Handsome and soft-spoken, with a foreign accent. Wasn't you, was it?"

"It might have been. You see my reason for finding out who really killed her."

"Poor cow," Nell said, pushing Dragan's hand and drawing away. "Never saw her. She died up Mudd Lane, didn't she? No one goes round there."

"Thanks for your time," Dragan said, stuffing the sketch back in his pocket.

Griz nodded to the women, who were looking her drab dress and gown up and down without noticeable favor. Nell's mouth dropped open at the courtesy.

"'Ere, Mister," Nell said, fluttering her blackened eyelashes. "Come back later, and you can spend some more of my time."

Dragan lifted his hat, unflustered, and drew Grizelda's hand through his arm. They walked away to more raucous laughter.

"Worth a try," Dragan said, clearly disappointed. "But I wish you hadn't followed me."

"There is no point in being prudish with me at this stage," she pointed out, which seemed to amuse him. "Perhaps we could speak to them again tomorrow. Now, which way is it to St. Martin's Lane?"

They walked briskly away from Covent Garden, each thinking their own thoughts.

"We may never find out the truth," Dragan said abruptly. "Can you live with that?"

She nodded. "I just don't think I can live without having tried. And I do think we will if we keep trying." She glanced at him with fresh curiosity. "She was our maid. I feel guilty for not looking after her. Why are you doing this?"

"Because you asked me. Because I knew her. Because, in spite of everything, I still hate injustice." His lips twisted. "And if the truth be told because I can't resist puzzles."

"Neither can I," she confided. Another thought struck her. "Do you play chess, Dragan?"

"Yes, when I can. Why, are you challenging me to a game?"

"I believe I am," she said happily. "Perhaps when this is done."

⋙✳⋘

GRIZ SPENT THE remainder of the afternoon in the library at home, writing out clearly what she knew about Nancy's death. Then she tore more paper up into quarter sheets and divided the information up under various headings such as Acquaintances, Opportunity, and Motive. Unsatisfied, she tore more paper and wrote down theories and speculations as headings, and under each, any facts that supported such ideas.

Having run out of space on the desk, she moved camp to the middle of the floor and spread everything out where she could see it, and shuffle all the pieces of paper as her brain thought through everything she had just written. Vicky didn't help by lying down on top of them, but having picked the dog up and plonked her to one side, she stared at the papers again.

She was still doing so when her mother wandered in, dressed for the evening.

"Good Lord, Griz, what are you about?" the duchess demanded.

"Oh! Sorry," Griz muttered, hastily picking up all the papers, but that didn't seem to be what was bothering her mother.

"You aren't dressed for the evening," she scolded. "Have you forgotten it is Azalea's party tonight?"

Griz smothered a groan. "Yes, I had, I'm afraid. But I don't have to go, do I, Mama?"

"Azalea will be disappointed if you don't."

Griz cast her a skeptical glance.

"Well, she will," the duchess insisted. "She is fond of you, and frankly, Grizelda, you are four-and-twenty, not four-and thirty. You are not yet on the shelf and need not behave like everyone's spinster aunt."

Griz regarded her with some suspicion. "I thought we had agreed I was happy on the shelf?"

"I remember you stating it," her mother retorted. "You are a duke's daughter and have every right to expect a good marriage."

"I don't expect it," Griz said bluntly, adding hastily, "I don't say I'm against it, but I refuse to go looking for it at parties where everyone is frivolous and makes such tedious conversation. I include myself before you scold me."

"Nonsense. How else do you expect to meet agreeable men?"

Over a murdered corpse in a Covent Garden back street. The shocking thought remained fortunately unspoken. But it was true that Dragan was the one good thing to come out of that evening. For her, at least. She wished Nancy had not died. But Dragan had come very suddenly to fill her world, with common purpose as well as humor and companionship and the excitement of physical attraction. *Dear God, that kiss…*

Appalled by even remembering such things in the presence of her mother, she jumped to her feet, her papers clasped to her breast. "I'll be as quick as I can," she claimed, dashing to the door. "Begin dinner without me if you need to."

CHAPTER FIFTEEN

"A RE YOU GOING out again?" Annie Cordell asked as Dragan ran lightly downstairs, dressed in his uniform. Her face fell further. "Oh. Are you going to a party?"

"As it happens, yes," he replied. "I'll just say good night to your parents—"

"Can I come with you?" she blurted.

He paused, blinking. "I don't think it's the kind of party where I can bring my own guests."

"Will *she* be there?"

"Who?" he demanded, opening the parlor door.

"Never mind," Annie muttered and brushed past him to run upstairs.

As he exchanged a few words with her parents, he couldn't help remembering what Griz had said at the inn. It made him uncomfortable, and he began to wonder if he could afford a cheap room somewhere that would keep him more or less out of Annie's way. Well, if he kept traveling by hackney, he would *never* be able to afford the rent. Perhaps he should speak to Cordell about working longer hours. If the doctor could afford to pay him.

Half an hour later, the cab dropped him in Mount Street, and Azalea welcomed him like an old friend.

"Ah, Mr. Tizsa! Or is it Captain?"

"Mister will do," he said mildly, bowing over her hand. "Thank you for inviting me."

"It's our pleasure—isn't it, Eric?" She turned to the man at her side. "This is Mr. Tizsa, whom I was telling you about, Grizelda's friend from Hungary. My husband, Lord Trench."

Dragan shook hands with Lord Trench, a tall, fair man with amiably smiling lips and a hint of cynical humor in his hooded eyes.

"Always glad to meet a friend of Grizelda's," he said, and Dragan passed on to make way for the couple behind him.

In the drawing room, a footman offered him champagne, which he accepted with a murmur of thanks while gazing about him in search of Griz.

There was no guarantee, of course, that she would be here. She had carefully arranged her life independently of the rest of the family, for the most part, and her feelings for Azalea were definitely mixed. He wondered whether she would be glad or appalled to see him here. Perhaps he should have told her, but until he had found himself putting on the uniform, he hadn't been sure he would come. He didn't really want to think about the reasons he was here.

However, he had the feeling she preferred to keep him away from family eyes—probably another sign of her independence—but since he had by now met two of her brothers and a sister, that boat had sailed.

A man's voice penetrated the tasteful music and the chatter in the room. Dragan could only make out the odd word—"army...come from...pretty...".

Casting a glance in the direction of the voice, he saw a British army officer in dress uniform, a blaze of red and gold braid, which made Dragan's look as if he'd been rolling in mud for weeks. Perhaps the British officer felt the same, for he was definitely looking Dragan up and down, while he spoke to a court of three admiring young ladies and a dowager.

Dragan strolled on and was glad to run into Timothy Worth.

"Tizsa, old chap, pleasure to see you here," Worth said, thrusting out his hand. "Do you know Royston and Gardiner?"

Worth's friends proved as amiable as he. While they chatted, he took in the rest of the room, establishing that Griz was not present. In fact, he could not see any of her family, although Lord Horace's assistant, Gabriel, was seated at the far end of the room, attentively bent toward a large-boned lady who might have been his wife.

"Mr. Tizsa!" Annabelle Worth greeted him as she joined their group. "What a pleasant surprise." Inserting herself between her husband and Dragan, she drew him a little aside. "How goes your investigation, sir? I called on Griz earlier today to find out, but she was not at home, drat her."

"We are not much further forward," he admitted, "but we haven't yet given up."

"Ah, look, there are the duke and duchess," Annabelle said, nodding toward the door.

A dignified couple somewhere in their late middle years had appeared. Lord Trench was speaking to the duchess. Lady Trench kissed her father's cheek and turned, speaking rapidly to someone he couldn't see, presumably Griz, since the taller figure of Lord Forsythe lounged behind her.

At the same time, movement within the room caught Dragan's eye. The loud officer had left his harem and was walking toward the door. Smiling, he made his bow to the duke and duchess. Now, Dragan could see Griz, and she took his breath away.

She wore the same rose silk evening gown as on the Hungarian evening, but her hair had been more elaborately dressed, with jeweled combs winking at either side and a necklace, surely of rubies or garnets, emphasizing the delicacy of her neck. She was not, he suspected, the most fashionable lady present, her full, elegant skirts not the widest, but even this could not detract from her sheer presence. This was the duke's daughter in her rightful environment, among her family, and she had never seemed so distant from him.

Before he could even register the pain, she turned quickly from her sister and gazed straight at the loud officer with her parents. And the expression in her eyes pierced him to the core. Not pleasure or annoyance. Fear.

It was only a momentary flash, but enough to cause an involuntary step toward her.

Annabelle caught his arm, preventing his instinctive charge to the rescue. By then, Griz was smiling. The officer took her hand, gallantly kissing it, and she laughed as he drew it free and walked on with a careless wave.

"Who is that?" Dragan asked sharply.

"Jonathan Galbraith. Her first love. Or at least first suitor. She dismissed him and never seemed to miss him. But she never looked at anyone else. Until..."

Until you? Is that what she would have said if he had not been drawing her toward Griz? A surge of yearning hit him, taking him by surprise, but he had no time to worry about such trivia while Griz was frightened or upset.

Annabelle bowed to the duke and duchess as they passed. Already engrossed with other people, the duchess spared her a quick, gracious smile in return. She did not even glance at Dragan.

Lord Forsythe was thrusting a glass of champagne into Grizelda's hand. The officer—Galbraith—was coming up behind her, his gaze flickering beyond her to Dragan and Annabelle.

Griz glanced up with a bright smile and took a step toward them. She blinked. "Dragan! I didn't expect you to be here."

His heart melted at the unguarded pleasure in her voice. The odd, slightly glassy look in her eyes vanished into a welcoming smile that deprived him of breath. How had she come to mean so much so quickly? Annabelle relinquished his arm, murmuring something to her friend that he barely heard.

Griz took his arm quite naturally, and they walked away at a tangent. She was trembling, as she had been the night of the murder, but she still smiled, nodded to acquaintances.

"In here," she breathed, leading him through an open doorway into another elegant room set up with rows of chairs. A pianoforte stood at the front of the room.

"I'm sorry," Griz muttered, sinking onto a chair that was out of sight from the other room. "I just need a moment's peace."

He sat sideways on the chair in front of her, resting one elbow across its back. "I take it that was the fellow who was not your stable boy?"

She smiled a little wanly. "Am I so obvious?"

"No, you carried it off very well. I'm just sorry he still troubles you."

She frowned. "Actually, I'm not sure he does. It was the shock, Azalea had only just warned me he was here, and then he stood right in front of me."

"Why did she invite him?" Dragan demanded.

"She didn't. He came home on leave, just tagged along with his brother, Lord Garrowdale. But as you know, she thinks he broke my heart."

"Instead of your trust."

"Exactly. I hadn't realized before the ways in which men could...subdue women. His strength frightened me. His betrayal shocked me. Seeing him again brought it all back. But you know, I don't believe he frightens me anymore."

He searched her eyes. Whether or not it was true, he admired her strength and spirit. Though to be sure, he would find great pleasure in ramming the bastard's teeth down his throat.

"You've never told your family, have you? Nor Annabelle Worth."

She shook her head. "I always knew...*felt* I was making a fuss about nothing. He only kissed me after all. I should probably have been flattered."

"No one should feel flattered by a forcible mauling," Dragan said impatiently. His lips twisted. "Though to be sure, I am in no position to cast stones of that nature."

To his surprise, a tender smile entered her eyes. She touched his hand resting on the back of the chair. "You are different."

He turned his hand, clasping her fingers. He heard the catch in her breath, read permission in her eyes, and leaned closer to kiss her parted lips.

"That's hardly the point," a man's voice said, disastrously close, causing them to spring apart. Dragan stood, moving more decorously away from her, as the duke himself walked into the room with another man of similar age.

The duke scowled. "Griz? What are you doing here?" His gaze lashed Dragan, who bowed politely.

"Oh, just talking," Griz said carelessly. "But don't worry, we'll leave you privacy for your own discussion. This is Mr. Tizsa, by the way. Sir, my father, the Duke of Kelburn, and Lord John Russell."

Both gentlemen registered the introduction with brief nods, though both clearly had more important things on their minds. Dragan was not surprised. Lord John Russell was the prime minister.

"Your mother was looking for you," the duke said pointedly.

"I expect she's lost her fan again," Griz murmured as they walked back into the drawing room.

Dragan, deliberately searching for Galbraith's bright red coat, noted the direction of the officer's gaze. At Griz.

"Lady Grizelda," said a polite voice to their right.

Gabriel, Lord Horace's man, was bowing to Griz, who responded immediately.

"Ah, Mr. Gabriel, how do you do?"

"Very well indeed. May I present to you my betrothed, Miss Derryn? Sir James Derryn's daughter. My dear, Lady Grizelda Niven. And Mr. Tizsa," he added with hurried disapproval.

Griz gave her hand to the other woman with perfect friendliness. "A pleasure to meet you, at last, Miss Derryn."

"The pleasure is mine," the lady said pleasantly. Her gaze seemed to have got stuck on Dragan, though she dragged it back to Griz in time to add, "Thomas has told me so much about you, it seems odd this is our first meeting."

"Lady Grizelda is a little like you, my dear," Gabriel said, "in that she does not spend all her life at parties."

"Got bored with them in my first season," Miss Derryn confided, adding hastily, "though this is most pleasant and so kind of Lady Trench to invite Thomas and me."

"Oh, well, he and Horace work so hard together that Mr. Gabriel is like one of the family," Griz said.

Is he? Dragan wondered curiously. The cold eyes and propensity for work did not inspire affection in him, and he couldn't help speculating as to what had brought this odd couple together.

"Might I hope you will come to tea one day?" Miss Derryn asked Griz.

"How kind, I would love to," Griz said warmly. "Oh, look, I think it is time for Azalea's soprano…"

"Who is Azalea's soprano?" Dragan murmured as they moved back into the room they had just left.

"Her musical discovery of the year. Don't worry," she added. "Azalea's taste is excellent. She has helped several singers and musicians in this way."

Griz was musical, too, he remembered. He would like to hear her sing and play. A whole intriguing world was opening up to him, with Griz at its center.

They remained together quite naturally until he realized they were approaching the duchess at the front row of seats. Griz introduced him without fuss, and the duchess gave him a gracious smile in return for his bow. For an instant, he wondered if it would cause too much comment if he sat beside her. And then he caught sight of the British officer, Galbraith, moving into the chair directly behind hers. Dragan sat down.

"Grizelda! I have not seen you in ages." A woman took the chair next to his, talking across him.

The sister-in-law, Lady Monkton, who, by annoying Lady Trench, was indirectly responsible for his presence here. She was a proud, handsome woman, not quite thirty, he guessed.

"Good evening, Augusta," Griz said cheerfully. "Do you know Mr. Tizsa?"

Lady Monkton smiled thinly as her gaze flickered over him. "I believe we have not been introduced."

"My sister-in-law," Griz murmured. "The Marchioness of Monkton. Where *is* Monkton?"

Lady Monkton waved one vague hand behind her. "Talking politics. So, Mr. Tizsa, you are one of Lady Trench's admirers?"

It was, he reflected, a blatant way to warn Griz away from him. The woman must have seen them together before this. Although he did not care two hoots for her opinion and assumed Lady Trench more than capable of taking care of her own reputation, he did not want Griz hurt.

"Isn't everyone?" he murmured.

Fortunately, there was no time for more because Lady Trench walked in front of them with a young woman dressed all in white, whom she introduced to the audience as "the finest singer I have heard in years." An older woman at the pianoforte began to play, and the singing began.

Griz was right. The soprano was talented and a pleasure to listen to. She had one of those voices that both soothed and exhilarated. He lost himself easily in the music, and yet his surroundings never quite faded. More than anything, he was aware of the young woman beside him, her breathing changing with the rhythm and emotion of the songs. And with that awareness came happiness, a realization that at this moment, there was nowhere in the world he would rather be.

Until, during the third song, he felt her tense. She was gazing determinedly at the singer, but her fingers had clenched in her lap.

He flicked his gaze behind her. The officer was sitting forward in his chair, his elbows on his knees, his chin resting in his hands. Very subtly, the bastard was breathing on Grizelda's nape. Even as Dragan watched, Galbraith raised one finger, about to brush it casually against her skin.

A more sophisticated women—Azalea Trench, perhaps—would have casually reached behind her head and batted him away or leaned forward herself to avoid him. But Griz was rigid, afraid to draw attention to what was happening, but unhappy.

Fury surged in Dragan. This Galbraith was clearly the kind of man who fondled women under the pretense of helping them. No doubt he groped maids and brushed up against women in crowds. Dragan's instinct was to leap over the back of the seat and knock him to the floor. But he had to protect Griz's comfort and her reputation. With difficulty, he controlled his disgust and merely shifted his chair.

The sudden movement stilled Galbraith's finger before it touched her. His eyes swerved and met Dragan's.

Whatever Galbraith saw there froze him, caused a deepening of color in the florid face. He curled his lip, trying for amused disdain. Casually, without hurry, he sat back in his chair, and Dragan returned his attention to the singer.

He felt the officer's gaze burning into the back of his head and was glad. A challenge had been given and accepted. More importantly, Griz began to breathe again.

And when they stood to applaud the singer, she had a determined look about her. While everyone complimented the singer and congratulated Lady Trench on finding her, Griz swung suddenly round to face Galbraith, her smile dazzling.

"I thought it was you! You must tell me what you have been doing all these years since we last met." As she spoke, she nodded invitingly to the end of the row. Galbraith, with a glance of triumph over his shoulder at Dragan, moved at once to join her.

⇶⇷

GRIZ HAD BEEN uncomfortable and then angry at Galbraith for spoiling the music, which had been bliss to listen to with Dragan so close beside her. That closeness had prevented her feeling unsafe, but it had done nothing to quell her anger. She had been grateful when Dragan had turned his head and somehow scared Galbraith off with his glare.

But she also knew Dragan would not always be there, that the problem was not yet over. And that she would not put up with it, even if it meant ruining Azalea's party—which, of course, she would do her best to avoid.

And so, she made herself smile at him and, ignoring Dragan, walked away with him. At the door, he touched her elbow, no doubt meaning to direct her into whichever direction he wished to go, but she gave him no chance, merely moving her arm away to smooth her skirts and walking into the heart of the drawing room.

She had no intention of going anywhere with him unattended.

She chose an empty chair in a group of four.

"I was almost afraid you had forgotten me," he said lightly, dropping into the chair closest to her. He smiled winningly. "So, I am doubly glad to catch up with my old playmate."

"We were never playmates," she said flatly. "I was a naive child. You were a grown man."

"Isn't that what you liked?"

"Probably," she admitted. "Being, as I said, a naïve child, foolishly flattered, and not quite aware of the subtle differences between *man* and *gentleman*."

He blinked, clearly thrown for a moment. Then he smiled again. Why had she never noticed that he smiled too much? Because she had imagined he smiled only at her. "You don't pull your punches, do you, little Griz?" he said with amusement. "I believe that is what I first liked about you."

"Oh, I doubt that," she said. "I suspect my parentage was the chief attraction." Beyond him, Dragan had caught Azalea's attention and was drawing her with him in conversation. Hastily, she looked away to find Galbraith regarding her with some indignation.

"That isn't fair."

She shrugged. "Perhaps not. If I'm wrong, I apologize. But here is what I wished to say." The room was filling up, and people would soon come close enough to overhear. "I don't forgive you for your attack on our last meeting—"

"Attack?" he interrupted, staring at her, while his hand reached up to the side of his head in an involuntary gesture of pained recollection. "You attacked me—with a candlestick, and it was damned painful."

"Good," she said. "Because if you ever dare to breathe on me in that disgusting manner again, I may not use a candlestick, but I will make certain no hostess of renown ever invites you anywhere."

His eyes widened. His jaw showed a tendency to drop before he wrestled his face back into a smile. "Oh, don't be like that, Griz. I was only playing."

She didn't smile back. "I don't like your games. I found long ago that I don't actually like *you*. So please, in the future, keep your distance."

She would have risen and walked away, but to her surprise, Azalea suddenly flopped gracefully onto the chair on her other side. Dragan perched on the arm, and Annabelle sat in the other, deep in some laughing conversation with a young couple Griz did not know.

"So, what do you think of my soprano, Griz?" Azalea asked lazily.

It was easy to answer that with an enthusiasm that drew in everyone but Galbraith, who, had no interest in anyone or anything but himself. He could not even depart easily, since he would have to have disturbed Annabelle and the others who had been drawn into the group.

Dragan had done this, she realized, almost with awe. To give her the protection of family and friends if she needed it.

After several bewildered minutes, Galbraith began to flirt with Annabelle and the younger lady and was soon supported by a friend Griz did not know but who was introduced merely as Paddy. Under the cover of general conversation, Galbraith said something to Paddy that she could not hear, although she noticed their gaze was on Dragan, which made her wary.

"Probably someone's cast-offs," Galbraith said scornfully, and Griz realized with fresh indignation that they were mocking Dragan's slightly threadbare uniform. She knew he only wore it because his one black coat was done, and an officer's uniform was considered acceptable evening dress. Of course, it was not as smart and shiny as Galbraith's.

"Can't say I recognize it," Paddy said, and catching Dragan's eye, he grinned. "Which regiment are you with?"

"None," replied Dragan. "It was forcibly disbanded, along with my country's independence."

"Mr. Tizsa is in exile from Hungary," Azalea observed.

"Really?" Paddy said. "Then allow me to shake your hand, sir!" Paddy stood to offer his hand, and everyone's attention was suddenly on Dragan, asking eager questions and professing admiration for his cause.

In the midst of it, with space now to escape with dignity, Galbraith took the opportunity.

Azalea closed one eye and leaned closer to Griz. "You should have told me," she murmured. "You should have told somebody. I thought you were in love with the lout."

"Oh, no," Griz said uncomfortably.

Azalea squeezed her hand in a rare gesture of affection. She glanced at Dragan, still fielding questions and adulation. "He is a good friend to you."

Griz smiled. "Yes," she said happily. "He is."

Dragan looked up and met her gaze—the briefest of glances, but one she would treasure.

"Well," Azalea said, rising to her feet. "It would appear the other room has been cleared for dancing. You must save a waltz for me, Mr. Tizsa. I hear you dance divinely."

"I can't imagine who told you that," Dragan said, amused.

"It wasn't me," Griz told him when he offered her his hand in silent invitation.

"I know that," he said meekly. "But I thought I would try to improve."

Griz laughed and took his arm, and, with several other young couples, they moved into the other room, and the trio of musicians were striking up a waltz.

"Thank you," Griz said with difficulty.

"There is nothing to thank me for. I apprehend you had already dealt with the problem. I only brought reinforcements. I hope you don't mind that I told your sister. I thought she should know."

Griz thought about it as he took her in his arms. "I don't believe I mind at all," she said in surprise.

It was time, she saw, that she should move on from a lot of her more childish issues, including the foolish jealousy of Azalea that had still reared its ugly head over Dragan. Despite her earlier discomfort over Galbraith, the world that night was a delightful place.

CHAPTER SIXTEEN

ONLY WHEN THE dance ended, and she noticed Monkton and Horace together, frowning in her direction, did she remember that she had spent virtually all of Azalea's party with Dragan.

"I had better show my face to my mother," she murmured.

"Thank you for the dance. Are you free tomorrow to return to Covent Garden?"

"Oh yes. I can bring the carriage and pick you up at ten. Are you leaving already?"

"Soon," he replied. "I have things to do."

Of course he did. She must not assume, she must *never* assume, she could monopolize him.

While sitting by her mother, who barely noticed her, she discovered an old friend close by, a tongue-tied young man who relaxed enough to speak only in the presence of people he knew well. His position was not improved by his mother constantly demanding his escort to parties and balls where he was never comfortable. With some relief, he asked Griz to dance, which she was glad to do.

"Thank God you're here," he said simply. "Otherwise, I should be pestered to marry Miss Watters."

"What is it about Miss Watters?" Griz wondered aloud, before she added hastily, "Do you *want* to marry her?"

"I'd rather marry you. *You* don't make me uncomfortable."

"Well, take my advice and tell your mother you don't want to marry anyone for at least five years."

It was always easy, she reflected, to give other people advice.

When the dance ended, she noticed Dragan heading out the door. He gave her a quick smile, which she returned, and then he was gone, taking the unexpected excitement of the evening with him.

As she dragged her attention back toward her partner, she noticed Mr. Gabriel among a more serious group of guests, observing her. She inclined her head, and to her surprise, he abandoned Miss Derryn to their friends and came toward her.

"Lady Grizelda," he greeted her. "I am glad to see you enjoying such a pleasant evening. You deprive yourself of too many such treats."

Grizelda laughed. "How can you say so, when you have seen me at two parties in one week?"

"Ah, well, I don't count the Hungarian charity as more than duty. Though perhaps you do?"

"It was fun," she said lightly. "Entertaining and informative."

He offered her his arm, a rare enough gesture to alarm her, although she took it and strolled with him around the room. "I count myself very much a friend of your family," he said at last. "So I hope you will forgive me for speaking freely."

"No forgiveness is necessary," she assured him.

"I am aware you have independent interests that do not necessarily coincide with your family's, and they have grown used to you going your own way, a most sensible lady as you are."

She blinked. "Thank you. I think."

"Your interests take you largely away from the society of your class. This inexperience combined with your good nature makes you vulnerable to those who would take advantage."

"I am not quite the helpless fool you think me," she said, more amused than offended.

"Oh, no, I meant no such thing," he assured her. "On the contrary,

I think you a most capable young lady in many areas. But I do feel compelled to warn you."

"Of what?" she asked, bewildered.

"Rather of whom."

Suspicion dragged down her brow. "Has Horace put you up to this?"

"Of course not. Though I know Lord Horace to be concerned, he, like the rest of your family, assumes there is no reason to intervene."

"I really doubt there is," Griz said discouragingly.

"I hope that is true. I see that you suspect I speak of your friendship with Dragan Tizsa."

"There is no need," she said flatly.

"But there is," Gabriel said with greater urgency. "The police arrested him for very good reason, and you not only extracted him from under their noses but seem to be constantly with him. My lady, I believe him to be a very dangerous man."

"Only to tyrants and his enemies in battle," she said lightly, although she began to draw her arm free, determined to end this tête-à-tête.

He caught her hand on his arm, staying her. "Please, hear me out, ma'am, before you continue this friendship. I do not even refer to his politics, though they are radical enough to appall the bulk of his fellow refugees. Do you not know he is still the main suspect in your maid's murder?"

Griz stared at him, disbelief warring with unease. "No, he isn't. Even before I knew him, I proved that."

"No, you proved it was unlikely, but if he took a shortcut, for example, through the carpenter's yard in Mudd Lane, it is still very possible."

"But the workshops were closed."

"Were they? All he would need was an accomplice or a key. Inspector Harris is looking into that now, along with other possibilities.

Which is why I warn you. It would really be best for you, for your family, to draw back from him."

Distress clawed at her stomach, not because she believed the accusation but because it was being made. "Then the police will prove themselves wrong. They are looking for someone, anyone to blame, and he is convenient. He could not have done this thing. He had no reason to."

"Hadn't he? He knew her. He went to meet her that night. You saw him leave the theatre just before her murder. She had told the world she was going to marry him—no one believes they did not have a liaison. It did not suit him to marry a housemaid, for he has pretensions to nobility in his own country, whatever his politics. And to thrive in exile, he needs a wife of much better birth. Or at least wealth. He has, after all, a handsome face and engaging manner to help him, along with the heroic battles in his past. Poor Nancy would have held him back, dragged him down. He is no stranger to killing."

"He is a doctor," she said between tight lips.

"We have only his word for that."

"And Dr. Cordell's," she retorted. "And among the refugees is at least one man who knew him as a medical student in Hungary."

"It doesn't matter." There was pity in his eyes, in his soft voice. "Doctors have killed before. That isn't the point at issue. *Please*, Lady Grizelda, draw back from him."

Finally, she disengaged her hand. "Thank you for your concern," she said coldly and walked away.

She didn't believe a word, but the shine of the evening had dulled. She wanted only to go home because her happiness, her joy, had been sullied. It didn't matter that they were half-truths and mistaken beliefs. He was in danger from the police, who were, no doubt, under a good deal of pressure to find the killer of a girl in the service of so powerful a family. It was more urgent than ever that they find the real killer before Dragan was arrested again.

Horace stood with a group of people, glass in hand, laughing. At the other end of the room, her father and eldest brother were deep in conversation with the more political types. She stopped in her tracks, causing two young men to almost walk into her.

After a flurry of apologies, she walked on, faster, then almost threw herself into the chair beside her mother.

Why had Mr. Gabriel spoken to her of this? She believed his concern was genuine, but surely if it had any basis, Horace would have forced this talk or put their father up to it. Horace did not like her friendship with Dragan either, but he hadn't tried to forbid it or warn her, although he must surely be aware of the same facts as Gabriel. Did they disagree on its importance? If Gabriel had learned more about Inspector Harris's inquiries, would he not have spoken to Horace rather than to her?

Something about the whole conversation felt…wrong. Her stomach wasn't twisting simply with fear for Dragan. Was Gabriel driving the case against him?

Why in the world would he do that?

➤➤➤◄◄◄

EMMIE, THE HOUSEMAID, had stayed up to help her out of her gown.

"You didn't need to," Griz said, still distracted by her own thoughts. "I am adept at wriggling in and out of clothes on my own."

"Why should you?" Emmie said stoutly, "when I am here. Besides, I like the practice. I would like to train to be a lady's maid."

"Have you spoken to Kettle?" Griz asked, focusing her attention. Her mother's dresser was clearly the best person to help Emmie. "I am not the best to help you in such a quest."

"But you liked the way I dressed your hair?" Emmie asked anxiously.

"Indeed, I did. In fact," she added, remembering it was true, "several people complimented me on it."

Emmie beamed. "Well, if you will put up with me, my lady, set me tasks and tell me when I'm wrong..."

"I'm happy to have you, Emmie, but you must speak to Kettle, too. In fact, I had better speak to Mrs. MacKenna. And my mother." She yawned. "Tomorrow. Thank you," she added as the maid lifted her gown over her head and threw it over the back of the nearest chair.

A thought came to her while Emmie wrestled with the other ties. "Tell me, did Nancy ever seem to have favorites among the visitors to the house?"

"Not really, my lady." A smile flickered over her face. "She was more interested in the family. In fact, we used to tease her because she would always jump up to show Lord Horace's visitors in or out."

Griz paused in the act of pulling on her dressing gown. *No. Oh, no.*

Perhaps Emmie saw the sudden distress in her face, for she burst out, "Not that we were implying any impropriety! His lordship is a handsome gentleman, and it wasn't surprising she noticed him. But we all know *he* never noticed *her.*"

"Of course not," Griz said calmly, although now she had even more to think about, and it was far more worrying. "Does Lord Horace have many visitors, then?"

"No, for he's usually out," Emmie said. "But Mr. Gabriel comes quite often, and occasionally other people from the office. Clerks," she explained with faint disdain.

"Clerks," Griz mused, happy to be distracted. "Could one of them have been Nancy's gentleman? Did she show any of them special attention?"

Emmie considered. "Not really. Not beyond being eager to take them to Lord Horace and show them out again."

Another question hovered on her lips, but she pulled herself up, approaching the issue in a more roundabout way.

"What duties do you have now that might be upset if you spend more time with Miss Kettle or me? Who keeps the main reception rooms and the library clean?"

"Just Janet and me, now Nancy's gone. Nancy used to help Janet in the library and me in the drawing room. I did the downstairs reception rooms, Nancy did the hall and the stairs, and we helped her when we could. I do the duchess's morning room. I can easily keep that up as well, helping you, my lady, especially if Janet will take over Lord Horace's study."

At last. "You clean there, too?"

"No, my lady, Nancy did that. Janet and me have been taking it in turns since she died. But Mrs. MacKenna is looking for a new maid to replace Nancy." Her lips trembled suddenly. "Not that anyone can, truly..."

Griz patted her shoulder. "Go to bed, Emmie. We'll sort it out tomorrow."

As she climbed into bed, she found it utterly frustrating not to have Dragan close by to talk to about her new suspicions. Then, the thought of Dragan in her bedchamber made her body flush from head to toe.

I must not love him, not like that. It would spoil everything.

Still, she could not stop the memory of waltzing in his arms, of the warm smile lurking in his haunted eyes, his devastating kiss...

Had that been gentlemanly? She had known him only a week, and she was not dispassionate about his possible involvement with Nancy or her murder. Did she just not want to believe? Or did she *really* know him well enough to judge?

Once she had worked out his innocence, her growing closeness with him had been driven by instinct. But she, who had been flattered and silly about Galbraith, could easily have been fooled by another, much more subtle man. Could he have courted her to keep her good opinion, even to bring her family onto his side to protect him from the law?

The thought made her blood run cold.

He had been breathless when he had arrived at the scene of Nancy's murder. Because he had run all the way through the carpenter's yard and around the theatre to catch up with her? Or because, as he had told her and the police, because he had been looking anxiously for Nancy?

Do I believe him because I think he has started to care for me? Because I think he is my friend? Or is he my friend because I have always believed in his honesty? He was, in many ways, a tortured soul, haunted by his lost cause and by taking lives in battle. That much, she could not doubt. And knowing that, could she really imagine him killing Nancy? Because she bore his child and was pressing him to marry her?

No, Dragan would not kill his own child or a helpless maid who loved him. He might not have returned that love—he had shown no profound grief at her passing—but he, principled and sick of death, would never have murdered her.

No, Gabriel had spoken to her, told her of the police's suspicions for a reason. And she could not believe that reason was Dragan's guilt.

AFTER A DISTURBED night and dreams full of vague, unspecific threats, Griz forced herself to rise and speak to Horace before he went out.

Vicky accompanied her downstairs, galloping ahead as though to persuade her to an early walk. Griz decided to take the dog to Nick for his walk, and Vicky seemed to cooperate, hurtling past the dining room and bolting down the next flight of stairs. There was an explosion of laughter as the dog collided with Nick, and then Nick's footsteps speeding upstairs in the wake of Vicky, who must have noticed Griz hadn't followed her.

On sudden impulse, Griz walked to the dining room door and

opened it, walking inside just as Vicky bolted across the landing. From the table, Horace scowled over his newspaper.

"Nick, is that you?" Griz called into the hall. "Come and take Vicky for me."

Since Vicky had bounded onto a chair with the table clearly her next objective, Griz grabbed her and waited for Nick to hurtle into the room, which he did, grinning.

"Sorry, m'lady," he said cheerfully. "She's just playing,"

"I know, but Lord Horace likes his breakfast in peace, don't you Horace?"

Horace lowered the newspaper, glaring at the boy. "Who the devil's this?"

"Nick. He looks after the kitchen fire and helps me with Vicky."

Nick, still grinning, made not a bad bow before taking the dog from her. Horace grunted and returned to his paper.

As Nick and Vicky left, Griz turned to the sideboard, blindly filling her plate. She felt horribly, traitorously disloyal, but the relief that Nick and Horace did not recognize each other made her knees tremble.

"Horace," she said, sitting down opposite him. "How far do you trust Mr. Gabriel?"

Horace's mouth dropped. "Implicitly."

"That's what I thought. You and he had to work instead of coming to the opera the night Nancy died. When did you leave the office?"

"About nine," Horace replied, then blinked as though surprised he had answered. "At least, that's when I got to my club. Griz—"

"Did Mr. Gabriel go with you?"

"Of course not, he's not a member," Horace said with quite unconscious snobbery. "He left earlier to call on Miss Derryn, as he had promised."

"Ah." She ate, thoughtfully aware of her brother's bewildered gaze upon her.

"Griz, what is going on in your head?"

"I'm not sure yet. You can go back to your paper now."

It took him almost half a minute, but he did eventually return to the newspaper. He was still reading it when Griz bade him a cheerful goodbye and left the room.

CHAPTER SEVENTEEN

S HE CAME UPON Dragan walking down Caroline Place with the
ladies of the Cordell family. He saw Griz at once, and with a mere
tip of his hat, left his companions and strode across the road to leap
into the carriage. There was no time to do anything but wave through
the window. And take in Anne Cordell's glower of displeasure.

He seemed to see at once that something was wrong, but he didn't
speak, merely looked at her and waited.

"I had some other ideas," she blurted. "Last night, Mr. Gabriel told
me the police still suspect you, that you could have killed Nancy and
escaped via the carpentry shop in the lane, then run around to find the
body after I did."

"Why would I do that?" he asked with a frown, then, "Do you
believe him?" His eyes were steady, unreadable, though his posture
had tensed.

Waiting to be hurt, perhaps.

Perhaps.

She dragged her gaze free. "That it's possible? It's easy enough to
check. That you did it, no. What really troubles me is why he wants to
convince me. Why does he care? He has no professional interest in
crimes of this nature and no expertise."

"Did you reach any conclusions."

She nodded. "That he would like to blame you without tarnishing
my family or me by association."

"He seems to be very protective of you all," Dragan said neutrally.

"Horace raised him from a much lowlier position. I think he would do anything for Horace."

"Including murdering Nancy? Why would your brother want Nancy dead?"

"Emmie—one of the maids who was Nancy's friend—said the other servants teased her because of her devotion to Horace. Emmie denied there was any impropriety. But…but what if there was? What if her child was—"

"With respect, a man in Lord Horace's position is unlikely to care two hoots for any scandal of that nature. He could easily pay to send the girl away and acknowledge the baby, or not, as he saw fit. It would not end his career or cause society to shun him. It was Nancy who would have suffered."

Having thought of all that herself, she merely nodded.

There was a pause. "For what it is worth, he does not seem the kind of man to philander with his mother's servants. Has he ever done so before?"

"Not to my knowledge. He has never seemed terribly interested in women. I mean, he flirts a bit with ladies of his own class, but if he has affairs of the heart, I always imagined they were conducted elsewhere."

"You were probably right. On the other hand, Nancy was suddenly interested in radical politics. Lord Horace is professionally interested in such matters, too."

Her eyes widened. "You think she was *working* for Horace?" She wriggled in her seat with excitement, causing her shoulder and hip to brush against his. Ignoring the shooting awareness, she said, "That would explain her going to so many meetings, talking to people and moving on, after, perhaps, reporting to Horace, which were worth investigating. Perhaps she was even killed by some radical who had discovered her perfidy…"

"Which brings us back to me," Dragan observed wryly.

"Hmm. I wish we knew why she wanted to see you. Perhaps she meant to tell you that you were in danger from Horace's department?"

"Why *then*, several weeks after I had last seen her? There was no reason for his department to be interested in me or the Cordells."

Griz frowned, remembering. "But he said—Mr. Gabriel said—that the other refugees dislike your radicalism."

"Some of them do. All we had in common was a desire for self-determination, for which we had to drive out the Austrians. But none of us have ever threatened the British government in any way."

She sighed. "I need to talk to Horace again, but I doubt he'll answer any more of my questions."

"Why, what have you asked him already?"

"Where he and Mr. Gabriel were when Nancy was murdered. Horace left the office—in Whitehall—and was at his club by nine. I imagine that can easily be verified, so he couldn't really have been in Covent Garden at half-past."

Dragan nudged her in a way that reminded her of her brothers when they were all children. "You see, you don't believe he did it. You're just upset because you feel guilty about suspecting him at all."

She regarded him ruefully. "Didn't you say we were all capable of killing in the right circumstances? I don't think these are the right circumstances for Horace."

He nodded thoughtfully. "And what of Mr. Gabriel?"

"He left the office earlier, but I had run out of goodwill to ask Horace what time he left. Horace did say he went to call on the Derryns. So, after we finish in Covent Garden, I thought I would go and have tea with Miss Derryn and find out what time Gabriel arrived and departed."

"Good plan."

"I do feel a bit of a traitor," she confessed. "Even for considering Horace."

"Do you want to stop looking into this?"

She shook her head. "How could I with such suspicions swirling in my head?" She sighed. "Besides, I'm not sure I *can* stop. It's a bit…addictive, isn't it? Even the unpleasant parts. Like craving alcohol or opium. Or perhaps that's just because—" *Just because you are with me.*

If they found the truth of Nancy's murder, there would be no excuse but friendship to meet.

"What?" he asked.

She shrugged. "Will we still be friends when this is done?"

As soon as she blurted the words, she wished them unspoken. To force or insist on friendship was anathema to her, and she had no desire to appear needy. Worse, the silence stretched between them, sinking her heart and causing every nerve to cringe. In desperation, she cast about for something light or witty to distract…

The touch of his hand on hers made her jump, her gaze flying back to his.

"Griz. Do you not think we are already more than friends?"

A smile seemed to surge up from her toes, flickering across her lips. His fingers curled around hers, and she clung to them, drowning in the heady warmth of his eyes.

The carriage stopped suddenly, right beside a halted vehicle pointing in the opposite direction. Griz remembered how much glass there was in the carriage and hastily withdrew her hand.

Or perhaps Dragan withdrew his, for he was taking something from his coat pockets. On the top of the little pile of similarly sized paper was his sketch of Nancy, which he must have cut from the notebook. He peeled it off and slid it to the bottom of his pile, revealing beneath a sketch of Horace that caught at her breath. The likeness was unmistakable, from the arrogant set of his shoulders to his amiable and yet somehow secretive eyes.

"Oh, no," Griz whispered, "you suspect him, too…"

"Of some connection to Nancy, yes. His employment and her mercurial interest in radical politics seemed too much of a coincidence. And I did wonder—I still wonder—why they came to the Hungarian evening."

He moved Horace to the bottom of his pile and revealed the much blander Mr. Gabriel, with his watchful eyes and thin lips. "If it has anything to do with Lord Horace, then it's perfectly possible Gabriel acted for him, either with or without his knowledge."

Griz swallowed. "Perhaps Nancy came to the theatre to renew her acquaintance with you because she was ordered to look into you or one of the other Hungarians. Like your newly arrived Mr. Lazar, who seemed to cause such a stir."

"Or perhaps she came to warn me."

"Not asking for your help after all," Griz mused, "but offering hers..." She dragged her gaze away from Gabriel's subtle face to Dragan's. "I deliberately let Nick and Horace meet this morning. I thought if they had seen each other in Art's company, they would give it away."

"And did they?"

"No. I could swear neither had ever laid eyes on the other."

Dragan nodded and removed Gabriel to the bottom of the pile. Jack Payne's ordinary yet determined face gazed up at her now. "Nancy may have worked for your brother, and yet her death has nothing to do with him or politics, but with unrequited love and jealousy."

"If I can suspect my own brother, then I can suspect an old friend," Griz said ruefully.

Dragan moved Jack to the bottom of his pack, revealing the last sketch, the harsh, semi-shaven face of Goddard, his mean eyes glaring out of the paper.

Griz shivered. "I can't work out how he is involved, especially if he didn't know Nancy. And yet, he does seem to be somewhere in all of this. I wish we knew what Art looked like, too. Do you mean to show these to people in Covent Garden?"

"I think we should."

"They are amazingly detailed," Griz said with all the wonder of a young lady who had failed miserably at sketching and water coloring, "especially considering you must have worked only from memory. The likenesses are so good. How did you learn to draw like that?"

He shrugged. "I just always did it. I was an observant child. A teacher at school encouraged me, taught me other techniques more useful to portrait artists than anatomists."

He put the sketches back in his pocket, his lips parted as though to say more. He seemed to bite back the words, then they tumbled out anyway. "I used to draw everyone. Friends in cafes plotting revolution, working men and peasants, marchers and leaders, soldiers, prisoners... I lost them all when I fled Hungary. I never meant to draw anything at all again, ever. Until that day in your house when I felt compelled to sketch Nancy."

A requiem. A tribute to a vital young woman who should never have died when or how she did.

Forgetting the windows once more, she laid her head against his shoulder. Just for a moment. An instant of mutual comfort. Then she straightened. "We're nearly at the market. Shall we alight here and send John home with the carriage?"

Crossing the bustling market toward the theatre, they were hailed by a sudden, "Hello there again, my darling. Couldn't stay away, could you?"

It was Nell, standing beside a flower girl with a bruised face. She seemed to have been hugging her and now, surreptitiously slipped a coin into the girl's hand, even as she swaggered across to Griz and Dragan. Other young women, dressed much in the same manner as Nell, were still with the flower girl, half-cajoling, half instructing.

"What happened to her?" Griz demanded.

"Walked into a door, didn't she," Nell sneered. "Told her she needed a new door that doesn't get in her way."

"One without fists?" Griz guessed.

Nell stared at her with rather more respect.

"How much money would she need to get out?" Dragan asked.

"It's courage she needs, not money."

"But the money would help," Griz said suddenly. "A barrow and flowers to sell in the wealthy neighborhoods." She pulled a note from her capacious cloak pocket and thrust it into Nell's hand.

The grubby, painted nails scratched in their instinctive grab at the money.

But Nell's eyes had narrowed. "What you giving it to me for? I'll only spend it on drink, or His Nibs will have it off me."

"Not if you give it to her now."

Without a word, Nell turned, stalking back to the group around the flower girl. Nell spoke rapidly, but the girl hid her hand behind her back, refusing to take the money, even while she glanced with fear at Dragan.

"...idiot," came Nell's rising voice. "It don't come from him. It's from her...suppose she don't like men too free with their fists."

Dragan's gaze burned into the side of Grizelda's face, but she did not look at him. The flower girl suddenly seized the money, thrust an armful of flowers into Nell's hands, and ran off with one of the other women.

And as Griz had hoped, Nell swaggered back to them, in company with another prostitute, by her dress.

"Millie's gone to help her get her things while he's out," Nell said carelessly. "She wants you to have these."

"Keep them," Griz said. "Sell them yourself if you like."

Nell's eyes mocked her. "Keep me off the streets?"

"Would it?"

"Nah. This is Junie. Show her that picture you had yesterday."

Obligingly, Dragan drew out his drawings like a pack of cards and showed Junie the picture of Nancy.

"Yes, that's her," Junie said, causing Grizelda's heart to leap.

"Who?" Dragan asked.

"Girl I saw come out of the opera house last Thursday night. Well before the end of the show. She looked around her, like, then hurried over *there*." She pointed to the right of the theatre, the direction Griz had followed.

"Was someone waiting for her?" Dragan asked with suppressed excitement.

"Yes, I think so. Young feller in top hat. Nob."

"Had this—er...*nob* come out of the theatre, too?" Dragan asked.

"Didn't see him. Didn't notice him until I saw her hurry toward him. Funny thing is, he didn't wait for her to catch up, just bent his finger like *this*." She stuck up one finger and curled it in the universal gesture for come here. "And she went. Followed him up there."

The girl's eyes focused on Dragan. "I saw another young fellow, then, distracted me on account of his handsome face."

"Who?" Dragan asked eagerly.

"You, you pillock," Nell said.

Junie sniggered. "You seemed to be looking for someone, too, but you went off the other way."

"Did you see this lady?" Dragan asked, touching Grizelda's arm.

"Don't recall it. But then, just after I saw *you*, I was distracted by a customer and didn't look no more."

"And this man she followed," Griz said eagerly, "what did he look like? Was he tall or short, dark or fair?"

Junie thought. "Don't think he was that tall, but then I wasn't that close, was I? And he never stood beside anyone else. Couldn't see his hair for his hat, so it must have been cut short. He moved funny."

"Was he lame?" Dragan demanded.

"Oh, no, not like that. He sort of...swaggered, but as if he was practicing. Struck me, he was very young and unsure but trying to look commanding." She cast a cheeky smile at Dragan. "Like you."

Impatiently, Griz swept Nancy's portrait off the top of Dragan's "pack." "Was it any of these men?"

Having asked, she was afraid to hear the answer. No one would have called any of the sketch subjects very young and unsure, but in that particular situation, about to take a life, surely anyone would be wary, uncertain...

She felt faint with relief when Horace elicited no response from Junie. Neither did Gabriel or Jack Payne. Or even Goddard.

It was Nell who jerked back as though struck when she saw the snub-nosed face of the prisoner. "What you got a picture of *him* for?"

"You know Goddard?" Dragan asked carefully.

"No, nor want to," Nell said with a shiver. "Saw him once, though, last year when his bullies were looking for girls. I hid. His Nibs is no gent, but God knows he's better 'n Goddard."

"Do you know Art Dooley, too?" Griz asked.

"Leave off, he's even worse. He even shops his mates to take over their manors. Or so I heard. Don't have nothing to do with these people." Nell caught the exchange of looks between Griz and Dragan and added urgently, "I mean it. If you think either of 'em murdered that girl—and I wouldn't put it past them—you leave it to the Peelers! You, handsome, look after your pretty lady." She cast him a grin. "And if you fall out, you know where to find me."

And Nell swaggered off, her hands full of flowers.

Griz took Dragan's arm, excitement tugging her onward because finally, they seemed to have learned something. "You were right. Someone *did* entice Nancy up to Mudd Lane, and from what Junie saw, he was a gentleman. Surely he must be her lover."

"But we're no closer to finding out who he is," Dragan pointed out.

"I'm glad it isn't Horace or Mr. Gabriel."

"It's still possible she wasn't close enough to see him clearly. Though it's true, she recognized Nancy."

As one, they were following the same path as yesterday, up the side of the theatre and through the back streets to Mudd Lane. Dragan appeared to be concentrating on something and said nothing as they walked until they reached the place of Nancy's murder. "Three minutes and forty-five seconds at a brisk walk. Let's go and talk to our carpenter again."

The carpenter scowled at them as they crossed his small yard and threw down his hammer. "What *now?*"

"Good morning and apologies for disturbing you again," Dragan said civilly, delving into his pocket. "Would you be so good as to look at these drawings and tell us if you've ever seen any of those gentlemen before?"

"If it'll get you out of my workshop quicker," the carpenter said ungraciously and deigned to look at each of the pictures as Dragan revealed them.

"Him," the carpenter said, pointing a calloused finger at Jack Payne.

Grizelda's stomach twisted. "Where did you see him?"

"In the Queen's Head. All by himself. Looked like he was crying into his ale."

"When was this?" Dragan asked.

"Not last night. Couple of nights ago."

Griz breathed a sigh of relief. "Was that the only time you saw him?"

"Only time I can recall it."

"What of this gentleman?" Dragan asked, revealing Goddard's face.

The carpenter shook his head. "No. Can I go back to work now?"

"I have one more request," Dragan said apologetically in the teeth of the carpenter's glare. "Would you allow me to run through your shop from the lane?"

"Dragan, you don't need to," Griz said, distressed, as she realized he meant to prove Gabriel's accusations one way or the other.

"If you knock anything over, you'll pay," the carpenter growled. He seemed to have decided they were lunatics and best not thwarted, provided they caused no actual harm.

"Agreed," Dragan said, drawing Griz back across the yard to the lane. He closed the gate behind them, and they walked the few yards to where the body had been found. "The gate should have been locked, and both doors to the building, so that should add a few seconds at the very least. But let's assume he had forgotten to lock everything. Can you count accurately in seconds?"

"Of course," said Griz, who, as the youngest of a large family, had often been forced to time races, tree climbing, and swimming competitions. She didn't want Dragan to have to prove himself, but she acknowledged this would be useful proof for Mr. Gabriel. And the police, should they try to arrest Dragan again.

He gave her his hat and a lopsided smile, which threatened to melt her from the inside out.

"Go," she said hastily and began to count while Dragan took off like a hare, bursting through the gate and pushing it shut behind him. It banged and swung open again. She had heard no such sound, so if anyone had left by that route, they must have taken more time to close the gate quietly.

She acknowledged these thoughts and the distant growl of the carpenter while maintaining her steady count. Concentrating on the numbers prevented her mind from dwelling on the idea of the murderer picking locks only yards from her while she had knelt by Nancy's only just lifeless body.

She was at four minutes and twenty-three seconds when Dragan sprinted around the corner of the lane and slowed to a brisk walk as he had appeared that night.

"Maybe someone could have done it in less," he commented, recovering his breath when she had told him. "But they'd have drawn a bit of attention."

"Either way, there was nothing like four minutes between my arrival and yours."

"Good. Now," he said, taking his hat from her, "let's show our pictures to the butcher and the baker and move on."

CHAPTER EIGHTEEN

Entering via the back premises of each shop, they showed Dragan's sketches and received little reaction, except the baker's wife, who remembered seeing Jack in the flower market looking sad and aimless.

Moving on from Mudd Lane to the street the killer had most probably escaped by, they knocked on doors and spoke to a wide variety of people who regarded them with curiosity or annoyance, according to their character. An actress told them she hadn't been at home last Thursday evening because she was working. She lingered over the drawing of Horace, worryingly, but said only she might have seen him in an audience at Drury Lane. An interested soldier on half-pay said apologetically that he'd been drunk and asleep last Thursday. A woman with a gaggle of children clinging to her skirts shut the door in their faces. An artist recognized none of the pictures but said he slept odd hours and probably had been awake last Thursday night.

"Good work, by the way," he added, handing the sketches back to Dragan. "Where did you study?"

"Pest in Hungary," Dragan said. "Thursday was the night a young woman was murdered in Mudd Lane. You might have heard of it."

"Oh, yes. I spoke to a policeman, but I had to tell him I didn't see anyone in the street. It's quiet around here."

"Did *anything* disturb you that evening?" Dragan asked. "Running footsteps, perhaps?"

The artist shook his head. "I didn't notice. I did hear a woman laugh and actually went to the window to look out. I suppose that was round about nine or half-past."

Could that have been Nancy? Why would she laugh? Was that why her killer had seized her by the throat? But Griz hadn't heard anything like that.

"Did you see anyone in the street?" Griz asked.

He shook his head. "No, there's no light here. The laughter probably came through an open window close by."

"Thanks for your help," Dragan said politely.

"Nobody saw him," Griz said discontentedly as they walked on toward the market once more. "He got clean away."

"Unless they were lying."

"Who?"

"The men we spoke to. Nancy could have regarded either the soldier or the artist as gentlemen."

"She could have gone to their rooms," Griz said with a spark of excitement. "Perhaps he killed her there, then dumped her body in the lane and ran back home." Irritably, she shook her head. "There was no time, was there? Not from when she left the theatre to when I found her. And none of them showed any recognition of Nancy. We're not much further forward after all, are we?"

"Oh, I think we are. Though we're no nearer finding her unknown gentleman, we at least know who he is *not*."

"Do we?" she countered. "The man Junie saw needn't have been Nancy's lover."

"It must have been someone she trusted, though, or she would never have followed him. But I suppose it could have been a friend of his, someone she already knew. Are you hungry?"

"Starving," she admitted.

To her surprise, he veered toward a stall at the edge of the market and bought a meat pie, and they sat on the edge of a pillar to eat it. It tasted surprisingly good.

"Do you think Jack has gone home after all?" she said as she wiped her lips on her handkerchief.

Dragan followed the movement with his eyes before lifting them with a certain determination to meet hers. "I can go and find out if you like."

"No, not yet. I think I'd like to talk to Miss Derryn first."

He stood, holding down his hand to help her rise. Perhaps he pulled her too quickly, for she took an extra, involuntary step forward, which meant she was almost touching him. She could feel the heat from his body, his breath against her face.

There was no one else in sight. She could think of no reason to move away.

His eyes were both warm and amused. Wordlessly, he took the handkerchief from her hand and wiped her chin. "You missed a bit."

With an embarrassed choke of laughter, she tried to take the handkerchief from him, but his fingers closed around hers, still holding it. She could not breathe. Her whole body seemed liquid with longing.

Slowly, he bent his head and kissed her. His lips were firm and tender, softly caressing, and hers parted in instant response. It ended too soon, but since he did not draw back, she lifted her face invitingly closer.

"Again," she whispered, and his mouth took hers with much more serious intent, strong and sensual, making her gasp as she melted into his arms. Her whole being thrilled and yearned, and she never wanted it to end.

For a while, she really thought it wouldn't, for he seemed excitingly reluctant to leave her lips. He held her tightly against him, and somehow, although she couldn't recall doing it, her arms were around his neck, one hand cupping his head, the other clutching his coat collar as if to hold herself steady as she fell. Her whole body seemed to sing.

Only voices approaching made her move, dragging down one

hand to his chest, where his heart thudded strongly against her palm. But she didn't need to push him. He released her mouth, letting his arms fall.

"You're right," he said unsteadily. "This is not the place."

She swallowed, allowing him to hook her trembling hand into the crook of his arm, over-aware of every movement of her body and his.

"Why do you kiss me?" she blurted, because she really wanted to know.

"Why do you let me?" he countered. His dark eyes had grown secretive again, and yet there was a challenge there, and she rarely refused a challenge.

She lifted her chin. "Because I like it." She knew she should have been appalled at admitting such a thing, particularly to a man she had known little more than a week. But she wasn't, especially when his eyes darkened, and she could see through the vanishing veil to his smile, to desire, and something much deeper that caught at her breath all over again.

His arm squeezed her hand. "So do I," he said softly.

And she found herself smiling for no reason at the couple who passed them going toward the back of the theatre.

He said, "Your family won't like this."

"Will you mind?"

"No." He didn't even think about it, which warmed her even further. "But I would like you to be happy."

It was odd, but no one had ever said that to her before. Her family had always been concerned with a good marriage in terms of rank and wealth rather than happiness. Despite what her mother had said yesterday before Azalea's party, she was sure they already had her earmarked as the spinster who stayed at home to look after the aging duke and duchess and help with her siblings' children. In truth, she was not discontented with her lot, with the independent and varied life she had made for herself. But the idea that she could share it with someone had never entered her head. Dragan had changed everything. She had never been so happy as in this past week following the horror of Nancy's death.

And now, the doors were opening to new hope that she was afraid to let in, hopes she had never acknowledged of love and children and happiness. Because she had never imagined anyone like Dragan.

She would keep those doors shut, she told herself sternly, and live solely in the moment. That was where true happiness lay. And she basked in it.

⇒≫✕≪⇐

"I THINK MISS Derryn might speak more freely if you're alone," Dragan remarked as the hackney approached Mayfair. "Especially if she knows her betrothed suspects me of murder."

"That might be true," Griz allowed, although she was reluctant to part.

"You can tell me about it tomorrow. Are you going to the soup kitchen? I'll collect you there if you like, and we can plan what to do next."

"Very well. I should probably go home and change in any case. I doubt the Derryns will be impressed by this dress. One can carry eccentricity too far."

"I don't think she would mind," Dragan said. "She struck me as a trifle eccentric herself."

She got down at the end of Grosvenor Place, parting from Dragan with no more than a touch of hands, leaving him to take the hackney home. Or wherever he was bound.

Half an hour later, dressed in a more suitable afternoon gown of blue embroidered in white, she left the house once more and walked round to Berkley Square and the Derryns' townhouse.

Griz, who had no patience with the silly practice of merely leaving cards on a first visit, asked if Miss Derryn was at home. One quick, supercilious glance at her card had the servant all but falling over himself in his hurry to lead her up to the drawing room. There were advantages to being a duke's daughter.

"Lady Grizelda Niven, ma'am," the servant announced reverently.

There were three ladies and a gentleman already in the room. A couple, whom she did not recognize, were clearly visitors like herself. Miss Derryn was seated beside a dainty, blonde matron, somewhere in her thirties, presumably her stepmother, Lady Derryn. Beside her, Mr. Gabriel's betrothed looked even more large-boned and gangly, but her face lit up on sight of Griz, and she leapt to her feet in welcome.

"Lady Grizelda! How kind of you to call on us. Allow me to introduce my sister-in-law, Lady Derryn. And Mr. and Mrs. Vanborourgh. Barbara, Lady Grizelda Niven. Her brother, as you know, is a colleague of Thomas."

Amidst the introductions and greetings, Griz was aware of Miss Derryn's slightly pathetic triumph in her visit. She suspected the connection validated the betrothal to Gabriel, which was, perhaps, a point of contention in the family.

Griz was given tea and made the kind of bland, small talk she most disliked. Fortunately, the Vanboroughs did not stay long after her arrival, and Lady Derryn, whose bosom friends they clearly were, left the room with them for a few moments.

"You dislike this kind of genteel gathering as much as I do," Miss Derryn said bluntly.

"Well, it depends on the company," Griz admitted. "But it rarely feels a natural way of getting to know people."

"You were different last night. More...at ease."

"I was in my sister's house," Griz said lightly. *And in Dragan's company.* Did it really make such a difference to her? To her basic happiness? Hastily, she turned the tables. "You do not like society's events?"

"I don't," Miss Derryn said bluntly. "I am a countrywoman at heart, more at home with dogs and horses than with people. I am no beauty, Lady Grizelda. I have no vivacity or charm. My London Seasons were a torture to me."

"Oh, and to me," Griz said fervently. "But I think that such feelings have little to do with how others perceive us. None of us are the best judges of our own beauty or charm. Mr. Gabriel, for example, clearly disagrees with your judgment of yourself."

Miss Derryn smiled, her slightly harsh face softening. "Thomas and I suit very well. Despite him being such a town dweller! For him, I am prepared to be an occasional town hostess, and through me, he has learned to enjoy the charms of the country."

"It sounds a perfect arrangement," Griz offered.

"We think it is. My family is more ambivalent." Miss Derryn gave Griz a wry smile. "You must be aware that while he is a gentleman by birth, he is well beneath me in rank. A Derryn should look higher, I am told, than a government clerk."

"I understand his prospects are good."

"It makes no difference. His father was a minor clerk, too. We are old, landed gentry with pretensions to the highest society. If I had not failed to catch the interest of any more suitable gentleman, my father would never consider this match. As it is, he forever points out what Thomas gains from it—entry to the highest society, which can only help his career. And my dowry, of course."

"You might point out he is forever in our house and a frequent guest for dinner."

Miss Derryn laughed, a harsh, braying sound. "It was considered a vulgar boast until you walked into the drawing room. I thank you for that."

"I'm glad if such a simple thing can help your cause. When do you plan to be married?"

"Next month, all being well."

"Well, we shall all pay you bride visits," Griz said lightly. "And before then, I'm sure my mother or sisters will invite you to dinner or the theatre with us. If we had only known Mr. Gabriel didn't come to the opera with us last week because he was calling on you, my mother would have invited you both!"

Miss Derryn seemed much struck by this, for she gazed at Griz unblinking before she said breathlessly, "How kind you are. I see now why Thomas likes you."

Which, of course, was flattering, if untrue, but not the way she had wished the conversation to go. "Horace works all hours," Griz pursued, "but between us, we must make sure he does not keep Mr. Gabriel too late. You might even have already been in bed last Thursday by the time he escaped the office!"

"Oh, no," Miss Derryn said as, annoyingly, her stepmother returned to the room.

"So kind of you to call," Lady Derryn said, seating herself with a smile. "We know, of course, what great friends your family has been to Thomas Gabriel."

"Oh, that works both ways," Griz said deprecatingly. "My brother forgets other men have lives outside the office! I was just saying to Miss Derryn that she and Mr. Gabriel could easily have been at the opera with us, but Horace kept him so long that it must have been— what?—nine o'clock before he arrived here?"

Lady Derryn's smile stayed in place a fraction too long. "Just after, I think." She did not look to her stepdaughter for confirmation. In fact, neither so much as glanced at the other, which was interesting.

Griz could ask no more without rudeness, but it certainly gave her cause to investigate Mr. Gabriel further. She was sure the Derryn women were hiding something, which could only be the time of Gabriel's arrival. But why?

GRIZ HAD GIVEN Nancy's letters, which she discovered behind the loose wall panel beside the maid's bed, to Mr. and Mrs. Barrow. But she had kept back the scribbled notes of addresses.

She sprawled now on her bed, with all the notes spread out for her examination. Some were in different ink and probably different pens since some of the notes bore thicker letters than others. On the other hand, she did think they were mostly in the same hand, and she didn't think it was Nancy's.

Gabriel's?

She gathered them up and slid off the bed. She had never seen Mr. Gabriel's handwriting, to her knowledge, but she was sure she would discover an example in Horace's study. And for at least another hour, Horace would be at his office in Whitehall.

She walked briskly downstairs to the ground floor and the smallish room at the back of the house that Horace used as his study. It was convenient so that he could work late without being disturbed or disturbing others.

He kept it very sparse and neat, with a row of pens and inks along the back of the desk and a shallow basket for documents on either side. The largest space, in the middle of the desk, was entirely clear, its polish gleaming in the late afternoon sunshine.

There were only a few papers in the left-hand basket and none at all in the other. His desk drawers were, as she had expected, locked. Horace's study was not a place to spy out his or his department's secrets. He was far too discreet for that.

Griz didn't want to know her country's secrets. She just wanted to find a note, however innocuous, in Mr. Gabriel's handwriting.

She picked up the first paper from the basket, a report from some underling. The one beneath was longer, several pages, but it was the note beneath that caught her attention.

Worth reading when you have time, but long-winded and not urgent.
G.

"Aha!" G had to be Gabriel. She set the document with its attached note on the desk and took the scraps of paper from her pocket. "Drat," she breathed, scowling at them. The pen had leaned less hard on the scraps of paper than on Gabriel's note, and they were straight where his writing sloped to the right. The tails of his letters had unexpected little flourishes, and his vowels were much fuller in shape.

Annoyed, she looked at the last document in the basket, on which were three notes.

For your comments, G.

Requested changes in the margins. Perfect otherwise, HN.

With requested changes, G.

Griz gazed at the middle line, initialed by her brother, and sank into Horace's chair. It was odd, but she had rarely seen Horace's writing. He had never written to her. His letters to the family from school had been read out by her mother or Azalea. And more recently, his infrequent letters from London to the country estates when she had been there had gone straight to her parents. She could not even recall seeing his letters waiting to be delivered or to be sent. But there it was now, one hastily written, initialed line. And it looked just like Nancy's notes.

Without warning, the door opened, and Horace strode in. He froze, startled to see her sitting at his desk.

"Griz? What the devil are you doing in here?"

There was no lie that could possibly work in this situation. In any case, she had always preferred the truth. "I was looking for an example of Mr. Gabriel's handwriting."

Horace's already prominent frown deepened. "Why?"

Since they were lying all over the desk, she said, "I was comparing them to scraps of notes that had been with Nancy's things. I thought she might have been working for him."

Horace's gaze flickered over the notes. Presumably, he recognized them. "It's none of your business, Griz."

"She was my maid," Griz said flatly. "She was murdered. And she was working for you."

He didn't deny it, merely said impatiently, "The two facts are not connected."

"Prove it!"

He scowled. "Stop being annoying. You will have to take my word for—"

"*Please*, Horace," she said fiercely. "I have never asked you for anything since I was twelve years old. I *need* to know."

"You've already worked it out," he snapped, dragging his hands through his hair. "She worked for me occasionally, attending meetings, warning me of anything dangerous that came up."

"She cleaned the study," Griz recalled. "You left her the addresses to find."

"On the desk. It worked well, meant there was no need for communication in front of the rest of the household."

"Were you her lover?" Griz blurted.

His jaw dropped. "What do you take me for? She was Her Grace's maidservant!"

Griz shrugged. "I know nothing of how you conduct your affairs."

"Discreetly and away from home," he said flatly. "Which is so much not your business that I shouldn't even need to say it."

"Well, the household noticed her penchant your company."

"For my study. She left brief reports here, too."

"Did you send her to the opera house? To Mudd Lane?"

"No." His lips twisted. "Actually, the last place I asked her to go was the Blue Horse."

"The Hungarian evening," she said slowly. "That's why you were there because she couldn't go. And that must have been why she wanted to see Dragan, to warn him... Horace, are you investigating him?"

"He and one or two friends have come to our notice," Horace said carefully. "But I cannot discuss that."

"You will have to. I like him. He is a friend."

"Don't you find him a dashed odd friend for a duke's daughter?"

"No," she said uncompromisingly.

To her surprise, he merely shrugged, and since she didn't have to fight for her friendship, she returned to the matter of Nancy's notes.

"Seven Dials," she said abruptly. "Why did you send her there?"

"I would never have sent her to such a place," he said, clearly affronted.

Griz raked through the scraps and found the alehouse address. "That is an alehouse in Seven Dials." Even as she said it, she realized the writing was in a different hand.

She hadn't noticed before. She had merely assumed it had just been scribbled in more haste than the others, but now that she truly looked...

She reached for the document with Gabriel's note, but Horace had already swiped the scrap of paper from her fingers.

"I didn't give her that. It's in her own handwriting."

Griz stared at him. "She sent herself to Seven Dials? Why would she there? Horace, do you have cause to know underworld characters like Art Dooley and Goddard?"

"Goddard dabbled in sedition, so yes. But I would never have sent Nancy into such a place. It was a damned rookery, and I doubt that tavern of yours is any better."

"It's run by his rival in Seven Dials. Art Dooley."

"Maybe it was just a name she heard and wrote down the address to give it to me. Perhaps he is up to the same tricks as Goddard."

Perhaps he was. After all, the unused pamphlets had ended up in Art's alehouse. But she could hardly tell Horace she had been there to witness that, not when he had been so appalled about the idea of Nancy going there.

"Do the police know Nancy worked occasionally for you?" she asked.

"No, there was no need. She was not in Covent Garden about my business. Her killer is some random cut-throat that they will find in time. Please, Griz, stop poking around!"

CHAPTER NINETEEN

NICK, WHO SEEMED quite contented with his life at Kelburn House, had clearly got over his fear that Griz would send him back to Art or someone very like him, for he accompanied her to the soup kitchen without fuss on Saturday. He worked with a will, greeting their "customers" with good cheer and just a hint of superiority. He even spoke to Mr. Wells, Bill, and the ladies without swearing.

It was Nick who saw Dragan first, dropping his broom and haring over to meet him. However, he skidded to a halt before anyone could imagine he might want to hug him and thrust out his hand, grinning.

Dragan shook it solemnly, and the boy immediately raced back to work. Looking amused, Dragan strolled through the hall to join her in washing and drying dishes. "He seems to have come a long way."

"He has. He barely swears at all now, and nothing at all has gone missing."

"Your Mrs. MacKenna must be a fearsome woman."

"She's strict," Griz allowed. "But she never bullies and does not tolerate such behavior in anyone else. He goes to bed every night warm and well-fed and unafraid. And he isn't afraid of working for it."

"Will you keep him on, train him in service?"

"I don't know yet. I was thinking of taking him to the country when we go in the summer. He likes working with horses. But he should go to school, too. It will be easier in the country to mix the two if he takes to the life."

He smiled. "How many other waifs have you taken in? Besides me."

She blushed. "You are silly. But oh, Dragan, I have lots to tell you! I'm nearly finished here. I thought we could take Nick to a tearoom as a reward for working so hard, and I'll tell you everything I've learned."

"I'll be happy to escort you."

Accordingly, they were soon seated at a quiet corner table of a cheerful tearoom, and while Nick ate steadily, Griz spilled out everything she had learned from Miss Derryn and from Horace.

He listened with steady attention, and when she had finished, sat back in his chair. "So, she worked for your brother and was warning me. But you think Gabriel did not visit his betrothed that evening?"

"Or that he was late, or something else happened. There was definitely a strange stiffness in both women's manner when I mentioned him calling there that night. But I couldn't poke further without appearing rude. I will pursue it, though."

"So, you think Gabriel was Nancy's gentleman?"

"You don't seem surprised."

"It would explain her murder. Presumably, he needs this marriage to Miss Derryn."

"I think so." Griz sighed. "The trouble is, she needs it, too. She is so happy to have him, it will hurt her if he is taken for murder. And then, the infidelity will not be easy."

"Do you think she knows?"

Griz frowned. "I think she knows something. Not enough to prevent her marrying him."

"It's a theory that works with what we know, but we have no proof. Also, how did she know I would be at the theatre that night?"

"Perhaps she didn't know. She came to meet Gabriel, saw you enter the opera house, and decided to warn you before meeting him. Only he was early."

"But the man Junie saw was not Gabriel."

"Gabriel's friend?" Griz suggested with less confidence. "In which case, someone else knows the truth. And we would have *two* people running away from the scene before I got there. Or a hired assassin we will never find."

"Junie thought him a gentleman. Besides, if Gabriel got someone else to commit the crime, why would he not have been with his betrothed? There is also the connection to Art, which is not yet obvious to me."

"Or me," Griz admitted, while Nick looked up from his cake at the sound of the name, looking from one to the other. Griz smiled reassuringly. "Art was building his criminal business, it seems, by shopping his rivals to the police. Gabriel was the one who insisted Goddard, the main rival, was spreading sedition. Horace didn't really believe it, but it was enough to persuade the police to raid the rookery."

"After which, the evidence of sedition disappeared," Dragan said slowly.

"And Goddard is prosecuted for all his other crimes. Perhaps because the pamphlets were planted, because they would be traced."

Dragan drummed his fingers on the table. "We need to speak to Art."

Both Nick and Griz stared at him. Griz said tartly, "Art tried to kill us just for asking questions. Why would he speak to us?"

"He wouldn't if he knew who we were," Dragan agreed. "But even at the time his men chased us from the alehouse, the reaction seemed excessive. Murdering two strangers and a child who made him money, just to prevent us knowing...what?"

"A connection to Nancy?"

"To the police," Dragan said. "As he saw it. To Gabriel, in fact. Art must pay Gabriel money. We need to know when and how, and that is our proof."

"Proof of corruption," Griz objected. "Not of Nancy's murder."

"Oh, I think Art might give that up if cornered," Dragan said distractedly. "He won't accept execution for murder if he can get a lesser sentence for lesser crimes." His eyes refocused on her, and he stood abruptly. "Shall we go?"

⨠⨠⨠⫷⫷⫸

"GO WHERE?" SHE finally asked when they had dropped Nick in Park Lane and watched him scurrying down the area steps to the kitchen. "And should I change?"

"Ah. I never thought of that. I'm assuming you know where Gabriel lives?"

She stared. "He has rooms near St. James, but he will be in the office."

Dragan's lips quirked, and with sudden understanding, her breath caught. She didn't know if it was shock or laughter.

"I can probably awe his landlady into letting us in," she admitted. "but he will be bound to find out. Unless we can make up some excuse."

"Hopefully, it won't matter by then."

"Give me five minutes, and I will meet you along the road in Grosvenor Square…"

It was slightly more than ten before she emerged from the house, dressed without ostentation but at least as though she could be a duke's daughter.

"I think you should be someone from his office," she said briskly when she had climbed back into the cab. "A cousin of mine, perhaps, sent to bring some important papers to Whitehall."

"I could almost believe you had done this before."

"Oh, no, I'm doing lots of things I hadn't done before I met you. Though I find myself hoping Mr. Gabriel *is* guilty now, or this would be an entirely unforgivable invasion of his privacy."

For a while, as their hackney negotiated the traffic in Piccadilly, she sat gazing at her hands, deep in thought.

"You don't have to come," he said abruptly. "I can barge in on my own. In fact, it would probably be best. I forgot these people are all known to you, friends even."

"Which is why I should be there," she insisted. "If we are wrong—though I have to say I don't think we are—then I shall apologize to him with great and humble sincerity."

"I won't," Dragan said. "I don't like the man, and I don't like his work."

She found she was frowning and smoothed her brow. "Does the same go for Horace?"

"For the work, yes. For his person..." He shrugged. "I have yet to exchange more than a bow with him, but I can't imagine he cares much for me either. What do you know about Gabriel's lodgings?"

"Bury Street," she said. "I can't recall the number, but it has a blue front door, and his landlady is called Mrs...Dashet!"

His eyes smiled, causing an inconvenient flight of butterflies in her stomach. "Is that her name or an exclamation of annoyance?"

She put out her tongue in a most unladylike gesture, and his gaze dropped and lingered, leaving her flustered.

The hackney dropped them at the corner of Jermyn Street and Bury Street, and they walked along the road in search of a blue door. Sadly, there were three. One Griz was sure was on the wrong side of the road. The second was opened by a stern woman who frowned at them and said no Mr. Gabriel lived there.

The third was opened by a clearly flustered woman of faded beauty, who fitted perfectly with Mr. Gabriel's occasional funny stories.

"Oh, you must be Mrs. Dashet!" Griz exclaimed, reaching for her blustering character. "Mr. Gabriel has told us all so much about you! Oh, forgive me, this is my cousin, Mr. Niven."

Mrs. Dashet looked bewildered for a moment, though the name

clearly meant something to her, for she murmured, "Oh! Oh indeed! Mr. Gabriel is not... How may I help you?"

"Mr. Gabriel sent Mr. Niven to collect a document he'd left in his rooms," Griz explained before Dragan could open his mouth and reveal his accent. She laughed. "I am only here cadging an escort to Bond Street. Grizelda Niven," she added, thrusting out a commanding hand, which poor Mrs. Dashet took with a flustered curtsey.

"Oh, well, do come in, ma'am...my lady. Perhaps you would care to step into my sitting room while Mr. Niven fetches..."

"Oh, no," Griz burbled with a laugh as she entered the hall. "I am most curious to see his rooms! You must know he is quite a family friend, is he not, Christopher?"

Dragan nodded and grinned and bowed Griz upstairs before him. Mrs. Dashet hastily led the way in a welter of breathless half-sentences and finally threw open a door on the first floor.

"Can I help you find anything?" she asked.

"Oh, no, Christopher knows where to find it, don't you, Chris? Oh, you wouldn't be a darling, would you, and bring me a cup of tea? I swear I am totally *parched*!"

"Oh, goodness, yes, of course, my lady! Just give me a few minutes."

Dragan exchanged speaking glances with her. "*She* is worse than the creature who sprang me from the police."

"Yes, she's vile," Griz agreed, striding across the room to the large desk that seemed a large part of his sitting room. "But at least she won us a few minutes in privacy. You look in his bedchamber."

There were no documents or even personal letters left on Mr. Gabriel's desk. The drawers were not locked, though they revealed little more. A few letters from Miss Derryn, which she did not read, another couple from distant family members. Of course, he was an only child, and his parents were dead.

"If you've time, Dragan," she called, pulling open another drawer, "look under loose floorboards or wall paneling near his bed."

"I hope Mrs. Dashet is deaf."

"No, but Mr. Gabriel said she was hard of hearing." She picked up a notebook in his drawer and quickly rifled through it. It seemed to be columns of numbers, income and expenditure, both now and projected figures for after his marriage. His salary was clear, and so little, she didn't know how he could afford even two rooms in such a good location as this.

Because there was some other income listed, perhaps from investments.

"Griz," Dragan called, and she quickly replaced the notebook, closed the drawer, and hurried into the bedroom.

He stood before a large, open wardrobe, staring downward. When she joined him, she could see why. He had lifted a panel on the wardrobe floor, and inside the revealed cavity was a small, neat pile of banknotes and a half-open purse containing gold sovereigns.

Griz swallowed. "Perhaps he does not trust banks."

"Perhaps he does not want anyone knowing what he has salted away or speculating how he acquired it."

"That does seem more likely in the circumstances. There is a notebook, too, that lists various incomes—he has more than his salary, and he projects spending a good deal when he is married, on a new house and entertainment. He'd have Miss Derryn's dowry, of course, but—" She broke off, hearing footsteps on the stairs, and darted into the other room, throwing herself into the armchair by the empty fire.

"Haven't you found it yet, Chris?" she demanded as Mrs. Dashet arrived, panting with the tea tray. Griz beamed at her. "Oh, how kind of you. This is just what I need. The document, apparently, isn't where Mr. Gabriel told Chris it would be. And it isn't in his bedside table either. Chris is looking in his other coat. Oh, and there's his overcoat, Chris, I'll wager he left it there! Thank you so much, Mrs. Dashet, don't let us keep you..."

"Utterly vile," Dragan said from the other room when Mrs. Dashet's footsteps sounded on the stairs.

Griz gulped down the scalding tea and hurried back to join him. "Did you look under the mattress?" she asked, pushing her hand beneath it and sliding it up to the pillows.

"No." He was standing right beside her, watching her, and suddenly, the scene seemed unbearably intimate. They were alone in a man's bedchamber, and she found herself wishing it was his. She wanted this intimacy, imagined it every day.

But not in the shadow of the man she was afraid had killed Nancy.

She straightened. "He wouldn't leave anything there, would he? Not when Mrs. Dashet could find it when she changes his sheets or turns the mattress." Hastily, she pulled open the drawer in the bedside table and wasn't surprised to see nothing in it.

Or was there? Something slid forward. A hairpin with a pearl at its head.

Slowly, her heart beating fast, she picked it up.

"A token from Miss Derryn?" Dragan suggested.

She shook her head. "No." She raised her gaze to his face. "It was Nancy's."

Triumph flared in his eyes. "Are you sure?"

"Yes. I gave it to her. At Christmas, because she had taken on the extra work of looking after me. She admired it, and I thought it was something pretty she could wear without causing too much comment..."

"Would she have given such a token to him?"

She flushed in spite of herself, trying not to look at the bed. "If she did, he would surely have hidden it with his money. I think she wore it to their...tryst. I imagine he found it after she left, and he slung it in here in a hurry, probably on his way out the door, and just forgot about it. Nancy was his tool, not his beloved." She swallowed hard and dropped the pin back where she had found it. "I think we should go."

Dragan was already walking toward the door. Feeling guilty for her character's behavior, Griz swiped up the tea tray and took it with her, a minor courtesy that seemed to stun Mrs. Dashet into silence as they made their escape.

She would tell Gabriel about this as soon as he came home, warning him to get rid of the one piece of evidence that incriminated him.

On impulse she turned on the doorstep. "Mrs. Dashet, I have a confession. We weren't looking for office documents but for a place to hide a small wedding gift. It is to be a surprise, so I beg you will not mention it to him. Then, when he comes across it on the morning of his wedding, he will be so delighted."

"What a kind thought!" Mrs. Dashet seemed to prefer this lie, so Griz only hoped she would stick to the secrecy.

"Well, my brother appreciates him so much," Griz said, patting Mrs. Dashet's hand before smiling gaily and touching her finger to her lips in a silent reminder of secrecy.

"Nice touch," Dragan murmured as they hurried along Bury Street.

"I wish I'd thought of it before... And at last, we have something that ties him to Nancy."

"But not to her murder." Deep in thought, Dragan strode so quickly toward Piccadilly that Griz caught at his arm to slow him down. He muttered an apology, still obviously distracted and thinking furiously.

"How much money was there?" she asked.

"Not enough to allow him to become a gentleman of leisure. Enough to buy better coats and pay his way among the monied classes. I think he has been doing this for several years."

"Taking bribes from criminals?"

He nodded. "We still have no real proof. A man's entitled to keep his money in his wardrobe if he wants to or to work out his finances with imaginary figures. He's smart enough to keep it all away from bank ledgers."

"I should tell Horace."

"Would he believe you? As it stands, we can't tie Gabriel to Art or even to Nancy's murder. We just know he *could* have done it."

"I could visit Horace's office," she said brightly, "look for colleagues who fit Junie's description of the man Nancy followed."

"What if Junie is just wrong?" he said. "I know she picked Nancy out and described some of what we *know* happened. But Gabriel isn't exactly a memorable fellow, at least not in appearance. He would have stood out to her as a gentleman, but her imagination could easily have supplied the rest. And she could very well have been drunk."

Griz blinked. "You don't know that."

"No, but she certainly reeked of gin at ten in the morning," Dragan retorted, "so it is a distinct possibility."

"Then we are *still* no further forward!"

"Oh, we are. Gabriel is definitely suspicious, and he definitely had ties to Nancy. If we can prove his ties to Art, I think the rest might follow."

"We could go back to the alehouse in Seven Dials," Griz said dubiously.

"Nothing so suicidal," he said at once. "Just a thought."

Avoiding pedestrians and vehicles on Piccadilly made it difficult to concentrate on anything else, so they cut up Berkley Street, past Devonshire House, to take a quieter route through wealthy residential streets toward Grosvenor Square.

"Isn't that your carriage?" Dragan said suddenly, and she looked across the road in time to see one of the arms-emblazoned town carriages rolling past in the same direction.

Fortunately, it didn't stop.

I might have got away with it.

This turned out not to be quite true, since her mother brought up what she had seen over dinner that evening.

It was one of the rare occasions when they dined without guests, not even Mr. Gabriel, which was a relief since Griz doubted she could have hidden her distaste. Even if he hadn't killed Nancy—and she was fairly sure he had—he had most certainly seduced a maid in her family's care and made her pregnant, making it impossible for the girl to get another decent situation or even a decent husband. He had betrayed Nancy *and* Miss Derryn.

Both Horace and Forsythe were present, though not Monkton or any of her married sisters.

"I saw you in Charles Street this afternoon, Griz," the duchess observed, fixing her with a serious glare. "My dear, I know you like to be independent and are no longer a young girl, but you are still a marriageable lady, and it is really not the thing to go gallivanting about the town with unknown young men, entirely unchaperoned."

"But I do know him," Griz said lightly. "So do you, Mama. You met him at Azalea's party."

Horace scowled and laid down his fork.

The duchess paused and dabbed her lips with her napkin. "The excessively handsome foreign gentleman...of course."

"A foreign gentleman under suspicion of murder," Horace said shortly.

"No, he isn't," Griz said, throwing caution to the winds. "*You* could have more easily done it than Dragan." In fact, he could have been the elegant, confident "nob" who enticed Nancy from the theatre toward Mudd Lane... Not that she truly believed that.

"That isn't funny," Horace said coldly.

"No, it isn't. Nor is accusing my friend of a crime you know perfectly well he did not commit. Dragan is a gentleman, unfortunate enough to be exiled from his own country, most of which regard him as a hero."

"Well, if you like him that much, invite him to tea," Forsythe drawled.

"I will," Griz retorted. She swallowed. "With Mama's permission, of course."

The duchess frowned at her in some consternation.

Unexpectedly, it was the duke who, reaching for his wine glass, said, "Yes, you better had. Let your mother look him over. Never known her to be wrong about a fellow yet. Except myself," he added with a bark of laughter.

CHAPTER TWENTY

D RAGAN, MEANWHILE, HAD indeed made his way to Seven Dials. He kept his collar up and his hat pulled down so as not to alert any of Art's men who might have recognized him from his last sortie into the neighborhood. He walked quickly, for he had no desire to linger in these mean streets after dark.

He nearly walked past the alehouse. Only the movement of the person loitering by the almost-invisible door caught his attention, and he swerved toward it. The unsavory individual by the door watched him with hostility, but Dragan avoided eye contact.

He swaggered in the door as though about to address his men in the moments before battle, and sauntered up to the counter where the same potman waited without interest.

Dragan drew the folded paper from his pocket and slid it across the counter. "For Art. See he gets it." Just to make sure, he pushed back his hat, waited long enough for the man's eyes to widen in disbelief, then laughed and strode out of the alehouse.

Again, he ignored the loafer at the door, just concentrated on his own brisk walk. All the same, the hairs prickled at the back of his neck, and every nerve was at alert, like moving through enemy territory you'd just captured.

For a moment, he even wished he'd brought his pistol, but there was no point. He'd only debilitate himself by firing it. Shadows had darkened with the lowering sun. Men who passed him or watched from doorways or lamp posts seemed more threatening than ten minutes earlier. He didn't relax until he reached the main road, full of traffic, and even then, he glanced over his shoulder as he strode on to safer territory and a hackney back home.

DRAGAN LAY AWAKE for a long time that night. Not, as he should have been, dwelling on Art Dooley and his possible tricks, or even what should be the next step if Art simply did not turn up. Instead, his mind was full of Griz, her quick, serious mind and sudden, dazzling smile. Her unexpected and entirely disconcerting leaps into alternative characters. The way her breathing changed when he touched her. The feel of her crushed in his arms, her soft lips open and passionate beneath his.

He had not known her two weeks, but the grey hopelessness of his exiled life had vanished like a spring cloud, reviving his dreams and his sheer love of life. There had been a good deal of wine and women in those heady, youthful days. But the failure of the revolution in which he had believed so passionately had not crushed his spirit. Griz had shown him that. Perhaps it had just taught him a little more realism, a different sense of responsibility that was no less important. He no longer wanted the charming, willing women who had passed through his life via his bed. But he did want Griz.

Her birth did not deter him. But her happiness did. Could she be happy with a poor man? A foreign exile her parents would never approve? On what he earned from Cordell, he could not even afford a tiny house, and Cordell could not afford to pay him more. It was possible Griz had money, of course, though it was likely her family would cast her off if she chose him, and in any case, his pride rebelled against living off his wife, his love.

Woah, there! Slow down. Even I cannot fall in love in two weeks, and she certainly can't. As for marriage…

His stern, if silent words, seemed to make no difference. She still filled his heart, his mind, and, when he eventually slipped into sleep, his dreams.

❯❯❯❮❮❮

AS USUAL, HE breakfasted with the Cordells, who were always alarmingly lively for early morning. Even on a Sunday, with church to look forward to.

A letter lay propped up against his plate.

"That was delivered for you," Mrs. Cordell explained. "By hand. A servant in livery, no less."

Margaret said, "It will be from Lady Grizelda!"

Annie curled her lip and stared at the paper as if she could make it burn. Yes, it was definitely time he left the Cordells.

He broke the seal on the letter and read the short note.

My dear Dragan,

We should meet today to discuss our strategy. I mean to call on Miss D. again, but I shall be at home until eleven o'clock if you are not busy. Let me know at your convenience.

My mother has also extended an invitation to tea, but I shall quite understand if you would rather not!

Griz.

Dragan frowned. What did she mean by the last sentence? That she didn't want him to go? That he was the sort of man who ran when parents were introduced? Not that he could blame her for wishing to put off such a meeting. There was time enough to deal with these matters.

He stuffed the letter in his pocket. Actually, it would be a good thing if she meant to be at home until eleven. It meant she was less likely to walk into Art.

He drank down his coffee gratefully and rose from the table with half a slice of toast in hand. "Forgive me, ma'am. I have to dash."

"Has she whistled for you?" Annie taunted.

"Anne!" snapped her mother.

"Oh no," Dragan said vaguely. "I have a previous engagement. But I should be home for dinner."

Having run out of money for cabs, he intended to walk to Hyde Park and so left himself plenty of time.

Nine o'clock was too early for the upper ranks of society to be active, but there were always people in the park, walking, exercising dogs or horses, or taking short cuts to avoid busy streets. He had chosen the Crystal Palace Exhibition building as the rendezvous because he would not stand out from all the other people who paused and lingered to stare at the amazing glass hall. He supposed there would be no work done on it today since it was Sunday.

Also, if he kept walking around it, he could see any of Art's murderously inclined friends long before they could be a threat. Although he had told Art to come alone, he had no guarantee that the criminal king of Seven Dials would pay any attention to his instruction.

It was a soft, drizzly day, but the weather had not deterred walkers and riders in the park. Dragan arrived at the Crystal Palace at about ten minutes to nine and immediately made a wide circle all the way around it. A young, courting couple stopped to gawp at it. But no one seemed to be approaching it directly.

Dragan kept walking, circling the building until on his third round, he came back to the front to see a man seated on the bench opposite. A quick quartering of the view behind showed no signs of cut-throats approaching from the river or the trees. Nor was anyone shinning up the steel supports to hurl glass at his head.

The man on the bench wore a slightly squashed top hat and a coat that seemed too tight across the shoulders. Both had probably cost a fair penny, as had the smart boots. But no one, let alone Nancy, would ever have accused this man of being a gentleman. There was an air of unkemptness about him and, as Dragan drew closer, a distinct smell. The man oozed Seven Dials and its insalubrious alehouses from his pores.

Dragan stopped and met the deliberately amiable gaze. "Do I address Mr. Dooley?" he asked civilly.

"You appear to have the advantage," the man said, not troubling to get up. His accent was Cockney, his manner mocking, if not quite sneering. "You the cove that summoned me here?"

"Invited," Dragan corrected mildly.

"Not my usual stamping ground. But it's very pretty, very pretty indeed."

"Would you care to take a stroll, see the building from all angles?"

"Lead on," Art invited. He stood, and Dragan walked with him, almost like two old friends out for a stroll. Almost.

"You took my young Nick away," Art observed. "I hope you ain't been bad to him?"

"I haven't dropped a ton of masonry on his head if that's what you mean."

Art let out a bark of laughter, as though Dragan had made a great joke. "He won't stay at an orphanage, you know. He'll keep running away, and they'll beat him. Workhouse is worse."

"I'm more interested in a housemaid called Nancy Barrow and a man called Thomas Gabriel."

"Never heard of them," Art said.

"Allow me to refresh your memory." He took the sketches from his pocket and showed him Nancy and Gabriel. "Gabriel here, occasionally influences the police to raid certain establishments, which always seems to work out in your favor."

"Then I'm much obliged to him, whoever he is."

Dragan raised his eyebrows. "You pay him without knowing who he is?"

Art stared. It wasn't a comfortable stare. Art had no doubt practiced to make sure it was as scary as possible. So had Dragan when keeping the worst of his soldiers in order, so he wasn't cowed.

"Who says I pay him at all?" Art demanded.

"He does," Dragan lied. "In a very neat little notebook he keeps in his rooms. For another thing, I'm pretty sure his days of such deals will end with his wedding. He's already done away with poor Nancy, and I suspect he's set you up to take the blame for that."

It was, of course, arrant rubbish. Dragan was fairly sure *he* was meant to hang for Nancy's murder. But it worked so far as to rile Art.

"Take the blame?" he exclaimed. "I barely knew the girl. Why would I kill her?"

"Barely," Dragan repeated, careful not to gloat.

Even so, Art glared at him again.

"How barely?" Dragan asked. "Did she bring messages to you? Collect a bit of money for Gabriel?"

"Who in hellfire are you, anyway?" Art demanded. "Peeler?"

"Lord, no. The Peelers don't like me. I just want the man who killed poor Nancy. Did she come to the alehouse?"

"God, no. Met her up the back of Covent Garden, once."

"Mudd Lane?" Dragan wondered. Art gave no sign of assent or otherwise, but it was likely, close to St. Giles as it was. Was that why she had gone so willingly the night she had died? She had been before and felt safe... "When?"

"Last year some time."

"To give her Gabriel's money?"

"I'm not admitting to nothing. I'll deny everything if the Peelers come near me."

"I know. I just want to hear the truth."

Art eyed him, then sighed. "Money might have changed hands, but I never touched her."

"And last Thursday, when she died, did you have plans to meet her?"

"What would I do that for? It was the next day before the Peelers took that rookery down."

Dragan's heart beat a little faster. "Do you still owe Gabriel for that? When do you pay him?"

"I ain't telling you. You'll bring the rozzers."

"Well, I will," Dragan admitted, guessing *rozzers* was yet another derogatory term for the police. "But now that you know, you can make sure you escape."

Art regarded Dragan with a faint, mocking smile, not entirely free of threat. Then he gazed around the park. The rain had stopped, though the sky had not lightened much.

"Not sure what I've gained by coming out here," Art remarked, "pretty as it is. Truth to tell, it's too open for me, and I wouldn't trust you, my friend, further than I could throw you. But since you're an amiable cove and a foreigner here, I'll give you some free advice. Don't bring me or mine into it. It won't be worth it for you, and it won't find who killed your girl."

Art tipped his hat in an entirely mocking kind of way. "Goodbye. You'd better pray we don't meet again."

As Art strode off down the path, Dragan stood still and watched him, glad to have had some of his suspicions confirmed but annoyed and frustrated not to have them proved. Well, he would just have to resort to his alternative plan and...

Abruptly, his thoughts were cut off with all the force of an ax. For coming along the path toward Art were the unmistakable figures of Griz and Nick, with the dog, Vicky, tugging Nick off the path and across the grass.

Without conscious decision, Dragan charged into motion, running along the path, terrified of what Art might do to Griz, whether by way of demonstration to Dragan or just sheer badness. At least Nick had his back to the villain and didn't seem to have seen him. As long as he didn't open his mouth, Art would surely ignore him, but Griz...

Art swerved off the path, on the opposite side from Nick. And strode away along the river, Dragan, weak with relief, slowed to a walk.

Of course. Art hadn't known Dragan. He was unlikely to have recognized Griz. It was his underlings who had pursued them through Seven Dials.

Griz, who must have seen him coming, sped toward him, her face anxious.

"Dragan, what is it?" she demanded. "What...?"

Dragan's attention was still on Art, who had collected company along the banks of the Serpentine and was now walking between them, still away from Griz.

"Who *is* that?" Griz asked, following his gaze with some consternation.

"Art," Dragan said shortly. While her mouth dropped, he watched Nick and the dog run up to greet him. Although he smiled, made joking comments, he was still quartering the park, making sure Art was not returning, that no other thuggish figures approached. He didn't want Art to even see him with Griz.

By silent consent, they did not mention Art in Nick's hearing but walked one more time around the Crystal Palace, with Nick exclaiming and awed. What Dragan itched to do was sit on a bench and make a sketch of Art while he was fresh in his memory.

As soon as Nick meandered out of earshot, Griz hissed, "What was Art doing here?"

"I asked him to come," Dragan confessed. "It seemed the safest place, and I didn't expect you to be out and about, let alone here, at this time. You said you would be at home until eleven."

"Vicky needs to walk, and so does Nick," she said impatiently. "Tell me everything."

In fits and starts as they started back toward the Grosvenor Gate, he told her about contacting Art via the alehouse and his frustrating conversation with the villain. "He as good as told me he did pay Gabriel to help get rid of his competitors and that he had met Nancy. I think she passed money between them once. I believe he still owes Gabriel, but he won't tell me where or when they're meeting."

She was frowning. "You should not have gone alone to Seven Dials. You should not have met him here. You know how dangerous the man is! Besides which," she added with growing indignation, "I wanted to be there!"

"You nearly were," he said. "I was never so scared in my life, which is why I didn't involve you in this."

"I don't like not being involved," she said crossly.

He nudged her arm. "I didn't tag along with you to visit Miss Derryn, did I?"

"No," she allowed, not entirely mollified. "But *she* presents no danger. I hope to see her again this afternoon. I think I should warn her about Gabriel. She will be devastated, I think."

"I'm going to follow Gabriel wherever he goes."

She blinked. "You can't, not all the time. Besides, he knows you."

"I think I can get a couple of people to help me."

She looked annoyed and hurt, and then she sighed. "I would stand out too easily, wouldn't I?"

"Like a beacon."

"Even in my dullest gown and cloak?"

"He knows you too well," Dragan said diplomatically, "and besides, he may well go places where a woman couldn't—or shouldn't!"

Her eyes widened at that, so he hastily changed the subject. "Do you want me to come to tea with your mother?"

"You might wish to," she said. "Gabriel and Miss Derryn will be there, too."

She said it with a certain satisfaction, but it left Dragan baselessly annoyed. Because she was treating him as her partner in this investigative venture, not as her friend, who should be invited to tea on his own account. Her...

He veered away from that thought because it was too soon and, frankly, too unsettling.

Nick joined them again, and they had left the park before Griz asked him what he intended to do now.

"Find a coffee shop or a tearoom and sketch."

She met his gaze, clearly knowing immediately who he meant to draw. "Do it in the house, if you like. After all, you are coming to tea."

CHAPTER TWENTY-ONE

I F HER MOTHER thought it odd that she accompanied Dragan into the drawing room early that afternoon, she hid it beneath a gracious smile.

In fact, Griz and Dragan had spent the day together. She had sat at his shoulder, watching as his pencil flew across the paper he had brought for the purpose, and Art's head and shoulders had formed with remarkable speed. She had barely registered the man walking toward her in the park, for her attention had all been on Dragan and why he was running. It had made her heart leap before the anxiety in his eyes had frightened her. But she could not help liking that protectiveness.

Art, on the other hand… His eyes looked mean and violent in the portrait, his face podgy with the prosperity he had stolen from others. She was sure he could have killed Nancy without a qualm, as he had tried to kill her and Dragan and even Nick, by proxy, just for asking questions—not about Nancy but, as they now suspected, about matters leading to Gabriel, the goose that was laying golden eggs for him.

Dragan had been happy to talk while he sketched, and they had discussed the investigation, sometimes veering at tangents into other aspects of their lives. She had been glad to learn something of his past, growing up in Hungary, about his easy-going parents and fun-loving brother, about his desire to make a better world for people. He said little about the revolution and the war to defend it, except the odd funny story that made her laugh.

Her own life, by comparison, seemed mundane and dull, but he appeared to be interested, and the time flew past. She fetched the notes she had made and spread them out on the floor in front of the fire, where they knelt and poured over them. With their heads together, their shoulders brushing whenever one of them moved, awareness flared between them. Once, he had stopped talking and just gazed at her, and she was afraid to breathe. Then he had blinked and returned to the notes.

"Yes, it all leads to Gabriel," he had said. "The pamphlets, the hairpin, Nancy's gentleman. Apart from the mysterious man Junie saw beckoning her. That bothers me."

"We can ask about his particular friends this afternoon. Subtly, of course."

As they walked into the drawing room, Dragan displayed no signs of nervousness or awe. It wasn't so much that he was used to high, aristocratic company—she suspected he was not, for his family had been very minor nobility—but that he simply didn't care about rank. He treated everyone with the same courtesy, from Art to her mother. She rather liked that.

The duchess clearly remembered him from Azalea's party and extended her hand with a welcoming smile.

"Good grief," Griz uttered before she could help herself because an unusual number of her siblings were present, not only Horace and Forsythe who lived there, but Monkton and Augusta, Azalea and Trench, even Rosemary and her husband, Sir Gordon Landon.

"What a pleasure to see you, too, Griz," Monkton said irritably.

"Sorry," Griz said, "I was just surprised. I didn't know we were having a family party." She introduced Dragan to everyone without fuss, by which time, mercifully, other guests had arrived.

Since the duchess kept Dragan by her side, Griz plonked herself down by Azalea and breathed, "What the devil is going on?"

"Consequences," Azalea drawled. "Several people have seen you jaunting about London with Mr. Tizsa, so inevitably, it gets back to your family. And you deliberately brought him to meet Their gGraces. Are we being presented with a *fait accomplit*, Griz?"

"I don't know what *fait* you think I've accomplished," Griz said crossly. "I just wanted Her Grace to stop worrying while we discover what happened to Nancy."

"That again?" Azalea gazed at her with a mixture of affection and helpless frustration. "Griz, it's not your responsibility. Leave it to the police."

Griz stared. "The police arrested Dragan."

"Have you considered that there was a reason?"

"Yes," she admitted. "But he didn't. You don't believe he did, do you, Zalea?"

Azalea opened her mouth impetuously, then closed it again. "Not really, no. In truth, I like him." She lowered her voice. "I just don't want him to hurt you in other ways."

"I don't know what you mean," Griz said with dignity.

"Yes, you do. With looks like that, he's had no shortage of women in his life."

"But he hasn't stayed with any of them, has he?" Griz retorted and used the arrival of Gabriel and Miss Derryn to jump up and move away.

In fact, she did not believe that Dragan had as many women in his past as Azalea seemed to believe. Not that he was an angel—there had been hints of a pleasurable student life in his tales, and in the remarks she'd heard at the Hungarian Evening. But he was so oddly unaware of, or perhaps just uninterested in, his spectacular good looks that she doubted he had ever used them cynically to get women into his bed.

She hastily dragged her thoughts back to Miss Derryn and Gabriel, greeting them with a friendly smile.

From Gabriel's unchanged and respectful manner to her, she was sure Mrs. Dashet had kept the secret of their visit to his rooms. The police needed to find Nancy's hairpin in his drawer. But there had to be a good reason to send the police there. Gabriel, after all, was a highly respected man with the patronage of Lord Horace Niven.

The duke appeared shortly thereafter, and while conversing politely with Gabriel and his betrothed, Griz kept half an ear on the nearby conversation.

"You remember Mr. Tizsa, my dear?" the duchess said. "Grizelda's Hungarian friend."

"Of course, of course," the duke said amiably. "How do you do, young man? I hear you are interested in politics, though I don't suppose they're very similar to mine."

"Oh, I can usually find a few points in common with everyone," Dragan replied with commendable diplomacy. "My countrymen greatly admire Britain's parliamentary system."

"But you would like someone like my coalman's laborer to be the prime minister," the duke mocked.

"I might like him to have the chance," Dragan said amiably. "I would certainly like him to be able to *vote* for the prime minister. Or not."

Grizelda's father gave a crack of laughter. "Not afraid to speak your mind, are you?"

"No, sir. I can't imagine you are either."

"Never had to be," the duke said thoughtfully. "I'm all for freedom of speech, myself, but everyone started to panic after the Chartist demonstrations in '48, and what with Europe in turmoil... I'll take a glass of brandy with you one day, young man, and we can quarrel without upsetting the ladies."

Griz breathed a sigh of relief and realized Gabriel and Miss Derryn were both gazing at her expectantly, clearly awaiting an answer. "I'm sorry, I missed that," she admitted. "I was afraid my father was about to annihilate Dragan."

Gabriel smiled faintly. "I think he has just promised to, hasn't he? When ladies aren't present."

It was one interpretation, Griz thought ruefully as Gabriel excused himself and moved on to speak to Lord Monkton.

"I'm glad you are here, Lady Grizelda," Miss Derryn said, "I did particularly want to speak to you." Her gaze flickered to the busy drawing room. "In private might be best."

"Come, then, we can easily slip away," Griz said, taking her arm and simply walking out the door. "And perhaps you should call me Griz. Everyone else does."

"But Grizelda is such a beautiful name."

"Do you think so? I always feel it sounds like some wicked witch in a fairytale. We can just go to my room. No one will disturb us there."

Griz was grateful to Emmie for tidying up as she led Miss Derryn into the small dressing room that she had turned into a comfortable—and usually messy—sitting room.

"My name is Penelope," Miss Derryn offered. "What a pleasant room."

"I used to sleep in it before Rosemary got married. What is on your mind, Miss—er...Penelope."

Penelope sighed. "I hope you won't take it amiss, but for friendship's sake and for the many kindnesses your family has shown to Thomas, I must speak."

Griz sat down in the chair opposite her and waited expectantly.

"It's about Mr. Tizsa," Penelope blurted. "I can see you are great friends, and he is obviously a charming and extremely handsome young man. And I am afraid... I am afraid he has expectations you would be unwise to fulfill."

"I don't believe he has any expectations at all," Griz said at once. Didn't he? Hadn't he kissed her, in *such* a way, and talked of her parents' disapproval?

"Thomas is afraid he has. Of course, Thomas cannot presume to speak about such matters to you nor even to Lord Horace. But consider Grizelda. If you married him, you could never provide evidence against him."

Griz blinked. "Why would I want to?"

"Because he killed your maid."

"No, he didn't," Griz said earnestly.

"But he did. Thomas explained it all to me. You don't have all the facts. Thomas does. Please, Grizelda, you must stay away from him. He is dangerous."

Something in Penelope's confident, downright voice sparked irritation in Griz. Perhaps it reminded her too much of her sisters and sister-in-law explaining to her what she could and couldn't do from their lofty heights as married women.

"That's funny," Griz said tartly. "Because I was about to explain the same to you about Mr. Gabriel."

That got her attention. Her large-boned face mottled unattractively. "What do you mean?"

Griz reined in her spurt of temper, tempering it with genuine sympathy. "That Mr. Gabriel is not the man you believe him to be. I think—I fear—that he has not always been faithful to you. But that his desire to marry you might nevertheless have led him to commit unforgivable—"

"*How dare you?*" Penelope sprang to her feet, her face now flushed all over, her eyes spitting. "How dare you say a word against him? This is not a game of retaliation! That because I warn you about a criminal, revolutionary foreigner who is clearly after your position and fortune, you feel the need to denigrate a good man who has always been your friend!"

Griz struggled to stand and faced her, but Penelope had the advantage of height and stared down at her with all the haughtiness of which she was capable. In addition, there was a deep, corroding disappointment, not with Gabriel, Griz saw, but with her.

"Penelope, my warning is genuine," she said urgently. "You must listen!"

"I won't. This Tizsa has already turned your mind so that you will listen to no one else. Heed my warning, my lady, before it is too late for you. As for Thomas, you would be ill-advised to attack him. I shall stand by his side, and I will fight like a lion. I shall return to the drawing room to pay my respects to Her Grace."

With that, Penelope Derryn stalked off, leaving Griz to the miserable knowledge that she had handled a tricky situation appallingly badly.

❯❯❯❮❮❮

THERE WAS LITTLE further opportunity for private speech with Dragan that afternoon. Only as he left did she find a moment on the stairs to say, "I tried to warn Miss Derryn and made a mess of it. Worse, you must take care, for I think Gabriel is out to prove you are the murderer."

"Well, he can't, can he?" Dragan said lightly.

"This is the man who has set up evidence to convict several criminals," Griz retorted, determined to make him take it seriously. "You must watch out for him and Harris."

"I will watch constantly," he assured her, which made her eye him with suspicion.

"You mean that literally, don't you? You are really going to follow him around London?"

"Don't worry," he said, taking his hat from the footman. "He'll never know I'm there. Griz—" He broke off, his free hand halfway to her face before he remembered himself and dropped it to his side. A tender smile flickered across his face, melting her heart. "Take care. I'll be in touch."

And then he was gone, leaving her to trail back upstairs to her family, who, as the last of the guests departed, turned their unanimous attention to Griz.

"He's handsome. I'll allow that," Rosemary said. "But he won't do."

"Who won't do what?" Griz demanded. "I have no idea what you're talking about."

"Yes, you do," Rosemary retorted. "And you know perfectly well he's unsuitable, too. I daresay that's half the attraction."

"Yes, I always choose my friends by the criteria of who will most annoy my sister," Griz remarked.

"He's poor, and he's foreign, with very questionable politics," Monkton pronounced. "A fortune-hunter if ever I saw one."

"Actually," Griz said irritably, "his *questionable politics* prevent him from caring about fortunes."

"Oh, please," Monkton replied, clearly amused.

"Monkton is right," Augusta pronounced, causing Azalea to gaze at her astonishment.

"Really?" she said reverently.

For a moment, Griz actually wanted to laugh, but then her father spoke up.

"For myself, I like the man, whatever his politics. But it makes no odds. He hasn't a feather to fly with and no prospects that I can see."

"He is a physician," Griz said. "Almost."

"A physician is not a suitable husband for my daughter," the duke replied.

"Of course not," Rosemary agreed.

Griz glared around them all. "Has it escaped your attention that no one but yourselves is speaking of marriage?"

"Well, he should be," Horace observed, "cavorting about the town with you! You have to stop encouraging him, Griz, for he won't do. For more reasons than you understand yet."

"If you are going to tell me he murdered Nancy—" Griz began furiously.

"Well, he probably did," Horace interrupted, "but even if he didn't, you have your name and your reputation to think about."

"If you're pining for a pretty face," the duke said kindly, "much better have Captain Galbraith, now he's back in London."

"I would not take Captain Galbraith if he was the last man in the kingdom," Griz said flatly. "And I repeat, why are you all talking about my wedding? I thought we were all agreed I would marry no one! If that changes, I shall let you know!"

With that, she stormed furiously out of the room. How dare they compare Dragan to Captain Galbraith? How dare they assume she was shallow enough to accept one handsome face in place of another? And how dare they even *think* that Dragan had killed Nancy when he was the only man among them doing anything about discovering who did?

⇛⇚

AFTER AN EVENING of frigid politeness with her family and an early night, she went into breakfast the following morning to join Horace, still rigidly polite.

She ate in silence, as did he. Only as she walked across the room to leave did he say sternly, "I hope you are not contemplating meeting Tizsa?"

"Why, yes, I am just packing for Gretna Green," she said and slammed the breakfast parlor door.

In fact, she took the carriage alone to Great Scotland Yard and asked for Inspector Harris. Almost immediately, she was bowed into his office, a room dominated by a large, paper-strewn desk and a bookcase containing rows of leather-bound volumes containing laws and statutes.

The inspector, looking slightly less harassed than the last time she had visited, bowed and invited her to sit.

"No dog this time," he noted.

"I learned from my mistake," she said meekly.

"I hope so."

Ignoring the ambiguity in his voice, she said, "I was wondering how you are progressing with finding Nancy Barrow's murderer."

"Well, as it happens."

"Oh, good," she said, crossing her fingers and hoping it was.

"Her friends—your other maids—believed she was seeing a young gentleman." Harris smiled thinly. "The same young gentleman you made a statement to defend."

"I stand by that defense," she said at once. "For I don't believe Dragan Tizsa was the young man she was seeing. Nor do I believe he killed her."

"Sadly, we must accept evidence, not your ladyship's beliefs."

"Good," she said at once. "Then you must accept that he could not possibly have committed the murder. As I said in my statement."

"I certainly accepted it at the time, but neither you nor I were then aware of all the facts."

Her stomach twisted. "To which facts do you refer?"

"You claimed, with perfect correctness, that Tizsa could not have committed the crime and escaped via the opposite end of Mudd Lane and been able to join you only a minute or so after you arrived on the scene."

"I did. You agreed. And in fact, we tested another theory, shortening the journey by cutting through the carpenter's shop, but it still takes too long."

"Agreed. But there is another way."

She frowned, taken by surprise. "What other way?"

"An old drainage tunnel entered from Mudd Lane and coming out close by the opera house."

"A tunnel," she repeated, flabbergasted. "But...surely that

wouldn't save enough time either?"

"Actually, it does."

"But you must have noticed yourself, he did not smell of drains!"

"Not obviously," he agreed, "yet still, it is possible."

She was silent, trying to absorb the danger this presented to Dragan, as well to justice. She licked her dry lips. "You did not mention a tunnel when last we spoke."

"I did not know of it," he admitted. "Neither did the constables who attended the scene. The plans of the drainage system were shown to me only recently."

By Mr. Gabriel! With difficulty, she kept the words to herself. She had no proof with which to accuse him, except a hairpin that only she could swear was Nancy's. And Gabriel was already clearly in favor with Harris for helping solve his case. She had to fight down fear while she tried to think.

"That is most interesting," she managed at last, rising to her feet. "I shall take up no more of your time, except to mention that you should probably speak to certain women whom you will find around Covent Garden...um... particularly of an evening. One of them, who is called Junie, saw a man beckoning Nancy to follow him up the side of the opera house, toward Mudd Lane. That man was not Mr. Tizsa."

To her surprise, Harris only smiled cynically. "And I suppose you asked her in his presence?"

"What difference does that make?" she demanded.

"All the difference in the world," Inspector Harris assured her. "However, I shall send someone to speak to your Junie and discover the truth."

"Thank you," Griz said, inclining her head and walking out.

Where, now, was the triumph she had felt the last time she had walked out of this building with Dragan at her side? Now, he was in more trouble than ever. At least Junie would win him some time. But they had to find the truth of the matter at once.

CHAPTER TWENTY-TWO

ON IMPULSE, GRIZ directed the carriage to drive past Horace's office in Whitehall. She imagined Dragan might be lurking there, watching to see if and when Gabriel might step out and follow him.

But amongst the people scurrying in one direction or another, or those who paused to talk in doorways, she saw no one she recognized. A plea to Horace at this stage would do no good. He would not interfere without evidence of an injustice. So she let the carriage continue home, peering anxiously out of the window for a glimpse of either Gabriel or Dragan. Which was silly. Even if they were outdoors, they could be anywhere, in shops or hackneys... Did Dragan even have enough money to follow Gabriel about in hackneys?

And what if Gabriel saw him? Would he confront Dragan? Trick him into some quiet corner and kill him, as he had Nancy?

Dragan had been a soldier. He had dealt with more dangerous adversaries than Gabriel and survived. But the knowledge did not stop her worrying.

Her hope, as she stepped out the carriage at home, was that there would be a message from him, giving her a clue as to his whereabouts. Or even that he would be there, waiting for her, with news.

He wasn't. Nor was there a note or message of any kind.

It was going to be a long day, and she could think of no useful way to fill it.

〉〉〉⫷⫷⫷

SHORTLY AFTER MIDDAY and a solitary luncheon, she began to make plans for informing the police a crime was being committed in Gabriel's rooms and hope that when they got there, they would find the hairpin that she and, at least Janet and Emmie among the servants, could identify as Nancy's. Proof of an affair, perhaps, but not of murder. She began to think that concealing Nancy's pregnancy from the police had not been the right thing to do.

In the same room as she had entertained Dragan yesterday, she pored over her notes once more, placing them in columns and using bits of string to connect items to other columns. Surely there was something there that would make the police act because if she sent them to Gabriel's rooms under the pretense of a crime being committed, they would undoubtedly walk away again when they discovered all was quiet. They had no reason to search.

Unless she ransacked the place to look like a crime? Leaving the pin in a prominent position? Though that was resorting to the sort of tactics Art and Gabriel used...

Peter, the footman, stuck his head around the door. "Miss Derryn, my lady."

"Oh!" In panic, she almost swept up her notes before she realized they might have finally convinced Penelope of her betrothed's guilt. "Show her in here, Peter."

She rose to her feet, straightening her shoulders to receive whatever fresh anger or accusation was flung her way.

But Miss Derryn flew into the room in clear distress, a handkerchief to her mouth. "I beg your pardon, Lady Grizelda," she exclaimed. "My outburst yesterday was quite uncalled for, and I was wrong, so wrong to—"

"Penelope, please sit," Griz said, going to her in some concern. "What is it? What has happened?"

"I cannot stop to explain, but I could not pass without apologizing for yesterday and to say...oh you are right and yet so wrong!" She turned on her heel, clearly about to dash off again.

"No, wait!" Griz caught at her arm. "What do you mean? If you have information, Penelope, you must tell me."

Penelope's eyes were wet and despairing. "I cannot stop. My stepmother is waiting for me. But yes, you have to know. I will *show* you." She broke free, clearly still agitated, and then at the door, cast a frankly pleading look over her shoulder. "Can you come to Covent Garden tonight?"

"Of course," Griz said at once. "To the opera house?"

"No," Penelope whispered in clear anguish. "Mudd Lane."

⇢⇥⇤⇠

GRIZ SPENT THE rest of the afternoon in an even worse state of anxiety. Penelope had dashed off, her nerves clearly in tatters, insisting only that she tell no one.

Griz had agreed in order to calm her, which had seemed to work, and had even won a wan smile from Penelope.

"It's not as if we shall be in any danger, not now. I just cannot bear... Oh dear, I must dash. Tonight then, Grizelda. You are so good..."

Naturally, Griz racked her brains in the intervening hours to work out what it could be Penelope meant to show her. Perhaps Gabriel had told her about the drainage tunnel Inspector Harris had mentioned as another way to shift the blame from himself to Dragan. Griz wasn't sure she wanted to inspect a drainage tunnel in the middle of the night. Or at any other time, really. But there must be some kind of evidence there, something that was clearly bothering her. Which surely meant the evidence was against Gabriel, not Dragan.

Or perhaps Penelope meant her to talk to someone, someone who knew something important, perhaps had even witnessed the crime.

Some memory was bothering her, too, something her brain couldn't quite locate, even when she read over all her notes yet again.

The promise she had made to Penelope also left her in something of a quandary. As a matter of course, she did not break her word, but on the other hand, it was common sense to let someone know where you were. Just in case there was an emergency at one end or another. However, her parents would never permit her to go alone to Covent Garden, let alone inspect a drainage tunnel, and she had to go.

From speaking to the residents of Mudd Lane and beyond, she knew it was actually regarded as a relatively safe and quiet environ. Nancy's murder was, therefore, something of a shock. Griz regarded the danger to her and Penelope as minimal. And she did not expect to be long.

If Dragan would only come, she would tell *him*, even if she would not let him come. Although, ideally, perhaps he could lurk nearby, just to provide an extra witness to whatever it was Penelope wanted her to see or hear.

But Dragan, infuriatingly, did not come. She thought of sending a note round to his lodgings with the Cordells, though she doubted he would go there if he were still following Gabriel.

Perhaps he would follow Gabriel here, for he occasionally came home with Horace.

He didn't today. Horace arrived home at six, alone, and shut himself in his study.

Eventually, Griz scribbled a quick note: *Mudd Lane with PD.* She tapped the feathery end of her pen against her chin, then added: *Did you know there's an old drainage tunnel that opens there? G.*

Hastily folding it, she decided not to write his name on it. But she told both the porter and Berry, the butler, that if Mr. Tizsa called, he was to be given it instantly. They each cast her a long-suffering look of reproach that told her they would, as usual, not mention the matter to her parents unless specifically questioned.

"Thank you," she said gratefully and hurried into the cab she had already sent Peter to summon.

* * *

DRAGAN HAD SPENT a dull day interspersed with mad moments of activity, following Gabriel to work, to teashops, and one hasty dash by cab across London and back. And finally, home to his rooms in Bury Street.

Since the quickest way to have been noticed was to be in the vicinity all the time, he had begged the assistance of a couple of Hungarian friends to spell him during normal office hours, which let him sit down and eat alone and think too much about Griz and not enough about Gabriel. It was depressing to think that it could take weeks before Gabriel would meet up with Art or commit any other incriminating act. For which he would, in any case, need witnesses. Who would take the word of a foreigner already suspected of murder?

All the same, he did not doubt he could bring Gabriel down physically, with Art's money in the man's possession, and from there, surely, the truth would out.

Gabriel did not stay long in his rooms but left again in evening attire. Dragan strolled after him at a safe distance, to the hackney stand, where Dragan gave his cynical driver the instruction to follow the cab in front. He was fairly sure the man insulted him in incomprehensible Cockney, but at least he obeyed.

Gabriel went to his betrothed's house in Berkley Square and dismissed the cab. Dragan got his to drive him further along the square, where he paid the driver off. If he got a hackney to the Cordells tonight, he thought ruefully, he would have no money to follow Gabriel tomorrow except on foot.

The streetlamps were lit here, so a lurking figure would be quite obvious. He resolved to stroll, wait, and stride briskly by turns, at least until he could be sure Gabriel was staying there for dinner.

However, he was still strolling from his cab toward the Derryns' house when their front door opened again, and a man in a top hat stepped out, closing the door behind him.

It wasn't Gabriel. This man was built along slighter lines and moved differently. He sprang down the steps rather than trod with Gabriel's firm step. Elegant and almost swaggering, the young gentleman paused under the streetlight to put on his gloves. Inevitably, he saw Dragan strolling toward him, but his eyes dropped at once to what he was doing.

There was something familiar about him, though Dragan couldn't think where he had seen him before. He gave the man a faint nod in passing, and the man nodded back and strode on in the opposite direction to Dragan.

Did Penelope Derryn have another admirer? Or was it her brother? More likely, for the man was oddly like her.

Dragan stopped dead and turned his head to stare. The man had vanished round the corner, but the impossible suspicion remained.

Abruptly, he sat down on the nearest step and dragged out his pencil, drawing the man he had just seen in his top hat and collar. The pencil seemed to obey his urgency and his perception, quickly creating the effete, elegant young gentleman's features. Leaving it, he hastily turned the paper and sketched Penelope Derryn, large-boned and awkward for a woman.

But they had the same eyes, the same bone structure.

The same height. The same shape.

And everything fell into place. Simple, neat, and appalling.

The door behind him opened, and a superior manservant instructed him to move along there before he was obliged to send for the constable.

Dragan needed no encouragement. He sprang up, stuffing the

pictures and pencil into his pocket as he strode away, making as fast as possible for Park Lane and Griz. His need to tell her, just to see her, superseded everything else.

The large house on the corner did not blaze with lights, so he presumed the family was out for the evening. He just hoped Griz had not accompanied the rest of the household.

The door opened quickly to his peremptory rap.

"Lady Grizelda, if you please."

"Her ladyship is not at home," the butler said loftily.

Dragan narrowed his eyes. Had the man been told by the family to deny her to him?

"But," the butler said, reaching behind the door to the little booth normally inhabited by the porter, "she left this for you, should you happen to call."

"Did she, by God?" Dragan almost snatched the note and read it by the light filtering out from the house.

Mudd Lane with PD. Did you know there's an old drainage tunnel that opens there? G.

Blood rushed into his ears. "Dear God… When did she leave?"

"About twenty minutes ago, sir."

Twenty minutes! While he had sat drawing pictures and walked round here when he should have followed—

"Tizsa?" said a surprised male voice, as Lord Forsythe, dressed for the evening, brushed past the butler. "You look as if you're about to murder poor old Berry. What's he done?"

"Nothing. Griz is in danger. I have to go."

"Danger?" Forsythe repeated, startled, seizing his arm to prevent his escape. "If ever there was a troublesome…I'll come with you."

And at last, Dragan could think beyond sheer instinct. "No. Fetch the police," he commanded. "Use the name of Inspector Harris—or Lord Horace if you need to. Send them to Mudd Lane, behind Covent

Garden, where Nancy Barrow died. And sir, it is *urgent!*"

"Use my carriage then," Forythe said, indicating the hackney that had just pulled up at the door. "Peter and I will summon the police."

Dragan might have thrown a grateful thank you over his shoulder as he flew down the steps. He meant to.

"Covent Garden! Quickly!" he yelled at the driver before hurling himself inside and slamming the door.

***

THERE WERE NO crowds in front of the opera house when he all but fell out of the carriage and thrust a pile of uncounted money at the driver. At once, he sped toward the road he had trodden so often since the night Nancy died.

"Looking for me, handsome?" asked one of the women lurking in the shadows of the square.

Too focused to acknowledge anyone, he ignored her, but another woman stood directly in front of him, forcing him to swerve. It was Junie.

"Here, don't ignore me," she said indignantly. "I saw that bloke again. And just a few minutes later, your beautiful lady went, too."

"Went where? Up that way? Going to Mudd Lane?"

"Maybe. She wasn't close enough to talk to, or I'd have warned her."

Hastily, he dragged his latest pictures from his pocket and showed the gentleman to Junie.

"That's him," she said excitedly.

"Bring everyone you can to Mudd Lane," he said grimly. "It's a matter of life and death. And watch out for a drain hatch."

Without waiting to see what she made of that, he sprinted up the side of the theatre and into the back lane that led to Mudd Lane.

CHAPTER TWENTY-THREE

Having learned from her previous trip to Mudd Lane in the dark, Griz brought her own lantern and lit it before venturing off the lit street where carriages once more awaited and heading toward the lane.

One of the things that had struck her during the afternoon was that it would have made better sense for Penelope and her to come together. But she supposed Penelope must be at the opera, probably with her family, possibly even with Gabriel, a thought that made Griz shudder. She just hoped Penelope could contrive to escape the theatre unseen by him.

She seemed to be the first to arrive, which didn't surprise her. As before, the dark alley was an oasis of quiet among the muffled merriment and other noises from surrounding streets, taverns, and the theatre.

Griz gazed at the ground as she walked, looking for the hatch that might open onto the tunnel.

A man stepped out of the shadows.

Griz froze. *Dear God, it's Gabriel.* She should have brought a weapon of some kind, a pistol...

"Grizelda," he said, and with relief, she realized it was not Gabriel at all.

Lifting the lantern a shade higher, she saw an elegant young man.

No, she didn't.

"Penelope?" she gasped. "Good Lord, I almost didn't recognize you!"

Penelope laughed softly. "You wouldn't be the first. But I couldn't take the chance of being seen."

No, but Griz had taken that chance on her invitation. Thrusting aside her moment of irritation, she said, "What have you found? What is it you need to show me?"

"This," Penelope said, reaching down to the ground at her feet.

Griz walked nearer, shifting the beam of the lantern, and saw that someone had already shifted aside the cover of a large, black manhole. "You found it? How did you know where to look?"

"Thomas told me, of course," she replied impatiently. "You know about it already?"

"The police told me this morning." She raised her gaze back to Penelope's face, pale and strong in the lantern light. She made a handsome young man. "Mr. Gabriel had told them about it. He seemed to think it was evidence against Dragan."

"Don't you?"

"No," she said frankly. "I think it's evidence of Mr. Gabriel trying very hard to blame Dragan. What other cause does he have to be poking into plans of old sewers? In fact, it proves *he* knew about the tunnel and probably escaped that way himself."

"Then let's go down and see if we can find evidence of either of them."

"Let's not. Let's send the police instead."

"You trust them?" Penelope sounded surprised.

"Not really," Griz was forced to admit.

"Well, I'm going down." Penelope crouched down, dipping one foot into the hole. "At least hold the lantern for me."

Griz shone the lantern on the hole, revealing a long, metal ladder. "Be careful. Some of the rungs look rusty."

"You will wait for me, won't you?"

"Of course," Griz said, watching her climb down. She did not care for dark, enclosed spaces, and there could be water and rats, and she could already smell something very unpleasant... *Damnation!* She sighed and took hold of her skirts, and began to climb down, grasping the rungs with one hand while she held the lantern in the other.

"I've found the ground," Penelope declared in triumph.

"Is it dry?"

"Yes."

Griz paused long enough to shine the lantern outward and down. Penelope stood in the ring of light in what looked like a brick chamber. Griz climbed down to join her and shone the lantern all the way around. Three tunnels led off the chamber.

"That one," Griz said, pointing to her right, "must lead to the theatre."

"Lead the way," Penelope invited, "since you have the light."

At that point, Griz would gladly have handed over this advantage. But, having shone it around the ground and the walls in search of any clue possibly left by Nancy's killer, she gathered her courage and plunged into the tunnel.

Almost at once, her foot struck something and knocked it over. Quickly, lantern swinging, she bent and felt for the object. Warm metal and glass. Another lantern. *Warm?*

Someone was only just ahead of them. Or...

All the hairs sprang up on the back of her neck as a horrible truth slammed into her. She whirled around, just in time to see Penelope coming at her with a glinting blade.

From sheer instinct, Griz threw up one arm to protect herself, and the knife struck the unlit lantern. Penelope cried out in pain, clutching her wrist, though she didn't drop the knife.

"The lantern is yours," Griz gasped. "You came down here earlier."

And now Griz had followed her, like a lamb to the slaughter. Penelope had known all she had to do was descend, and Griz would inevitably go, too.

In the madly swinging light from the lit lantern, Penelope's face looked nightmarish, the eyes insanely focused on Griz. "Of course I did, just to make sure it was safe." She raised the knife again. "Even that wasn't the first time."

"You killed Nancy. You were the 'man' who beckoned her." Griz jerked back as Penelope's free hand suddenly snaked out toward her throat and again used the lantern as a shield.

"It's fascinating, isn't it?" Penelope sneered. "I make a gangly, awkward woman but an elegant young man. Who would connect the two?"

"Not I," Griz admitted, wondering desperately how long she could fend her attacker off and then how she would get the blade away from her. Without the knife, she had more chance, though Penelope was bigger and possibly stronger. "Why did you kill my poor maid?"

Penelope's lips curled back in a snarl that seemed quite separate from the eager watchfulness of her eyes as she waited for the shielding lantern to lower. "Your *poor maid* was a whore. She was carrying my Thomas's child, threatening my marriage and his career."

"He told you about that?" Griz asked in such surprise that she almost dropped the lantern and had to jerk it back up when Penelope lunged.

"No, the whore told me herself, seemed to think I should help her." Penelope laughed. "So I did."

Pity and unexpected fury surged up. "That was why she answered you when you beckoned, why she wasn't afraid to follow you in the dark, even disguised. She thought you were helping her." Slowly, carefully, Griz bent her knees, lowering her lit lantern to the floor. "You meant to bring her down here, too, but I was following, and so was Dragan. You had to leave the scene without the body. I heard the hatch scrape. Only I had no idea what it was."

The other woman watched her like a snake, ready to strike. Only when Griz began to straighten did Penelope make her move, again reaching for the throat. Griz even felt the grasping fingers graze her skin before she slammed up her free hand, knocking Penelope's arm up. She even swung the shielding lantern, forcing Penelope back through the mouth of the tunnel into the entrance chamber.

"And you won't leave it alone, will you?" Penelope said bitterly as they again stood facing each other, breathless and watchful. "You're trying to ruin Thomas, even blame him for this murder. But I won't allow it. I won't allow anyone to take this happiness from me. We might have been friends, you and I, but now you have to die."

"There is no point," Griz told her. "Dragan will still come after him. And find out about you."

"*Dragan*," Penelope mocked with a sudden bark of laughter.

"Are you going to kill him, too?" Griz taunted.

"Don't be silly. I won't have to. He will hang for Nancy's murder, and for yours, and no one will pay any attention to what he says. A foreigner, a revolutionary, an unprincipled fortune hunter."

"Unprincipled?" Griz moved into the wall at her left shoulder as Penelope tried to rush her from that side. "That's quite an accusation from a woman who has already committed murder."

"Of a whore," Penelope said contemptuously. With a sudden change of tactic, she lunged to Grizelda's other side. Griz swished the lantern, knocking the knife aside, but not before the cold steel had touched her skin.

Damn, it cut me... But she could not look, could not lower the lantern. In desperation, she swung it at Penelope's head, again forcing her to fall back. But there was nowhere for Griz to run. She'd never make it up the ladder before Penelope caught her, and running into a dark tunnel with a murderer at her back was not a situation she cared for either.

Already, with lightning speed, Penelope was again reaching for her throat, forcing her back against the wall.

And then, miraculously, the woman stilled, clearly listening.

Griz was afraid to breathe. Something moved above, at the opening. A breeze, blowing gravel against the ladder? Or…

It was now or never. Taking advantage of Penelope's distraction, Griz flew at her, head down like a charging bull. She struck her in the stomach, taking her by utter surprise and toppling her over, while Grizelda's spectacles flew off into the darkness.

A sob of relief escaped Griz when she heard the heavier thud of the knife falling and skittering across the ground. But beneath her, Penelope struggled, knocking the lantern against Grizelda's temple. Griz threw it to one side, the better to grasp for the other woman's wrists.

Penelope's body heaved, rolling Griz over on to her back, and they scrabbled at each other's hands for an instant, both trying to get a grip of the other. Then Penelope's hand closed around her throat.

Just as she did to Nancy. In panic, Griz grasped Penelope's wrist, tugging and bucking in vain to dislodge her. This was what Nancy had suffered, too.

A dark figure loomed behind Penelope, blocking the pale light from the tunnel, and abruptly, Penelope was plucked from her like a rag doll.

As Griz scrambled to her feet, Penelope fought furiously against her captor, lashing with elbows and feet, and then she cried out as her arm was yanked up her back.

"Be still," Dragan said sternly. "It's over."

In spite of everything, a huge smile split Grizelda's face. "I knew it was you," she said happily.

But more people were swarming down the ladder, distracting her. They were women. Noisy, gaudy, bright, and utterly astonishing in this place.

"Griz, are you hurt?" Dragan demanded, his voice urgent, fearful.

Her wrist was stinging, slippery. "Oh," she said in surprise. "I forgot about—"

Dragan must have relaxed his hold because without warning, Penelope bolted from him, straight for the tunnel. She swiped up the lit lantern as she went.

"Don't worry, we'll get her," one of the women—Junie?—said grimly, and as one, they all ran after her like hounds after a fox.

Griz blinked up at Dragan. It wasn't quite dark because lantern light shone dimly down from the opening above. He took her wrist, raising it to examine the damage.

"A shallow cut," he said with shaky relief, wrapping something—a handkerchief?—around it. But he didn't tie it, for he suddenly crushed her in his arms instead. "Dear God, Griz…" And his mouth almost crashed down on hers in a fierce, desperate kiss that she couldn't have resisted if she'd tried.

She didn't, for everything in her leapt to meet his sudden passion. Her mouth wide open under his, she surrendered and cooperated, flinging her good hand upward to clutch his nape, straining against him in a wild release of joy and arousal.

There may have been muffled footsteps, voices, above. Had the light brightened? She didn't care. In the distance, from the tunnel, came screeching and laughter and crows of triumph. The women had caught Penelope. Somewhere, Griz hoped they wouldn't hurt her, but mostly, she hoped Dragan would never stop kissing her.

"Well, it's not the emergency I came for," said a dry, familiar voice above them. "Not sure what the police can do about it."

"Stand aside, sir!" That surely was Inspector Harris.

Reluctantly, Dragan released her mouth but kept his arms around her while policemen swarmed down the ladder, filling the chamber with men and light.

Inspector Harris handed her the spectacles that had flown off her nose in the tussle with Penelope.

"Thank you." Still dazed, she shoved them back on her face and saw that the men weren't all policemen. One of them was indeed her brother Forsythe, whose voice she had already heard. The other was...

"Mr. Gabriel," she said warily.

"I found him already at Great Scotland Yard," Forsythe said cheerfully, "trying to persuade the inspector into action."

"I knew when I went to the house," Gabriel said, "and she wasn't there. She did it the last time, too. Invited me and then was not there. I think she was giving me an alibi in case my connection to Nancy was discovered. But when she wasn't there tonight...I could no longer stay silent. It wasn't a one-time-only jealous rage. She is capable of any evil, and I would not see it..."

"And your own evil?" Dragan asked.

"He has already confessed it," Harris said impatiently. "We brought him in the hope he would help in capturing Miss Derryn."

"I was merely earning a little extra money for myself by redistributing the wealth of a few criminals," Gabriel said, almost pleading. "It did no real harm."

"But it did, and you always knew it did," Griz said. "Otherwise, you would have told Horace. And do you really think there was *no harm* in casting the blame on Dragan?"

"A revolutionary," Gabriel said with a dismissive wave of one hand. "Arguably, he deserves all he gets. But I could not let you die. Or anyone else."

"Did you know Nancy was pregnant?" Griz blurted.

Gabriel closed his eyes and nodded. There was real grief there, genuine anguish—yet another tragedy.

Griz dragged her gaze free, glad of Dragan's firm arm around her shoulders. "Inspector? There is a knife of some kind behind us on the ground. I think it is what killed Nancy. She tried to kill me with it, too."

"I have it." The inspector seemed more concerned with the gaggle of women emerging from the tunnel with Penelope captive among them.

Penelope's gaze flew to Gabriel, at once tense, terrified, and hopeful.

"She called your maid a whore," Junie informed Griz. "And now it's real whores who hand her over to the law. You're welcome, Inspector."

"And stay out of the way of her feet when you take her up the ladder," another woman advised.

"Thomas," Penelope begged.

"Not this time," he said hoarsely. "This time it's all over. For both of us."

Two policemen went first, then Penelope and another constable, keeping a wary distance from her feet. But she seemed dazed, as though all the fight had gone out of her. Harris waved Gabriel toward the ladder.

Gabriel paused, again looking back at Griz. "Tell Lord Horace I am...sorry."

She nodded curtly as Harris pushed him on.

"How did you even know where to find me?" Griz asked suddenly.

"I followed Gabriel to the Derryns' house," Dragan said, "and almost as soon as he'd gone in, *she* came out. I almost didn't recognize her as Miss Derryn. I went to warn you and got your note. Fortunately, your brother was around and went to fetch the police while I rushed over here."

He didn't even ask what she'd been thinking about to come here alone to the scene of a previous murder. He, too, had assumed Miss Derryn too innocent, too much the victim in Gabriel's crimes. But he had come for her. He had sent her powerful family to summon the police and elicited even the aid of the ladies of the night, all to help her. He had undoubtedly saved her life.

He cared.

She rested her head against his shoulder. "Let's go home," she whispered.

CHAPTER TWENTY-FOUR

BOTH FORSYTHE AND Griz insisted Dragan come into the house, which, of course, was in an uproar, since the servants had informed the duke of Forsythe's expedition to the police to save Griz.

They walked into a drawing room full of family. In a rare show of public affection, her mother embraced her. So did Azalea and Rosemary—clearly summoned from their own homes in the crisis—and Horace. Even Monkton patted her shoulder while her father was pushing glasses of brandy into everyone's hands, including Grizelda's.

And the tale was dragged out of her and Dragan, a brief and hastily edited summary of the investigations that had led to tonight, followed by the night's adventures. There were gasps and groans and cries of horror and then relief. And then, finally, there was silence.

The duke broke it. "I don't approve. I don't approve at all. You. Griz, had no business interfering in any of this, and nor, sir, did you. But we can't change that, now. All I can say is that we owe you, sir, a huge debt of gratitude for Grizelda's safety. For her very life. I shall not forget that."

Everyone nodded solemnly. Only Dragan looked uncomfortable.

"Mr. Gabriel says he is sorry," she told Horace.

Horace shook his head. "I never suspected him for a moment of anything underhand. Even the leaflets in the rookery. I was completely taken in. *I!*"

"I believe he was sincere in his work," Dragan said. "He really does hate the idea of revolution, and I'm sure he worked hard in his efforts to avoid the danger. He just saw no harm in lining his pockets at the same time, if it helped him aspire to a position closer to yours." He smiled faintly. "You see, equality would solve all that nonsense."

The duke let out a bark of laughter. Azalea emitted a slightly shocked giggle. Even Horace gave a sardonic grin.

"Well, thank God all is resolved," the duchess said. "Where is it you lodge, Mr. Tizsa?"

"Kensington, ma'am."

"Well, you can't possibly go all the way back there tonight. Not after what you have done. Pull the bell, Azalea. You must stay in the guest bedchamber, sir. And you should find there everything you need for your comfort. Shall we have supper?"

HER FAMILY'S GRATITUDE to Dragan had taken her by surprise, but when she finally found herself alone in her bedchamber, undressed and pulling on her nightgown, she was surprised by her dissatisfaction. She was glad of their warmth to him and their temporary forgiveness of her. And after those moments with the murderous Penelope Derryn, she was very thankful to see them all again.

And Dragan, if not quite accepted as an equal, was at least welcomed as a good person to know, a man of unexpected—to them—knowledge and humor. They had surrounded her, too, jostling each other for who sat next to her. At one level, she had truly enjoyed the impromptu family party, more than she had enjoyed any such gathering for years.

But what she had really wanted, what she still wanted, was just a few moments alone with Dragan. To be sure those wild, possessive kisses signified more than relief in her survival. But mostly, just to see him, just to take one more moment to bed with her.

The best guest bedchamber was where Monkton had used to sleep before he set up his own establishment when he married Augusta. It was only across the passage.

She brushed out her hair, listening to the growing silence in the house, knowing if she truly meant to say goodnight to him in private, she would have to do it soon, or he would be asleep. Perhaps he already was.

She dropped her hairbrush and rose, fetching her dressing gown from the back of the door. Her heart thundered as she struggled into it, tied it, and opened the door a crack.

All was in darkness. The servants had gone to bed. As she opened her door wider, the light from her room fell across the landing to his closed door. She didn't need light to find her way, so she closed her door behind her, walked through the darkness, and tapped lightly.

She didn't know now if she would be glad or sorry if he did not answer.

The door glided open silently, and Dragan stood there bathed in the warm glow of a single lamp. He was half-undressed, in his shirt-sleeves, tieless, shoeless. And not appalled at all.

The tenderest smile curved his lips, flooded his eyes as he drew her inside and closed the door. And then he took her in his arms, kissing her as she longed to be kissed, with deep, aching sensuality.

"Griz...Griz, do you love me?" he whispered against her lips.

"Oh, you know I do. Would I be here if—"

His mouth fastened tighter, drowning the rest of her words. "Will you marry me?" he asked an instant later. "I have nothing, but will you?"

She cupped his cheek to draw his mouth back to hers. "Of course I will." Lost in his wild kiss, it was some time before she caught at his head, pushing him back. "Wait... you have not... Do you love me?"

"Insanely," he whispered, seizing her mouth once more. "It is too soon, too mad, but I always knew."

"So did I," she said in wonder and kissed him again.

His hands swept down her body, making her gasp, and then her dressing gown was on the floor, and he was pulling her nightgown up over her head. Her glasses went with it, and she didn't care, for she was in his arms with a dizzy sense of flying, and then there was cool linen at her back, and hot, male flesh covering her front.

Excitement soared. His hands caressed everywhere, sweet and tender, arousing a hunger she only half-understood. How could there be such intense pleasure in the moment, along with such blinding need for more?

The skin of his shoulders and back was heated velvet beneath her greedy fingers. And below the soft skin, hard muscle thrilled her. So strong, so lean and flexible as he kissed her throat, her breasts, and his fingers stroked between her thighs, making her gasp with wild, new bliss.

But there were more than fingers there, and it seemed so right, so desirable that she wasn't even shocked when he slipped inside her. It helped that he was kissing her lips, that his rippling back and rear distracted her until there was only him, only tides of wonder and pleasure. And rocking, shattering joy.

⇛⇛✷⇚⇚

"DID YOU JUST take my virginity?" she asked. One had to be sure.

Breathless laughter shook him. "Yes. Now you have to marry me."

"Now *you* have to marry *me*."

"I'll settle for that." He shifted his weight, drawing her with him, still joined. The sheen of sweat stood out on his golden skin, catching the glow of the lamp. "When we are married, I will take a lot longer about it. We have so much to share."

"I like the sound of that," she said, suddenly shy, despite the current intimacy.

"Your family still won't like it," he warned.

"They will learn to," she said comfortably.

For a while, they lay in sweet silence, in each other's arms. There had never been happiness like this.

Eventually, as she felt drowsiness begin to overtake her, she moved.

She had thought he was asleep, but his arm moved at once, holding her in place. And his eyes were open.

"Will you stay?" he murmured. "Just for an hour."

She settled back down, smiling into his shoulder. "Yes."

⟫⟫⟫⟪⟪⟪

SHE STAYED FOR four. Dragan knew because he woke as she slid out of his bed before dawn. He didn't stop her. She was his, but he would not embarrass her before the household. And they could each do with another hour or so of sleep before they faced the fight with her parents.

He smiled into the pillow, desiring her with a sweet, lazy lust. She was wonderful, his Griz, giving and passionate and beautiful. Oh yes, they would have such times together.

If she could stand the poverty.

Tomorrow's fight. And there had never been anything or anyone more worth fighting for.

⟫⟫⟫⟪⟪⟪

THREE HOURS LATER, he and Griz stood before the duke in His Grace's library. He had just asked formally for her hand.

The duke gazed from one to the other in some consternation. "When do you wish to marry?"

"As soon as possible. This week, next week. No later than next month."

"But you have no means to support a wife," the duke pointed out. "Do you?"

"No," Dragan admitted. "Not really. Dr. Cordell pays me a little as his assistant, and I hope to work more for him in the immediate future. In the longer term, I mean to take the final medical exams."

"I suppose you could live here if you are set on this course…"

Griz looked stunned by such an easy admission. "I also have a little money," she said. "saved from allowances, and if you were to keep that allowance going, Papa, we could afford a small house. Probably."

The duke eyed her just a little sardonically. "To keep up appearances as my daughter? It had probably better not to be too small a house, then."

"I do not wish to be beholden," Dragan said stiffly, aware that he nevertheless owed Griz some degree of the comfort she was used to. It just went against the grain to live off her.

"We can sort that out later," Griz said, catching his fingers to implore his silence. "Then you do not object, Papa? We have your permission, if not your blessing?"

"I don't like it," he said. "You knew I wouldn't."

"Yes, but you want me to be happy and out of your hair," she wheedled.

"Yes, I do. But *will* you be happy? You barely know each other."

Griz laughed. "That's the odd thing, Papa, we do."

Before the duke could reply, the library door opened, and Lord Horace walked in.

"Ah, Tizsa, they said you were in here. Good morning," he added to his father and sister. "Am I interrupting anything?"

"Tizsa has just asked for your sister's hand."

"Just as well from what Forsythe told me," Horace said bluntly.

The duke blinked. "You are advising me to agree to this mad start?"

"You might as well, for she'll do it anyway," Horace said. "Besides, seems to me they understand each other, and she's been a lot happier since they met. He might not prevent her crazy starts—in fact, he'll probably join in—but he seems more capable than we are of bringing her off safe."

"Why, Horace," Griz said in some surprise. "You *do* observe human nature."

The duke scowled. "He doesn't even have a decent suit to marry her in!"

"Oh well, I daresay wedding gifts will take care of that," Horace said vaguely. "But actually, I was looking for you, Tizsa, because I have a proposition."

"What kind of proposition," Dragan asked dubiously.

"I was impressed—my superiors were impressed—with the way you ferreted out the truth about Gabriel when the rest of us suspected nothing but that something wasn't quite right somewhere."

"Thank you," Dragan replied. "I think."

"We—Her Majesty's government—would like to retain you to investigate similar problems that may arise."

He felt Grizelda's gaze on him, suddenly anxious. "What sort of problems?" he asked flatly. "I'll not denounce people for speaking their mind against the government or help oppress people without hope."

"I don't ask it of you," Horace said in apparent surprise. "I want to throw a few discrepancies at you. Discrepancies in my department and others, so that we can root out any...entitlement."

"Corruption," Griz corrected.

Horace scowled. "If you will. I doubt it will be constant work, however, so we're also happy to recommend your discreet services to others who will also pay."

Dragan liked puzzles. Even as he meant to pursue his final exams and some kind of career in medicine, he had been aware of his restless need of distraction. In Hungary, he had absorbed the revolution and war and his interest in art. And here, in his new life with Griz, there would be more puzzles.

His fingers entwined with Grizelda's and held. He smiled. "Then, on agreed terms, I am happy to oblige."

Griz laughed with sheer delight and hugged him, and he knew that against all the odds, he had found his new home.

About Mary Lancaster

Mary Lancaster lives in Scotland with her husband, three mostly grown-up kids and a small, crazy dog.

Her first literary love was historical fiction, a genre which she relishes mixing up with romance and adventure in her own writing. Her most recent books are light, fun Regency romances written for Dragonblade Publishing: *The Imperial Season* series set at the Congress of Vienna; and the popular *Blackhaven Brides* series, which is set in a fashionable English spa town frequented by the great and the bad of Regency society.

Connect with Mary on-line – she loves to hear from readers:

Email Mary:
Mary@MaryLancaster.com

Website:
www.MaryLancaster.com

Newsletter sign-up:
http://eepurl.com/b4Xoif

Facebook:
facebook.com/mary.lancaster.1656

Facebook Author Page:
facebook.com/MaryLancasterNovelist

Twitter:
@MaryLancNovels

Amazon Author Page:
amazon.com/Mary-Lancaster/e/B00DJ5IACI

Bookbub:
bookbub.com/profile/mary-lancaster

Printed in Great Britain
by Amazon

36885883R00155